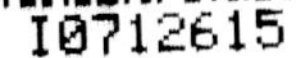

Books by Susan Quilty

Novels
The Insistence of Memory
To the Left of Death

The Psychic Traveler Society Series (Young Adult)
Healers and Thieves
Family and Foes
Elders and Aliens

Short Fiction
Audrey and Esther Geekify Greenville
Freely Written Vol.1

THE PSYCHIC TRAVELER SOCIETY
BOOK 3

ELDERS
AND
ALIENS

SUSAN QUILTY

First printing, 2023

Cover Design: Susan Quilty
Publisher: Bitter Lily Books, LLC

ISBN: 979-8-9889837-0-5
ISBN: 979-8-9889837-1-2

Bitter Lily Books, LLC
Ashburn, Virginia

SusanQuilty.com

Learn from
your elders

Follow your
own path

CHAPTER 1

A CHANGE IN PLANS

The voice in Amanda Jones' head was calm but insistent. She silently responded, then flicked on the windshield wipers as she prepared to make a right turn. She was getting good at multitasking between the world around her and the occasional psychic message from a fellow traveler. Driving in the rain was a new challenge.

"I should have driven us home," Patty Jones muttered from the passenger seat. Her hands were clasped on her lap as she shifted forward to get a better look at the storm clouds overhead.

"Mom, please," Amanda sighed, gripping the steering wheel. "I can handle a little rain."

They were quiet then, listening to the patter of raindrops and the swish of the windshield wipers. Patty insisted on turning the radio off whenever Amanda drove. Amanda didn't argue about it, though she'd had her learner's permit for over six months and listened to music every time she drove with her aunt. Judy said it was good to practice in *real-world* conditions. Amanda knew it was better to keep that method between them.

"I know what you can handle," Patty responded gently.

Amanda bit her lip, realizing her mom was trying to show she understood how hard it must be to balance high school with the secret life of a psychic traveler.

The rain fell harder as they neared home. Amanda wondered why Rory had messaged her. It wasn't unusual to hear from her training agent, but when she heard Amanda was driving, Rory had said they would talk later.

"Is Cameron coming for dinner?"

"Would that bother you?"

Amanda turned into the apartment parking lot and considered the question.

Cameron had been her first training agent. Now, after a diplomatic coup had upended the Psychic Traveler Society, Cameron had a seat on the new High Council. He also appeared to be dating her mother, though neither of them had confirmed that with Amanda. Not that she'd asked.

"He's been so helpful to me since… Oh, careful!"

Amanda eased into a parking space while her mom glanced rapidly at the cars around them. Though Amanda had never come close to hitting a car, Patty perpetually braced for a first accident.

"It's fine." Amanda slipped the car into park and shut off the engine. "I like Cameron, and we can go over plans for my trip."

She hopped out of the car before Patty could reply. Her mom had come to accept Amanda's role as a psychic traveler and trust Rory as her training agent, but she was not happy that Lucas would be joining them on this trip. Despite his part in saving her from the former High Council's schemes, and his new appointment as Director of the Psychic Traveler Society, Patty did not trust Lucas Flynn.

Amanda pulled up her hoodie and quickly crossed the parking lot. Patty hurried to follow, trying to awkwardly angle an umbrella over both of their heads. Once they were in the building, Amanda patiently held the elevator while her mom shook her umbrella outside the building's covered front door and neatly secured it with its attached strap. Lightning flashed outside the glass doors and a shiver ran up Amanda's spine.

Riding up to their apartment, Amanda remembered a very different elevator trip. The one where Aunt Judy had just confirmed her psychic travel abilities and was about to explain the secret world of the Psychic Traveler Society. It had only been 15 months since that crazy day, but Amanda felt like an entirely different person.

"Are you home yet?" Rory's message whispered through Amanda's head.

"In the elevator," Amanda answered silently, watching the numbers above the doors light their progress from floor to floor.

"Meet me in the house," Rory messaged. *"Before you talk to Cameron."*

"Amanda?" Patty peered at her daughter's face intently. "Are you here?"

"Obviously." Amanda shrugged. They both knew that wasn't obvious at all.

"Okay…" Patty accepted her answer reluctantly. Then added, "You were so quiet."

"I can be quiet and still be here," Amanda reminded lightly. She was careful not to sound defensive, knowing it would sound like a lie. Besides, she wasn't lying. Sending a psychic message wasn't the same as visiting the mindspace. With a message, she could be present in the world while a small part of her mind glimpsed the hazy house she'd once thought was a daydream. Like picturing a scene from a movie while still carrying on a conversation.

"I know," Patty said, though she didn't sound certain. "I'm still getting used to all of this…"

Amanda instinctively reached for her mom's hand. She gave it a reassuring squeeze without taking her eyes from the steadily climbing numbers.

Discovering the world of psychic travel had devastated Patty. Amanda remembered watching her mom lie on the couch day after day, unable to process the idea of psychic travel, let alone the thought of her own daughter magically transporting herself to strange new worlds.

Amanda had found it all hard to believe at first, too, even after stepping through a door in her daydream house and finding herself in the purple-hued world of Terra-V. She'd thought she was losing her mind until Aunt Judy showed up to explain how it worked.

Judy was a psychic traveler. Amanda's dad had been a traveler, too. He'd died when Amanda was young, but she remembered his bedtime stories about fantastic worlds and the amazing people who lived in them. Her favorite stories were about Terra-V, more formally known as Terra Violavita.

Though she hadn't known Terra-V was a real place until she stood in the purple grass, watching the tuntum trees slowly twist toward the ground in the darkening twilight. She could still hear their sound. *Tuntum. Tuntum.*

When they entered their apartment, Judy and Cameron were already there. Dinner was cooking on the stove and music was streaming through the TV. The three-bedroom apartment had once been Judy's alone. The Psychic Traveler Society had paid for it when they sent Judy to work as Amanda's integration counselor. Now that Amanda was a more established traveler, she worked with a training agent. Rory went with her on off-world trips and helped to guide her education through various PTS centers.

"How was the dentist?" Cameron asked. "Healthy teeth all around?"

Amanda shrugged off her coat and ducked into her bedroom, leaving Patty to praise her lack of cavities. There wasn't much time before dinner. Amanda dropped her backpack on her bed, then sat beside it with crossed legs and closed eyes. In an instant, her mind had traveled into the Victorian house known as the birdhouse.

The birdhouse had nothing to do with birds, and it did not exist in the physical world. It was a psychic way station built in the shared mindspace by the last psychic architect, Edmund Robinson. Travelers could send their minds into the birdhouse, or any other building in the mindspace, and then use one of the many doors to physically transport themselves to another location.

Rory waited for Amanda in the small den near the front door.

"What's going on?" Amanda sat in the chair beside her, noting Rory's tight jaw and sharp eyes. Though that wasn't an unusual look for her.

"It's not a big deal." Rory paused and Amanda tensed. "I wanted to be the one to tell you. The High Council is postponing your trip to Crystal Caverns."

"Again?" Amanda pressed her lips together and shook her head. "But we were supposed to go over winter break, until that Vertex protest thing happened. If we don't go now, I won't have another holiday for a month. Presidents Day, I think. Can't we go on a regular weekend?"

"A three-day weekend is better," Rory answered. "We're not sure how long it will take. Plus, we'll be better prepared for your trip by then."

Amanda narrowed her eyes.

"Why aren't you fighting this? Why isn't Lucas?"

Though Lucas' position as Director gave him a fair amount of authority, he still had to answer to the High Council, and he loved pushing back on every disagreement. Especially about the pace of Amanda's training.

Beyond making history as the youngest psychic traveler, Amanda had shown signs of becoming the next psychic architect, a traveler with the ability to build mindspace houses and connect doors to new worlds. Yet it had been nearly 100 years since the previous psychic architect and their training was shrouded in mystery.

They'd recently learned that Edmund Robinson had created a quest he called the architect's journey and left information about it with his closest off-world allies. Lucas and Amanda were keen to track down the steps she'd need to complete the quest. The High Council said they should tread carefully, as Edmund couldn't have known the next potential architect would be a teenager. Or a *child*, as they usually put it.

Rory leaned in, letting sincerity soften her eyes.

"We want you to come with us, Amanda, we really do."

"Wait! You're still going? Without me?"

Rory winced at the betrayal in Amanda's voice.

"It's just a recon mission. We're going to check out the route to the Pyuran forest and see what else we can discover about the legends."

"Without me!" Amanda fumed. There was a knock on her bedroom door, hazy and distant from her mental place in the house but filtering in because her physical body still sat on her bed. She ignored it, glaring at Rory instead.

"I know you want to go," Rory said calmly. "And you *will* go, once we have more information."

The knock on her door repeated. Amanda mentally popped out of the house, snapping, *"In a minute!"* at the closed door, then jumped back to her place beside Rory.

"If you and Lucas want to go without me. You could just say it."

"Amanda, please," Rory tried to explain, but Amanda didn't wait to hear her out.

"It's fine." She crossed her arms against the ache of disappointment. "You don't want a *child* getting in the way. Too bad you're kinda stuck with me since it's the architect's journey, and I'm the one who's supposed to be going."

When Rory tried to respond, Amanda shook her head and said she was being called to dinner.

With her mind back in her body, she wiped hot tears from her eyes, grabbed her phone from her backpack, and called, "Okay, come in."

When Cameron eased into the room, he found Amanda hunched over her phone, thumbs in place as if she'd been texting.

"I'm in the middle of something."

"What's wrong?" Cameron asked, showing concern Amanda didn't want.

"It doesn't matter," she snapped, still staring at her phone.

"Okay." Cameron hesitated. "I won't take long, but this is important."

"Let me guess," Amanda began icily. "My trip is postponed. Again."

Cameron studied Amanda's angry profile.

"Who told you? Rory or Lucas?" His tone was light, conciliatory even, but Amanda shrugged and refused to meet his eyes.

"No one," she sniffed. "I'm psychic."

§

The cafeteria was deafening as Amanda took her seat next to Drew. Normally, the noise jarred her, but today it felt good to be swept up in the activity. She didn't want to think about psychic travel, now that her trip was off, and being present with her friends felt like waking up to a life she'd half-forgotten. Even their everyday dramas—which typically irritated Amanda to no end—were more interesting as she tried to catch herself up.

"Rehearsals ran so long last night! *Je suis fatiguée!*" Trina mock complained while pushing spaghetti around her plate. She'd had to switch from Spanish to French to fit theater into her schedule and had started dropping French phrases into every conversation. "I've been off-book for weeks, but I don't know how our scene will come together by Saturday!"

"It will be perfect!"

Amanda studied Brooklyn, who was beaming at Trina's side. Brooklyn had been following Trina like a puppy since their first theater class, and Amanda wasn't sure what to make of her.

"What time does it start again?" Drew asked, catching Amanda off guard.

"Matinee at two, evening at seven," Trina answered on cue. "We can get dinner in between but have to be back by 6:15."

"That works for me," Nick agreed easily. "I can drop Trina at the theater at one and pick everyone up in time for the matinee. That gives us, what? A little over an hour for dinner in between?"

"About 90 minutes," Brooklyn corrected. "If the first show lets out by 4:30."

"We haven't ended on time yet!" Trina wailed. But Brooklyn patted her arm saying, "Stop worrying! It will be perfect!"

Amanda leaned toward Drew, putting a hand on his arm. "You're going?"

"Oh, um, yeah," Drew hesitated. "I mean, you were going to be out of town…"

"I hate that you're going to miss it!" Trina interrupted, clearly listening in. "It's my first One Act Festival and my best friend is out of town."

Amanda caught a flash of irritation pass over Brooklyn's face, but she didn't have time to process it. There was a rhythm to the conversation, and Amanda didn't want to fall out of step.

"Actually, my trip was canceled," she admitted, bracing herself for Trina's squeals of joy.

"So, you can come? You *have* to come!"

"Yeah, of course," Amanda laughed. "I mean, if there's room for me?"

"Sure," Nick offered. "My car seats five, so that's Trina, Drew, Brooklyn, you, and me."

"And you're coming to both?" Trina clarified nervously. "Matinee *and* evening? You have to if you want to see all of the plays!"

Amanda already knew that. The One Act Festival was an annual event where each senior theater student staged a one-act play, handling the casting, sets, and direction themselves. The plays were split over matinee and evening events, then swapped the next day, giving more chances for the audience to see them all. Trina had small roles in two of the plays.

"My parents will be there Saturday night and for the Sunday matinee," Brooklyn volunteered. "I told them they'll miss half the plays that way, but they only care about the play I'm in. *C'est trés mignon!*"

"It's meat?" Nick asked, drawing laughs from Brooklyn and Trina.

"Cute!" Trina corrected. *"Mignon* means cute."

She rolled her eyes at Brooklyn as if it were so hard to be the only two at the table who spoke French. Amanda tried not to make a face.

At a table behind theirs, Amanda caught Trey watching her before turning back to his friends. He'd been hanging out with a different crowd since Trina broke up with him, and Amanda was glad she rarely had to deal with him. Even knowing she'd been able to easily fight off Trey's creepy advances in the past, she didn't feel safe around him. Amanda glanced at Drew, relieved he hadn't noticed Trey watching her.

Trina had begun listing which members of her family planned to be at which performance. Brooklyn hung on her every word, but Amanda felt herself pulling away, drifting from her friends, as she wondered why Rory and Lucas were really going on this trip without her.

Drew leaned close, putting his arm around Amanda's low back, and whispered, "I am glad you're coming with us."

"Really?"

His dark eyes pulled Amanda back into the moment.

When he lightly kissed the side of her neck, Amanda looked at the scuffed table and felt her cheeks flush. She wondered if Trey was watching and wished Drew wouldn't do that in public. But Drew's gentle smile chased away her embarrassment. She smiled with him, and just when she started to think it might not be so bad to miss her trip, Brooklyn's bright voice cut through her happiness.

"It would be so much easier if we were those time traveler people!"

Amanda's head swiveled to face the group. Drew's hand tensed against her back.

"They aren't time travelers," Nick corrected. "They travel to *places* not different *times*."

"That's not what I heard!" Brooklyn insisted. "I heard they can blink out of existence and show up anywhere else. Anywhere could be another time."

A cold prickling ran down Amanda's collarbones. The room felt too warm.

"Oh, please!" Trina rolled her eyes. "None of that's real."

"It is!" Nick argued hotly, his face taking on an earnest intensity. "My brother's friend's neighbor saw one disappear right in front of him! He was out walking his dog when this big guy stepped out of the shadows, grinned at him like a psychopath, and just—Poof! Disappeared."

A hush fell over the group. Amanda's throat was too dry to speak. She was half aware of Drew's hand stroking her back soothingly as her mind flashed through possibilities.

There had been rumors of some travelers—members of the Vertex, a group that wanted to go public with their abilities—pulling stunts like that lately. The High Council had even issued reminders for public discretion. Though this was the first time Amanda had heard about it outside of her psychic traveler world.

"*Trés drôle!*" Trina scoffed, breaking the silence. "Your brother's friend's neighbor? It's always a friend of a friend of a friend…"

"*Un ami de un ami de un ami…*" Brooklyn giggled.

"He did see it!" Nick insisted angrily. "And he's not the only one. It's all over the internet. Not just disappearing

either. Some of them have talked to people. They call themselves travelers…”

Amanda froze. She kept her face relatively calm but had
to force herself to take a strained breath. White noise spread
through her mind in a screaming panic.

“Oh, well then, if it’s on the internet!” Trina laughed
sarcastically and Brooklyn joined her, not caring that Nick’s
face was turning red.

“Okay, let’s take it easy…” Drew broke in, trying to
diffuse the conversation.

“Whatever!” Nick’s head shook from side to side in a
tight jitter. “You’ll see. They’ve been hiding among us for a
long time, but they aren’t going to keep hiding forever.”

“Who are *they*?” Amanda heard herself ask the question
and was surprised at how calm she sounded.

Nick paused to size her up, weighing whether she was
really interested or just wanted to mock him. Amanda willed
her expression to stay neutral, curious but not *too* interested.
Nick nodded once, satisfied with whatever he saw.

“Aliens,” he answered gravely. “The travelers are aliens.”

Chapter 2

Threats and Promises

"I'm well aware of the rumors, Amanda." Cameron sounded weary as he shuffled and arranged stacks of papers on his large wooden desk. "We talked about it over dinner just last week."

"I know, but this was at my school."

Cameron frowned at a stapled report with bright red sticky notes attached to its margins and hesitated before placing it on one of the larger piles. He looked strange behind a desk. Amanda was used to him being off-world, dressed as a knight in the purple-hued forests of Terra-V. He was a man of action, not of paperwork.

"I don't like it either." He sighed heavily.

"They're getting most of it wrong," Amanda offered, sorry to bring him more problems. "But some of them, like this guy named Nick, are really worked up about it."

Cameron reached for a pen and paper. "What's Nick's last name?"

"Kersey," Amanda answered hesitantly. "Why? You're not going to talk to him."

"No," Cameron agreed. "But we can quietly look into him. Make sure he isn't a threat."

"That sounds grim." Amanda tried to ease the moment, adding, "Isn't spying on kids more of an *old* High Council move?"

"It's my job to keep you safe." Cameron visibly stiffened, his jaw clenched and eyes flashing.

"I know that." Amanda held up both hands. "It was just a joke."

"Keeping you safe is not a joke." Cameron's voice shook slightly. "The Vertex is not a joke. We're facing some very real threats, and I need you to take this seriously."

He stopped talking and looked out the window.

They were at PTS headquarters in Chicago. Not long ago, Amanda had been intimidated by this building and by the High Council. She'd been intimidated by Cameron, too, though that was hard to remember now. Even when she was stung by his sharp reaction to her bad joke.

"I am taking this seriously," she reminded him. "I'm the one who came to you."

"I know," Cameron agreed, still looking out the window. The surrounding buildings against a blue sky created an impressive view.

"Well, okay, then." Amanda crossed her arms, waiting for Cameron to say more, though she was surprised by his next words.

"It's hard to keep my guard up around you."

"What do you mean?"

"We've been through a lot," he explained, facing Amanda with bittersweet eyes. "Terra-V, helping your mom, and… well, everything. It's hard not to be protective of you. But I do try to set that aside and treat you the same way I would treat any traveler coming to talk to me as a member of the High Council."

"Oh." Memories washed over Amanda. The sweet scent of pineapple hinted as she pictured Cameron dressed as a knight, riding his feathered horse by her side on the open road in Terra-V. "A little protective is okay. I mean, I'm not just any traveler and you're not just a High Council member. You're my… uh…"

She stopped talking. Their eyes met uncertainly.

"I don't know what to call you," she admitted. "My advisor? My teacher?"

She didn't add, *my mom's boyfriend?*

"Your friend?" Cameron suggested with a smile she knew well.

"Yeah, I guess." Amanda wanted to agree, but the word felt too small, and she didn't know how to express that without making the moment even weirder.

"Well." Cameron cleared his throat and neatened a stack of papers. "Beyond our personal relationship, it's still true you aren't just any traveler. You're on a path to be the next psychic architect, and that makes you a special case."

"Right." Amanda nodded.

"Someday, you'll have a seat on this council and responsibilities beyond any other traveler. Part of my job is to prepare you for that future, but I don't want to rush you. I'd like to keep you safe in the shadows until your training is complete and you're ready to step into that role. But I'm afraid this mess with the Vertex will threaten that."

"I get that," Amanda said carefully, appreciating his honesty. "And I know it's weird that my psychic abilities kicked in so early, instead of in my twenties like everyone else, but maybe there's a reason for that. They wouldn't have started if I wasn't ready to use them."

Cameron's gaze drifted back out the window.

"You feeling ready isn't the only issue," he said with a heavy sigh. "This society is a mess. Not just because we're restructuring after the coup but because it's a vastly complex, international organization that hasn't been overhauled in centuries.

"And that's further complicated by the corruption that shaped the last High Council. Corruption that goes back decades. Maybe even a century."

"You aren't responsible for that," Amanda reminded. Though they both knew he had supported the previous regime, not wanting to believe Lucas and his rebels' claims until he was forced to face the growing evidence.

"Thank you," Cameron smiled sadly. They also knew she had listened to Lucas before he did, which had helped him come around to the truth. "Either way, I'm responsible for fixing it now. Because we're the country with the last architect and the next one."

A subtle hum buzzed through the room, the copier outside Cameron's office churning out papers that would soon be added to his overflowing desk. It reminded Amanda that Cameron's time was in demand, and they wouldn't be left alone much longer.

"But that's good," she insisted, leaning forward intently. "I can help you so much more once I complete my training and become the official psychic architect."

The smile faded from Cameron's tired face, and she saw a wall go up. The professionalism he wanted to keep between them.

"I know you want to help—"

"Don't do that!" Amanda interrupted. "I'm not a child. You need all the help you can get, and my architect training is part of that."

A knock sounded on Cameron's door. Sitting tall, he crossed his hands in his lap and met Amanda's pleading eyes with steady honesty.

"I'm not treating you like a child. You may not want to hear this, but this society does not need a psychic architect right now."

Amanda pulled back as if he'd slapped her face.

"We will someday," he continued, "and when we do, your skills will be invaluable. But for now, we have more important matters to deal with than making connections to new worlds. Amanda, we can't keep up with the connections we already have."

The truth of his words sunk in like cold rain.

A second knock brought Cameron to his feet. He cracked the door just enough to request a few more minutes. Amanda heard the murmured conversation behind her but was too caught up in her own feelings to process what they were saying.

When Cameron returned, he stayed close to Amanda, leaning against the front edge of his desk.

"The Vertex is determined to pull us out of the shadows, and they're using the chaos of this change in power to push that agenda. Travelers who were once against them are now saying it might be better if the world knew about us. If we can't contain them—if we can't maintain the secrecy of this society—our entire world will never be the same."

Amanda nodded slowly. She'd heard Cameron and Lucas argue this topic and run through possible scenarios, both good and bad. But she had never considered how it might impact her training. Her role had always seemed too important to be pushed aside. Even the High Council's position in the United States depended on their country being home to a psychic architect.

"Wait!" Amanda held up one hand, the thoughts still whirling through her mind. "You do need me to complete my training. And soon!"

Cameron glanced toward his office door. He had other responsibilities, and she was losing his attention.

"The High Council is only set here because Edmund Robinson was American, and it will only stay here if the next architect is American. That's me! I need to finish my training before a traveler in another country discovers they have architect potential."

"Amanda." Cameron reached toward her, then thought better of it and clasped his hands in front of his legs. "There hasn't been a new psychic architect in nearly 100 years. In the very unlikely chance that another turned up now, only the High Council can authorize an architect to begin training. No other potential architect will replace you. And if they did…"

Amanda held her breath, watching Cameron's gaze drift to an empty space above her head.

"Well, maybe it would be better if some other country took over for a while."

$

Amanda's cell phone read 5:23 AM. The numbers were sideways since it was perched on a charging stand, and her head was still pressed into her pillow. She didn't want to be awake this early or need to be awake this early, but she was wide awake with no hope of falling back asleep.

Rory and Lucas would be leaving for Crystal Caverns soon. They might even be in the house already. She could picture them in the second-floor bedroom. The blue bedroom. One she'd always liked, even before she knew where its doors led.

As she lay in bed, half-asleep, Amanda imagined the room more clearly. A plush blue carpet stretched across the floor, its pink and white rose design picking up the delicate flowers on the pale blue walls. A canopy bed with blue and white linens filled most of the space, while an upholstered chair sat in one corner, and a beautifully carved armoire centered between two white doors. Across from the foot of the bed, a marble-framed fireplace gleamed between another set of doors.

Amanda had once opened the door to the left of the fireplace, knowing it led to the starting point of her trip with Rory and Lucas. No one saw her, and she never stepped through the door. But she'd been amazed by the sight of this underground world.

Officially, the world was named Li-ugn Xinh, an approximation of its native name, but Crystal Caverns was the name given by Edmund and it was easy to see why. From its door, beautiful caves stretched into shadows, lit at intervals by shafts of light filtering in through cracks in the planet's surface. The light sparkled as it reflected against massive crystals glowing pale blue, pink, and aqua.

Amanda's Off-World Geology class had taught her that the glow of the planet's crystal structures came from a phosphorescent reaction. Its science was well understood. Yet when she opened the door to the caverns, Amanda could only see a world of magical beauty.

Picturing it now, as she drowsed in bed, Amanda felt a sharp sting of disappointment. It wasn't fair that Rory and Lucas were going on this trip without her. She imagined them standing in the blue bedroom as they checked over their gear. They'd be dressed in black tactical clothes and boots, like Lucas had been wearing when Amanda first met him, and they'd have backpacks slung over their shoulders. Amanda could see Rory's hair braided neatly at the back of her head, not a strand out of place… though her collar was flipped up on one side where it had been shifted by the strap of her backpack…

Amanda stood in the blue bedroom, staring at the back of Rory's neck. Her feet were bare against the thick carpet. She wore an oversized t-shirt over plaid pajama bottoms.

Lucas smirked her way, his gleaming eyes sliding past Rory, and his head cocked to one side.

"Come to see us off?" he asked casually, while Amanda felt her face burn.

Rory's shoulders stiffened. Her head shook slightly before she turned to face Amanda's unexpected appearance. Her stoic expression hid whatever she was feeling.

"I, uh…" Amanda swallowed hard and raked a hand through her tousled hair. She looked at her bare feet and felt two sets of eyes taking in her rumpled pajamas.

"I had to tell you something." Amanda stood tall despite the cartoon cow grinning from her bright blue t-shirt. "Before you leave."

"Okay." Rory waited for the news Amanda hadn't made up yet. Lucas leaned back on his heels, his crooked smile showing the same amusement he found with everything in life. Even things like this, Amanda thought sourly. Things that weren't funny at all.

"They think we're aliens!"

Amanda's blurted words hung in the space between them. Rory frowned, and Lucas' smile froze, giving a nearly imperceptible sign that she'd gotten his attention. Amanda tried to seize the moment, stumbling blindly toward whatever had hit a nerve with him.

"My friends at school," she clarified. "They're spreading rumors about us. About travelers. They think we're aliens who can travel through time. Or, well, some of them think we can time travel. But not everyone…"

"And you needed to tell us this now?" Rory's expression softened as she narrowed in on Amanda's tense face.

"Yes, because I…" Amanda paused, thinking wildly. "Because I'm going to Trina's play this weekend, and it will probably come up again. Cameron said to ignore it and let him handle it, but…"

"Amanda," Lucas interrupted softly. "What do you need from us?"

His calm intensity let Amanda's muddled pretenses and confused worries fall away. Despite her anger at being left out, Amanda trusted Lucas. The truth she'd been struggling to see bubbled up effortlessly.

"I need to be ready."

He nodded in instant understanding, and Amanda felt an invisible cage release its pressure on her heart.

Rory needed to hear more.

"Ready for what?" She stepped closer to Amanda. "What do you think is going to happen?"

Amanda put both hands to her forehead, trying to marshal her thoughts. The worry was clear in her mind, but she didn't know if it would make sense to Rory.

"I need to be ready for my friends—for the whole world—to find out about us. About psychic travelers." Her words sped up, tumbling out as quickly as they came up. "When everyone knows, I can't be the girl who may or may not be the next psychic architect. I need it to be settled. Everyone needs to know... No, *I* need to know who I am and where I stand."

Rory nodded. Amanda didn't know if it was agreement or comprehension. A trembling weakness fluttered through her stomach.

"We know this is important to you," Rory said carefully, shifting to make space for Lucas beside her. "It's important to us, too, and we want you to succeed. We also know that things are changing in the society... and we don't know where that change will lead."

Lucas had resumed his sardonic slouch. He raised an eyebrow at Amanda, silently asking a question she didn't understand. Rory transitioned into a familiar speech.

"It doesn't help to worry about things that haven't happened yet. I know you want to be prepared. I'm the same way. But there's value in knowing where to focus your energy and what to leave to other people. Right?"

She pivoted to include Lucas, giving him space to back her up. Instead, Lucas shot her an apologetic smile and shrugged with his hands raised.

"I'm not good at the party line," he laughed, making Rory's lips press into a white line.

"It's okay." Amanda jumped in before an argument could break out. "I'm just tired."

As soon as she said the words, she felt the exhaustion in her body. It had been a tense week, and she'd been plagued by bad dreams for days.

Turning her back on Lucas, Rory rubbed Amanda's arm sympathetically.

"I do get it," she said softly, lowering her voice so Lucas wouldn't hear. "You want to take on everything. But sometimes you need to rest and not take on the weight of the world, right?"

Amanda nodded and apologized for bothering them.

"You aren't a bother," Rory insisted, sounding more like an older sister than a training agent. "But you should go back to bed. Get some sleep before school."

Though Amanda agreed, she was looking past Rory to the spot where Lucas leaned against the fireplace with one arm across his waist and his other hand cradling his chin.

He was clearly amused again, though the topic felt entirely serious to her. In a flash of insight, Amanda wondered if maybe Lucas appeared the most amused when he wasn't amused at all.

§

They were halfway through the last play of the afternoon performance. It was a play-within-a-play, a comedy, where everything was falling apart on opening night. Trina had just taken the stage, rushing in as the disheveled make-up artist wielding an oversized powder puff. She was chasing the star of the show, who had shown up late after a series of slapstick mishaps, and the audience was in hysterics.

Amanda was proud of Trina's comedic talent and loved sitting with Drew and a group of their classmates. It was her first high school play, and she was surprised to find the theater packed with students, parents, and even some senior citizens bused in from their retirement community.

Trina lifted her arm, powder puff poised to attack, when she froze mid-sentence. Something off-stage had caught her attention. Amanda sat up, alert, as three men walked somberly onto the center of the stage. They were dressed in black with their pants tucked into combat boots and an identical V-shaped tattoo on their upper arms.

The actors stepped aside uncertainly. The audience waited, thinking it was part of the show. Amanda stood shakily, locking eyes with the man in the center. Without saying a word, all three men vanished into thin air.

Chapter 3

Moving Forward

The High Council held Amanda's briefing in their private conference room instead of their formal chambers. It was the same meeting room where Amanda had met the previous High Council when her psychic abilities were discovered. Though the atmosphere had changed with the new council members.

Instead of facing Amanda from across the table in one line, the seven council members were seated around its rectangular sides, allowing space for Amanda, Rory, and Lucas to join them. The latter two had cut their trip short at the news of the Vertex's latest demonstration. Cameron sat across from Amanda, next to the current council chair, Lenora Nagy.

"Have we identified the demonstrators?" Cameron sounded tired. He had been pushing for answers since Amanda messaged from the school auditorium.

"Damian Stringer, Syd Warrick, Kip Manco."

Lucas indicated the photos his assistant was passing around the table.

"Several parents were recording the play."

Amanda glanced at the photos. Their faces were still burned into her mind, along with the panic that had followed their disappearance. Everyone had begun talking at once. Some ran out of the auditorium, others ducked for cover or clutched together in fear. Trina had stood like a statue under the stage lights, her face pale under her heavy makeup.

The Vertex had staged this stunt at her school. In front of her friends, with her in the audience. It didn't feel like a coincidence.

"We've seen the videos," Lenora responded tightly.

All of the council members turned to Amanda. Rory pressed her lips together and dropped her eyes to the table. Lucas exhaled slowly, his eyes drifting to the ceiling.

"What?" Amanda met their stares defensively. "What's in the videos?"

Cameron cleared his throat and glanced toward a monitor mounted on the wall.

"You stood up," he told her carefully. "Before anyone else. Before they disappeared."

Looking around the table, Amanda saw various shades of discomfort and concern.

Patty's angry voice burst through the silence. "They did this at her school!"

All eyes shifted to the wall-mounted monitor. Patty and Judy sat side-by-side in their apartment back in Virginia. The council members often used video conferencing with government officials who did not have psychic travel abilities. Yet not all of them were comfortable with Patty's insisted presence in this meeting.

"We are aware of that," Lenora agreed.

"But what are you doing about it?" Patty demanded, clearly agitated as Judy sought to quiet her with murmured words and soothing hands.

"We'll get to that," Cameron interjected, drawing a frown from Lenora.

"Get to what?" Amanda tried to sound calm. "Why does it matter if I stood up?"

"You recognized them," Rory answered softly. "You knew who they were before they disappeared."

"Well, yeah," Amanda's face prickled. "They had the Vertex tattoo… but who cares if I stood up? That doesn't prove anything?"

"It stood out."

Amanda recognized Rory's flat tone. It meant, *don't fight me on this. We'll talk about it in private.*

Lucas tapped a photo and said, "This was a warning."

He leaned back in his chair, drumming his fingers on the table from his relaxed slouch.

"They know where Amanda goes to school. They want us to know they have no problem exposing her." He ignored Patty's strained gasp and slowly sat upright, turning his head to face Amanda. "This isn't the last you'll see of them."

Hurried conversation broke out across the table. Amanda heard overlapping snippets.

"We can relocate her… Arcadia… But her mother… No one believes them… It's only a matter of time…"

"Enough!" Lenora broke through the din and closed her eyes. She couldn't have been more different than her predecessor, but she understood the importance of keeping order in the council. When she opened her eyes, she narrowed in on Amanda.

"What do your school friends think of the Vertex?"

Amanda shifted in her seat.

"They think they're aliens."

"Aliens?"

A subdued murmur spread around the room.

"Aliens," Amanda repeated. "Like, from another planet."

Lenora nodded with pursed lips.

"It's one of the leading rumors we've heard," one of the members volunteered while sifting through some papers in an open file.

"Heard or started?" Lenora asked dryly, but another member was quick to correct her.

"That's not one of ours. We put out stories of performance artists, internet pranksters, and bad actors from enemy countries. Nothing about aliens."

"And contaminated drinking water," Lucas reminded, settling into his slouch. "You spread the idea that normals who saw travelers disappear were suffering the effects of contaminated drinking water."

"Well, yes, in one particular case…"

"Enough!" Lenora called for silence with raised hands. "Have these demonstrators been detained?"

Lucas let his eyes go out of focus as he listened to a message in his mind. "We have Warrick and Manco. Agents are in pursuit of Stringer."

Amanda saw disgust in his tense jaw. It hadn't been long since Lucas was the one being pursued by the previous High Council. A council that had selectively captured travelers, using drugs to thwart their ability to psychically escape. She had been held briefly and still had nightmares about waking up in that drug-induced fog.

"We also have the Disclosure Protocol."

Lucas' quiet words filled the room. No one spoke or moved until Lenora folded her hands and answered Lucas in a clipped tone.

"This isn't the time for that."

"This meeting or this point in time?" Lucas shot back, sliding a set of pictures forward. As the rest of the council looked between them, many seemed to agree with Lucas' suggestion. Their restraint to speak was palpable.

Lenora kept her eyes on Lucas, despite directing her words to Amanda.

"Thank you for meeting with us, Amanda. The details you provided were helpful." Her attention shifted to the monitor on the wall, including Patty as she continued. "We are aware of your concerns and are carefully monitoring the situation. For now, you will continue at school as usual, hiding any knowledge of psychic travel or who was behind the event at your school play."

"That's it?" Patty questioned from her glass screen. "What if this Vertex group goes after Amanda? Lucas said they are a threat!"

"Would you prefer we remove Amanda from your home?" Lenora asked coldly. "Dr. Webb would be happy to have her live in Arcadia while we sort this out."

Patty gaped at the council as Judy gripped her hand. Amanda didn't know if she was more shocked by Lenora's callous tone or her suggestion. *Live in Arcadia?*

Turning from the monitor, Lenora spoke more gently. "Go home, Amanda. We'll be in touch soon."

§

"You are *not* going to live in Arcadia." Drew sat on a couch in the party room. His forearms pressed against his upper legs and a shake of his head emphasized his words.

"No, I'm not." Amanda perched beside him with her legs hugged to her chest and her toes hanging over the seat cushion.

It had been nearly three weeks since her meeting with the High Council. The local news had called the Vertex stunt a prank, like other events that had happened around the country. The story briefly hit the national news but faded as days passed without another report of mysterious people disappearing into thin air.

When Amanda pushed, Rory had explained that the Disclosure Protocol was rumored to be a top-secret plan for admitting the existence of the Psychic Traveler Society. But she didn't know anything else about it. "Above my pay grade," she had joked, then told Amanda not to worry because no one was in a rush to open that door.

But Amanda knew that wasn't true. The Vertex wanted to come clean, and online discussions on secret PTS sites showed a lot of other travelers were thinking about it, too. Amanda wanted to rehash those debates with Drew, but he was fixated on the idea that the Vertex might be targeting her as part of their plan.

"They wouldn't hurt me," she insisted. "They just wanted to make a point with the High Council."

"By threatening to do what? Expose you as a traveler? What would that even mean to people?"

Amanda couldn't meet Drew's eyes. The idea of being exposed as a traveler already kept her up at night.

"They haven't been in the news in weeks," she reminded. "Lucas is working with them, negotiating some kind of deal, and he's good at that kind of thing."

Drew still hunched forward with his arms on his thighs. Amanda matched his position and nudged his shoulder.

"I'm not going to live in Arcadia."

Drew nodded thoughtfully.

"Yeah, well… I can see why you'd want to."

"Want to what?" Amanda searched his face for signs of being serious. "You think I want to live in Arcadia?"

"Maybe." Drew's leg shook with a nervous jitter. "It's all futuristic there. Cool buildings, smart people, actual aliens visiting the city."

Amanda didn't know what to say. Arcadia was a cool city to visit, but there was no reason to live there when she could visit any time she wanted. That was hard to say though, knowing how desperately Drew wanted to visit Arcadia. Or Terra-V. Or any of the worlds Amanda could now explore without him.

"Besides," Drew added bitterly, "Martin is there to keep you company."

"Mitra," Amanda corrected with annoyance.

"Whatever." Drew shrugged and his leg bounced more rapidly, but Amanda refused to take the bait. She didn't want to defend her friendship with Mitra again.

Instead, she put her hand on his shaking knee and said, "I don't want to live in Arcadia."

Drew smiled sheepishly.

"Because you'd rather be here… with me?"

His hopeful smile brought a flush to Amanda's cheeks.

"Maybe." Her eyes flitted away, but Drew ducked his head to catch her gaze.

"Only maybe?" he teased, and Amanda laughed.

"Partly," she admitted with a smile. "Here with you, and Trina, and my mom, and my aunt Judy…"

"But mostly me," Drew insisted, laughing as he leaned in for a kiss.

"Partly you," Amanda laughed, kissing him back until Judy's voice startled them both.

"Oh, sorry!"

Amanda lurched away from Drew, self-consciously wiping one hand over her mouth. Drew eyed her sharply, then settled into a mask of calm.

Judy waved away any embarrassment, sat on a chair beside them, and rested her clasped hands on her lap.

"The council made a decision. They want to move forward with the architect's journey."

The room fell away as Amanda processed her aunt's words. She was going to Crystal Caverns. She would prove herself as the next psychic architect.

Drew's fingers wove between Amanda's as he lightly squeezed her hand.

"But there's more," Judy added. Her smile faded into a grim line, draining Amanda's joy. The last time she'd seen that expression was when one of her favorite mentors had suffered a stroke.

"What? Is it Gerald?"

"Oh, no!" Judy reassured. "Nothing like that! No one is sick or hurt. It's just…" She examined her hands before going on. "You know that my job is to bring new travelers into the society. Help them learn the ropes…"

She trailed off, but she'd said enough.

"You're leaving." Amanda could barely speak over the lump in her throat.

"It's time." Judy nodded sadly.

As she looked away, Amanda's eyes settled on the blue streaks in her aunt's dark hair. Judy had always been the cool aunt with her piercings and tattoos, vintage rock tees, and sly confidence. Amanda had looked up to her long before learning about psychic travel. After living together for a year, she couldn't imagine not seeing Judy every day.

"You know the basics," Judy reminded. "And a lot more than that. You have Rory, Cameron, and Lucas, your mom. You've moved beyond me, and there are others who do need my help."

Drew squeezed Amanda's hand again, this time in sympathy before asking, "Where are you going next?"

Judy brightened at the question.

"Phoenix. There's a young man there, early twenties, who recently showed up in one of the houses. I've met him already. He's smart and kind, and terrified by all of this." She waved her arms wide to indicate the whole psychic traveler world. "And this is a particularly hard time to be coming into these abilities."

"Yeah, it is a hard time." Amanda sat up straighter and dropped Drew's hand. "It's a really hard time, actually, and..." She stopped herself when she saw the concern on Judy's face.

As much as she wanted to keep her aunt close, she couldn't bring herself to play up her own risk. Even with the threat of the Vertex and the uncertainty of her new journey, she had enough people in her corner.

"And that new guy is lucky to have you." Amanda's voice broke and Judy leaned forward to hold her hands.

"It won't be that bad," she promised. "I might not live with you for a while, but we're travelers. We can meet in the mindspace in an instant."

She snapped her fingers and Amanda smiled bravely.

"Yeah, that's true," she agreed. Though she knew it wouldn't be the same.

§

Alone in her room that night, Amanda toyed with the idea of living in Arcadia. She'd spent a lot of time there over the last year, working with Mitra and exploring the city. Arcadia was unlike other worlds she'd visited because it had been settled by human travelers who had cut ties with Earth centuries earlier.

From what she'd learned, an architect had discovered the uninhabited world in the 13th century, and a group of well-educated travelers from many countries had moved there to escape the violence of the Crusades and other medieval atrocities. They somehow found a way to sever their proximal door connection, keeping other travelers from following, and no one heard from them again. Until hundreds of years later when Edmund created a new door to their world.

By that time, Arcadian society was well established and psychic travel had faded into an origin story that few believed. Their modern society revolved around science and technology. They'd achieved space travel and established alliances with aliens on neighboring planets.

Settling into her pillows, Amanda remembered her earliest visits to Arcadia. It was after she'd fulfilled the Vherahna's prophecy in Terra-V and proven her architect potential by accidentally creating a new door between their worlds. She'd been assigned to work with Arcadian scientists, particularly Mitra, who was a prodigy like herself.

Despite his age, Mitra ran his lab with confidence. Older scientists deferred to his expertise, and he took their respect in stride, showing no concerns about being the only teenager in their ranks. Amanda wished she could feel that confident as the only teenager with psychic travel abilities. Instead, she always seemed to be second-guessing herself or saying something stupid when she was in a group of important travelers.

It was his confidence she admired, Amanda told herself, picturing Mitra's piercing blue eyes and self-assured smile. She often felt awestruck by his casual genius, her stomach fluttering and face tingling as he explained the science behind Arcadian technology. But she also felt comfortable around him now that their friendship had deepened.

Mitra was the one who had finally told Amanda the truth: In the years since Edmund had reconnected their worlds, Arcadians had tried to reawaken their dormant psychic traveler genes. They'd accessed a mindspace, but it was separated from the one used by psychic travelers on Earth. There were no houses or doors in their mindspace, only an endless void where they could psychically meet but do nothing else. They hoped Amanda's emerging architect abilities could help them.

Late one night, during the height of the PTS rebellion, Lucas had brought Amanda to Arcadia in a desperate attempt to connect their two mindspaces. She had stood in a dark field, with Mitra by her side, trying to recreate the powerful energy she'd used when accidentally making her new door to Terra-V. Rory had intervened, thwarting the misguided attempt, and Amanda was now embarrassed by what a foolish stunt it had been.

Yet her relationship with the Arcadians had continued with hopes of someday helping them regain their psychic travel abilities. If she lived there, she could focus on that more fully. She could work with Mitra every day instead of once a week.

Amanda curled under her covers and imagined Mitra surprising her at home with breakfast from his favorite café. She'd ask him in, and he'd laugh at her tangled bedhead and rumpled pajamas. There was something warm and cozy about the idea of him seeing her in her pajamas, fresh from a night of sleep in her own Arcadian apartment.

Like a scene from a movie, Amanda imagined telling him it was too early to be awake. Mitra would flash her a crooked smile and suggest they eat breakfast in bed with the sunrise shining through the glass walls and birdsong greeting the day.

As her fantasy took shape, Amanda could picture them in a huge bed made up with crisp white linens and a matching duvet. It was just breakfast with a friend, she told herself, but as she imagined the cozy scene, she felt her heart racing and her belly melting.

Amanda sat upright in bed.

Her daydream shattered with images of Rory bursting in on them. Of course, Rory would be there. Amanda would never be sent to live in Arcadia all alone. And Rory would look at her with disgust saying, *"What are you doing? What about Drew?"*

Confused by the direction of her thoughts, Amanda told herself it wasn't a fantasy about Mitra at all. She simply liked the idea of being on her own. Being an adult without everyone telling her what to do. Mitra had been swept up in that because he lived in Arcadia, and Drew didn't. In real life, it would be Drew bringing her breakfast. Drew leaning close to make her skin twitch.

She turned out her light and pulled the covers over her head, hoping for a dreamless sleep.

CHAPTER 4
CRYSTAL CAVERNS

Pink, blue, and aqua light spilled across Rory's features and added a pastel shimmer to the whites of her eyes. Amanda glanced frequently at her as they walked, wishing she could see how her own face looked in the pale glow of the immense cave.

They had entered Crystal Caverns and were now being led toward a large settlement by their anthropologist guide, Amit Singh, and their interpreter, Victor Frye. Both travelers had spent several years working in this world, though they had different feelings about their assignments.

"Don't expect too much from the Ooliani," Victor said as they headed into a narrow passageway. All around them, the walls glittered with embedded crystals. A faint, high-pitched hum echoed off the stone, growing louder as they continued forward.

No one responded to Victor's unsolicited advice, but that didn't discourage him.

"Everyone likes to personify them. It's like when Goodall saw those chimps using sticks to eat ants and tried to call them human."

Amit clenched his teeth to avoid an argument.

"See, when an animal does some simple thing, it's easy for us to read into it. That's a weakness we have as humans. We're always assuming everything is like us, and no one wants to admit the cold fact that not all animals qualify as intelligent life."

"You think the Ooliani are animals?" Amanda asked, once it was clear no one else was going to challenge him.

"We're all animals, kiddo. But personifying an animal doesn't make it our equal."

Amanda frowned.

"Doesn't *personify* only apply to non-living things? Not animals?"

Amit let out a sharp laugh.

"She's got you there, Vic."

"Fine, anthropomorphize." Victor waved off Amanda's correction. "You know what I meant."

"And you're a linguist, too," Amit continued, adding a low whistle. "Aren't you supposed to be good with the words?"

"There's not much for a linguist to do here," Victor complained. "The Ooliani barely have a language to study. They know a few of our words, we know a few of theirs. If they're even saying what we think they are. It's like apes and sign language."

"Enough," Rory warned before Amit could challenge that point. "We're almost there."

They were silent for several paces with only the hum of the caves growing louder. Then Victor said, "Just don't get your hopes up. Edmund had some wild claims about a connection with the Ooliani, but I say he just had a good imagination."

"What does that mean?" Amanda asked, risking Rory's annoyance.

"Well, for one thing, old Edmund claimed the Ooliani told him things no one else ever heard them say. Claimed the Pyura Elder talked to him, too."

Rory stopped walking so abruptly that Amit nearly ran into her. She stepped close to Victor and stared him down, saying, "You aren't here to give your opinion. You're here to interpret. That's all."

Victor took a half-step back and needlessly straightened his shirt.

"Fine, I won't make conversation."

"Good." Rory resumed her steady stride.

Amanda wasn't used to having an assigned PTS interpreter during an off-world visit. In Terra-V, many Vherahna and Churukh people spoke English, and travelers who lived there knew enough Churukh to get by. In Arcadia, translator technology interpreted for everyone. Amanda wondered if Arcadian technology would work with the Ooliani and whether that would put Victor out of a job.

Their visit to Crystal Caverns hinged on some diary entries a researcher had found while looking into Edmund's architect's journey. It was one of Edmund's favorite worlds, though most travelers hadn't seen much appeal beyond the beauty of the caves.

From what they could tell, cave systems covered most of the known world. Above ground, there were windswept plains and pockets of fire-ravaged forests, as well as a large sea with a rocky coast. Some scientists theorized that the upper planet had once been more like Earth until an extreme event devastated the environment.

The Ooliani lived in the caves and only ventured above ground when it was safe to hunt and fish. Ooliani priests also made pilgrimages to seek an entity known as the Pyura Elder. The same entity Edmund mentioned in his diaries, leading the High Council to hope for a connection to the architect's journey.

After several minutes, a bend in the cave opened onto a stone overlook high above a sprawling underground village. Incredibly tall columns of phosphorescent crystal reached from the dirt floor to the ceiling of the immense cavern, making contact between thousands of narrow stalactites that glittered in shafts of light from cracks in the rock above. The vast area between the columns appeared to be neatly sectioned, though it was hard to make out the details.

Squinting, Amanda watched Ooliani tribe members move around the cave floor or climb steep stairs to reach passageways set at regular levels along the rock walls. She was so intent on peering at the people below, she jumped when an Ooliani party crested the stairs beside them.

The Ooliani had a humanoid appearance but with a short stature and nearly translucent skin. Their wide pupils stared through the dim light, rimmed by a thin glow of pastel green. Each wore a small cluster of shining crystals on a leather cord around their neck. Crystals were sewn to bands around their wrists and ankles and even woven through their pale hair.

Before her PTS briefing, Amanda had imagined the underground world would be chilly, like the caverns she'd visited in the Blue Ridge Mountains. Instead, warm air currents rose through fine cracks in the stone floor, just as light seeped in from above.

In her black tank top, canvas pants, and boots, Amanda felt overdressed beside the Ooliani's bare feet and ragged cotton shifts.

Amit stepped forward and said, "Hey, Laum," to the Ooliani at the center of the group. He nodded to the others in turn, saying their names: Nayum, Shrium, Mayam, and Ch'tai. Victor followed suit, though his words were cold and clipped. He made no effort to introduce Amanda, but Laum quickly turned their wide eyes on her and spoke in a short series of soft, echoing sounds.

Sighing, Victor said, "Slower, please."

Amanda listened with interest as Laum repeated their message. She knew the Ooliani lived in tribes throughout the Crystal Caverns and had no outward gender roles. There were biological differences for procreation, but Amanda had been told that was beyond the scope of her mission.

"They want to know why we brought a child," Victor relayed, after a brief exchange. Watching Laum's expression, Amanda guessed Victor hadn't gotten that right.

"Explain that Amanda is Edmund's successor," Rory replied with a hint of irritation.

Victor stumbled through a series of sounds. Amanda heard her own name just as she and Laum locked eyes.

Though she couldn't explain it, Amanda felt a whispering sensation as she studied Laum's bottomless pupils. The hum of the cave closed in, echoing inside her skull.

"Edmund, Aman," Laum said slowly.

"AmanDA," Victor corrected, putting more stress on the last syllable of her name.

"It's okay," Amanda cut in. "Aman is fine. It's not like Laum is their real name." She added the last sentence without thought but knew it was true.

"Their real names are too hard to pronounce," Victor said dismissively.

"So is Amanda," Rory shot back. "For them."

Amanda tuned out their bickering and smiled at Laum. There was a message in their eyes. Amanda understood that the Ooliani tolerated their human visitors because they were interesting. Simple-minded but unthreatening.

"You think we're the simple ones?" Amanda asked, feeling that part of the message very clearly.

Laum nodded once and said, "Small words."

Amanda laughed, even more aware of the high-pitched hum echoing from the surrounding crystals. There was something in the hum, a vibrational quality that reminded her of the tuntum trees on Terra-V.

"You don't use words," she said haltingly. That didn't sound right to her. She'd heard them speak to each other in strings of sounds that seemed to be words, but she could sense that those sounds were linked to another energy. Something that carried more complex messages.

"Edmund, Aman," Laum repeated with a firm nod. The other Ooliani nodded in unison.

Rory watched the exchange intently.

"We should get on with this," Amit suggested, noting the anger spreading across Victor's face. He then rubbed his hands together nervously, and the Ooliani flinched, muttering lightly.

"They don't like that," Amanda told him.

"Oh, sorry!" Amit lifted both hands, palm up, then dropped them self-consciously.

"Now you speak Ooliani?" Victor asked sarcastically before turning to Rory. "Are you serious with this?"

Laum frowned heavily.

Amit glanced from them to Victor and muttered that he should let it go.

"Let what go?" Victor turned on Amit. "Pretend that I don't see what's happening here?"

Rory tried to quiet Victor, but he shook off her hand.

"Not all of us are on board with this new society of yours. You and Lucas Flynn. Cameron Minett. Overthrowing the council, working with the Vertex. Now you're setting this girl up to be the next coming. Edmund's successor! And you expect us all to just fall in line."

Rory held her ground inches from Victor's red face. Her nostrils flared and her hands tensed by her sides. Yet her voice was calm as she said, "Go home, Victor."

Amanda forced herself to breathe.

Amit opened his mouth to speak, but Victor didn't give him a chance. He threw one hand in the air, spun on his heel, and thundered down the dark passage.

"Should I go after him?" Amit asked, but Rory shook her head, adding, "You can translate well enough."

Though Amit paled at her suggestion, the Ooliani seemed relieved to see Victor leave.

"I'm sorry for his behavior," Rory told them. "Do you understand why we're here?"

Amit tried to translate her words. Laum looked past him, studying Amanda intently.

"I don't speak your language," Amanda apologized.

Rory encouraged her to try, and a cold sweat broke out across Amanda's upper lip and collarbones. The heat rising from the cavern floor seemed to swirl around her body like steam from a bowl of soup.

Though she didn't know a single word of Ooliani, Amanda gathered her hopes and expectations for this mission. She thought of Edmund's diary entries and willed Laum to understand how important it was for her to find whatever message Edmund may have left for her here.

A moment later, Laum faced Rory and said, "Seek Elder. Elder talk Aman."

"It's true." Amit's whispered words floated past Amanda, landing with a certainty she couldn't explain. Stories of Edmund's friendship with the Ooliani were true. She could feel it in her bones. They were in the right place. She would find the Pyura Elder and receive Edmund's message. Her architect's journey was about to begin.

§

The wind-swept plains were a shock after the warmth of the caverns. Amanda zipped her quilted jacket higher on her neck, scanning the hard-packed ground ahead of her and the rocky shore off to their right.

Occasional gusts of winds blew across the plains and out to sea, bringing a stinging cold to their faces and hands. Turning back toward the caverns, Amanda saw a rocky hill that spread for miles, gradually increasing in height until it reached a far-off ring of mountains. Thick clouds made it hard to see how high the mountains stood, but they seemed impossibly tall compared to the flat plains near the sea.

The open area around the cave entrance showed no signs of life. The ground was free of grass and the bushes close to the rocky hill were dry and brown. Yet Amanda had learned in her mission briefing that nuts and berries could be harvested from deep within those seemingly dead bushes. The sea also was a source of food with seaweed and small fish.

In the far distance, Amanda could just make out the edge of the barren forest where they would search for the Pyura Elder. She paused at that idea, struck by the wonder of standing on an alien planet, and in awe of the marvels that filled the life of a traveler.

The Pyura Elder was an entity beyond her imagination, though its youngest form was remarkably similar to a sea creature found on the coast of Chile and Peru.

Like Pyura chilensis on Earth, the Pyura in this world were filter feeders, living off smaller organisms in the sea. From the outside, they looked like rocks. Inside, they held fleshy organisms that could be considered a delicacy. Early travelers named them for these similarities.

Yet, unlike their Earthly counterparts, these Pyura would slowly evolve into creatures that could scuttle from the coast and make their way into the distant forest.

Pyura that survived their journey could continue to evolve, eventually growing a more upright form to walk among the fire-ravaged trees. Edmund's diaries said that worthy Ooliani priests could communicate with the Pyura Elder and that he had also been given that gift.

Gazing at the coast, Amanda shivered in expectation. Her encounter with the Ooliani had been encouraging, though the memory of Victor's disbelief cast doubt on the connection she'd felt.

"But where do you stand?"

Amanda shook off her worries, realizing that Rory had begun questioning Amit about his political position.

"Honestly?" Amit shrugged. "I spend most of my time off-world. Here, typically. It takes a long time for changes that high up to trickle down to a backwater like this."

"Meaning?" Rory pressed.

"Meaning I stay out of the politics. As long as I can do my work, and publish my findings, I don't exactly care who's on the High Council or sitting in the Director's office. Now, change up the head of the PTS Off-World Anthropology Department and you'd get my attention!"

Rory wasn't satisfied with that answer, but she let it go, saying they needed to get moving.

As they walked, Amit shared his knowledge of the Pyura Elder.

"Very few Pyura make it to the elder stage, from what we can tell. But they wander the forest alone, and it's nearly impossible to tell them apart."

"What are they like?" Amanda asked, uneasily scanning the rocky coastline.

"Well, it's hard to say. I've explored the forest several times and have only seen two elders. Or the same one twice. There's something hypnotic about them. They just sort of stand there, swaying, but moving so slowly you barely notice. Until you realize they've gradually backed away while you were caught up in staring. Makes studying them a challenge."

"I'd like to see the Pyura," Amanda said. "Along the coast, I mean."

"Once we get closer to the trees," Rory agreed. "We'll need to refill our water before entering the forest."

As they neared the coast, Amanda heard a faint hum rising from the water. Its high pitch reminded her of the tone she'd heard in the caverns.

Rory's eyes swept the shoreline, picking up on Amanda's agitation.

"What is it?"

"It's that hum. Doesn't it remind you of the sound in the caves?"

Rory and Amit exchanged a look of confusion.

"You don't hear it? It's really faint but almost the same as the hum underground. You know, that vibrating sound that was louder near the Ooliani village?"

As Amanda spoke, it became clear that neither Rory nor Amit knew what she was talking about. She thought of the silent communication between the Vherahna and the tuntum trees, wondering if the tone in the cave was related to the messages she'd picked up from Laum.

"Fascinating," Amit whispered, seeming to make the same connection.

"Ooliani priests communicate with the Pyura Elder," Rory offered tentatively. "It could be a… vibrational form of telepathy."

"It wouldn't be the first case we've seen off-world," Amit agreed. "Though it's strange that Amanda can hear it when no other travelers have had that experience with the Ooliani or any Pyura. Except maybe for…"

"Edmund," Rory finished his sentence with a gleam of understanding in her eyes.

Amanda studied the rocky shore and considered the possibility. If Edmund's psychic architect abilities let him communicate with the Ooliani and Pyura Elder in a way no other travelers could, that might explain why he'd leave a message for the next architect with them.

They continued to the water's edge where various sized rocks filled in most of the shore.

"Be careful where you step," Amit warned. "The Pyura are nearly identical to actual rocks and stepping on them firmly will crack their outer shells."

He crouched near a group of rocks sitting in the shallow tide and gently lifted one for Amanda and Rory to see.

"If you take a close look, there are markings here and here that give the Pyura away. Turning it over, you can also see these ridges that draw water in, kind of like gills."

He flipped the rock-like creature onto its back and the dull hum that only Amanda could hear screeched to a distressed whine. She waved her arms, gesturing for Amit to stop.

"They don't like that!" Her voice shook as she put a hand to her heart and told him to put the Pyura down.

"Okay! Okay!" Amit paled as he quickly resettled the creature in the shallow water. Rory studied Amanda with concern.

"Are you okay?"

"Yeah, I'm fine." Amanda brushed off the question, feeling her sudden pang of anxiety fade away. "It was just… They… I don't know how to explain it. There wasn't a message, like with Laum, but I could feel their fear."

Rory patted her arm reassuringly, looking out at the long stretch of Pyura mixed in with the rocks. A wave splashed over their boots, and Rory led Amanda to drier land. Amit followed, eager to set the record straight.

"I didn't mean to hurt them."

"I know," Amanda told him, still a little unnerved by the experience.

"You said you could feel their fear." Amit peered at Amanda's pale face intently. "Did you mean the fear of the one I was holding or more of them?"

"All of them," Amanda answered dully, before turning her back on the incoming tide. "Can we just get the water and go?"

Rory and Amit pulled out their special filtration bottles and crouched to fill them, being careful of the surrounding Pyura. Amanda distanced herself from the sea, looking toward the barren forest that now loomed about 100 yards away. She couldn't tell if the murmuring behind her back was the hum of the Pyura or a whispered conversation between Amit and Rory. Either way, she blocked it out.

Nearing the forest, its damage was striking. Towering trees were charred black. Brittle, broken limbs dangled and fell to the littered ground. Brush and fallen logs showed no sign of life. Yet like the bushes near the cave entrance, the forest contained hidden sprigs of plants gradually growing under the seared debris.

Ooliani hunters knew how to scavenge for nuts and berries, but to Amanda, the damaged forest only darkened the sadness she'd felt since hearing the Pyura cry out in fear. She was glad their hum had faded by the time they reached the forest. Amit, however, thought her ability to hear Pyura could make tracking an elder much easier.

"I've wandered the forest for days before coming across an elder. If you can hear them from a distance, that will give us a definite edge."

"Or it will sense me and keep its distance," Amanda countered, wiping away Amit's eager smile.

When they were sufficiently deep in the forest, Amit suggested they settle in for a rest break. They found a small clearing where they could sit on some fallen logs. Amit slipped away for a nature break, and Rory began unpacking a few meal kits.

"How are you doing with all of this?" Rory asked, without looking up from her task.

"I'm okay." It was only partially true, but Rory wasn't one to push, and Amanda appreciated that.

"You'll have a lot to tell Drew when we get back," Rory offered, pretending not to notice when Amanda stayed quiet. She sat beside Amanda on one of the logs.

"I don't know," Amanda began slowly, and Rory waited. "Drew is kind of upset about that thing where the council said maybe I should move to Arcadia for a while."

"Ah." Rory studied the back of a meal pack as if she hadn't read it a hundred times before.

"I told him that is not going to happen," Amanda continued. "But he thinks I would want to move to Arcadia. Because it's better than our world. He thinks everywhere I travel must be amazing."

"And you don't want to tell him about another amazing place?" Rory asked. "You don't want him to be jealous?"

Amanda sighed, then shifted uncomfortably at Rory's choice of words.

"He's not crazy about Mitra either."

Rory nodded, knowing she was in delicate territory.

"There's no reason for him to be jealous," Amanda said quickly. "Of anything."

"Or of anyone?" Rory prodded after Amanda went quiet again.

"Yeah." Amanda nodded. "I mean, Drew and I are dating and I'm not going to, like, cheat on him or anything. And he should know that."

"He does," Rory said plainly. Then added, "Mostly."

Amanda frowned and picked up a meal packet from Rory's open bag.

"Look," Rory told her. "Drew trusts you, but he's afraid he won't live up to your off-world excitement. Mitra is mixed up in all of that."

"I get that!" Amanda put down the packet. "But it's like Drew always wants me to be thinking about him, about us, and sometimes I just…"

She stopped talking and Rory suggested, "You have other things to think about?"

Amanda hesitated, uncomfortable saying it out loud.

They both looked up as Amit came into view with loudly crunching footsteps.

"We'll always hear him coming," Rory muttered, making Amanda grin.

She was about to give a joking response when a distant hum caught her attention. She stood up, peering deeper into the forest. Amit rejoined them and glanced at Rory questioningly.

"Do you hear something?"

"The humming," Amanda answered vaguely, still scanning the trees. "It's soft but getting louder. Closer, I think."

Rory moved to Amanda's side while Amit pulled a small pair of binoculars from his pocket.

"There!" He nodded toward the trees ahead of them. "An elder is coming straight toward us. I've never seen one move with such purpose. We should go meet it."

"No," Amanda said, her eyes fixed on the same spot. "Give them space."

After a few tense minutes, a dry rustling parted the brush at the edge of the clearing and a stony figure emerged. The Pyura Elder had the same stone exterior as the younger Pyura, yet it was about four feet tall and walked on two sturdy legs. Its large head was nearly the diameter of its body and half its height. Though there was no visible neck, the head turned slightly as it scanned the travelers. Slits seemed to roughly indicate eyes and a mouth, while arm-like shapes hung motionless beside the rocky, slumped torso.

Welcome, Architect.

The words floated through Amanda's mind. It was similar in sensation to the messages she had felt from Laum, but this time with clear words. Closer to the psychic messages sent through the mindspace by travelers. Before she could consider how the elder was communicating, the message continued.

We have carried a message for you from Edmund. Are you prepared?

"Who are you?" Amanda asked, unsure if she needed to speak aloud or only think her reply.

We are one. Eternal. Observing and sharing messages to those with the heart to hear. Are you prepared?

Wind rattled through the desolate forest as Amanda stared into the rock creature's expressionless face. She hoped she was ready but felt a shudder of fear as she turned to the others and said, "Grab a pen or something. I'm getting a message from Edmund."

The Pyura Elder waited. Amit fumbled in his pack before pulling out a digital recorder. Rory edged to Amanda's left, maneuvering herself into a better defensive position, though the elder seemed to take no notice of her.

"I'm ready for the message."

We will share this message from Edmund. There was a pause and the whispery voice shifted, taking on the quality of an old man. *I am Edmund Robinson, the last architect of the noble Psychic Traveler Society. This message is for my successor, the next to share the sensibility of the architect. You may be wondering why I did not simply include this message in my letter, instead of sending you on the quest to this world. Some messages are better kept off paper.*

"He says he left me a letter," Amanda repeated for the benefit of the recorder, hoping it wouldn't disrupt the message. Edmund's voice continued smoothly.

For thousands of years, the initiation into our select circle has begun with oral instruction. As I grow older, I become more certain I will not meet you in this life. Hence, the happy opportunity of discovering an ability to send you a message through the Pyura Elder. You will have questions about this method, which will become clear in your later instruction.

"I'll learn how the Pyura works later," Amanda said quickly, trying not to miss a word.

For your initiation, I will rely on my closest allies who reside in four remarkable worlds. Perhaps you have met some of them already. In the case that my allies have not survived the time between my passing and your calling, they have agreed to pass my instructions to their successors.

Amanda briefly summarized his message, trying not to be distracted by her own questions about its meaning. As he went on, she repeated key phrases and hoped that would be enough to remember the full message.

An architect's acumen encompasses four realms of study. Empathy and perception to see what cannot be seen. Creativity and truth to build what already exists. Courage and restraint to live with bravery and boundaries. Knowledge and wisdom to wield power sparingly.

My allies on Terra Violavita, Arcadia, Optimae Viridi, and Stellaria will be your guides. Offer them each a Pyura relic. When you have completed each of the four trials, your initiation will be complete. The trials are key to your training.

Fare well on your architect's journey.

A shift in energy suggested that Edmund's message had finished. Amanda blinked to clear her head, then refocused on the Pyura Elder.

Would you hear our message again?

The elder waited as Amanda explained the experience to Rory and Amit.

"It's not what I expected," Rory said, studying the elder carefully.

"It's incredible!" Amit reacted with more enthusiasm. "You have to listen again. This time, repeat every word as well as you can."

Amanda turned to Rory, who shrugged and said, "Might as well get it all down clearly."

"Yeah, okay," Amanda agreed.

She wanted to hear Edmund's message again, but her mind and heart were racing. She was standing in a charred forest on an alien planet listening to a psychic message from a traveler who had been dead for a hundred years. It was unreal and overwhelming. And one thought floated about the rest. *"What was that part about four trials?"*

CHAPTER 5

GATHERING SUPPORT

"There's no letter from Edmund?" Drew sat beside Amanda in the media room where they were supposed to be working on homework or group projects. He was eager to rehash the details of her trip. She was leery of talking about psychic travel at school.

"Not yet."

"But they're looking?" Drew pressed.

"It's been nearly a hundred years," Amanda reminded him, but Drew was skeptical.

"Seems like a pretty important thing to hang onto."

Amanda agreed. A team of PTS historians had been established to support Amanda's quest. They were pulling together everything they knew about Edmund, but there was no sign of a letter he had left for his successor. They wouldn't have found their way to Crystal Caverns at all if it weren't for mentions of the Pyura Elder in his diaries.

"Nothing about these trials either?"

Amanda shook her head and scanned for students sitting within possible earshot.

In Terra-V and Arcadia, Alira and Doctor Webb had already confirmed they had instructions from Edmund that were meant to be kept secret until *the time was right*. After her meeting with the Pyura Elder, they further confirmed that receiving a relic was part of that evaluation, though they both declined to say more until meeting Amanda in person. The historians on her team were contacting the leaders of the other two worlds as well.

"They can't be that bad," Drew reassured. "I mean, calling them *trials* sounds intense, but Edmund wants you to pass them, right?"

"I guess."

Amanda didn't want to talk about the trials or the new worlds she would visit. Now that the High Council had decided to start her architect training, everything was moving quickly. The support team was already scheduling specialized training sessions and off-world briefings. Since no one knew what to expect, they were also increasing her physical training routine and her sessions with their leading psychic engineers.

"You're worried?" Drew asked, seeing a shadow pass over Amanda's face.

"Not exactly," she said slowly. "It's just that… Well, this is going to take up a lot more of my time for a while."

"Oh."

They sat on the same side of a table, books spread out to discourage anyone from joining them and notebooks open to look like they were working. Drew leaned on an elbow and looked at Amanda with the crooked smile that always lightened her mood.

"I get it. You're afraid you won't have time for me. But I'm in this with you. Like when it all started. Who was with you the first time you went to Terra-V?"

Smiling softly, Amanda remembered sitting on a park bench while Drew led her through a guided meditation he had found online. It was back when they thought Amanda's daydreams were some kind of psychological upset, not a way station to other worlds.

Drew pulled out another notebook and opened it to a dog-eared page. He had divided the paper into four quadrants, each with a list of what they knew about the worlds Edmund had chosen for Amanda's training. Amanda straightened in her seat.

"You shouldn't have that here!"

A month had passed since the One-Act Play Festival, but rumors around school had only increased. It didn't matter that the Vertex had been less conspicuous since then. Small incidents were still in the news. Many proved to be hoaxes, but that didn't change their classmates' sense that something special—something dangerous—had happened at their school.

"No one is listening to us," Drew insisted, glancing at their classmates talking softly all around them. He went on to describe how they could list the highlights on this page and start separate pages for each of the worlds as they learned more.

"I wish I'd gotten a look at those relics. Can you bring them home before you deliver them?"

Edmund's mention of Pyura relics had puzzled Amanda, but Amit had known exactly what he meant. The Ooliani had a collection of relics in their sacred shrine. Fossilized Pyura that had been polished until they gleamed, showing streaks of phosphorescent crystal like the structures in the caverns.

After she met with the Pyura Elder, the Ooliani let Amanda choose four relics to bring on her journey. She chose lemon-sized fossils that fit in the palm of her hand and left them with her support team.

"Probably not. They're being documented and studied."

Drew's crooked pen lines and scribbled notes floated in front of Amanda's tired eyes. She didn't have the heart to tell him that her support team was tracking and analyzing every step of her journey with sophisticated computers and mountains of off-world data.

"Well, there's one to deliver before each trial," Drew noted, tapping on the page. Amanda leaned over to see that he'd written the names of each world in the four sections along with a to-do list below each that started with *deliver sacred relic.*

"Right," she agreed uneasily, her mind drifting back to her evening with the Ooliani.

The cavern had gleamed around them, casting its eerie pink and aqua light across the open space where a fire burned in a large, hollow dish of smooth rock. Pastel clouds of smoke from the fire had picked up tiny particles in the light as they floated toward cracks in the ceiling high above. It was a sweet, tangy smoke, scented with dried seaweed and precious herbs foraged from the desiccated forest.

Laum had invited Amanda to browse the vast collection of relics and take the four that spoke to her. The warmth of the cave, as well as her mental and physical exhaustion after their trek to the forest, had put Amanda in a drowsy state. The relics had seemed to shift and shimmer before her in the soft, smoky light.

As if in a dream, she saw her own life reflected in the Pyura. As a baby, she'd been resting on the shore, filtering the world around her like water from the sea and unable to move without external hands picking her up to be placed in the next patch of water. Then slowly she grew, expanding her freedom and gaining the strength to crawl toward the forest where she could make her own way through the world. As the idea grew, she imagined Edmund's trials as the next phase of her own evolution. Her chance to leave the comfort of her familiar shore and share in the deeper story of the select circle of psychic architects.

"Did they say anything about the trials?"

Pulling free from her reverie, Amanda blinked in the fluorescent light.

"Who?" When she realized Drew was asking about Alira and Doctor Webb, she shook her head. "Nothing yet. I guess I'll learn more when I bring them the relics. It's all being arranged now."

Her head hurt from the glaring overhead lights. After two days of briefings, she was tired of going over every detail of her trip.

"Hey." Drew nudged her shoulder reassuringly. "We've got this. I can't go with you, but I can help you work it out. Be the objective outsider. You'll need that, right?"

Despite his confidence, Drew's right eye twitched.

"Yeah, of course," Amanda reassured, nearly leaning in for a kiss before remembering they were at school.

Though she appreciated his support, Amanda couldn't bring herself to say that it wasn't that easy. Even the PTS historians' vast resources were surprisingly limited when it came to psychic architect training, and it appeared Edmund had devised his architect's journey with only the help of off-world allies. Allies who were going to put her through initiation trials, whatever that might mean.

Drew placed his hand over hers, lightly curling his fingers through hers and stroking her hand with his thumb. A passing student smirked at them, and Amanda pulled her hand away. She flipped a page in her history book without reading a word.

"You have the engineers to help, too," Drew reminded after a stretch of silence. Amanda turned another page in her book. "They might not know about Edmund's plans, but they know more than the average—"

He stopped talking as another student passed by.

"I know," Amanda agreed in a tight voice. "I just don't want to talk about this here."

"Yeah, sure." Drew turned a page in his own book and started reading at random.

Across the room, Amanda saw some of their friends at another table. Trina wasn't in this class, but Brooklyn was chatting to Nick, who didn't seem to be listening. Instead, he was watching Amanda intently.

Since the play, Nick had gotten more vocal about his belief in the aliens traveling among them. Most everyone laughed him off, but he only shrugged and said they'd find out eventually.

Now that she'd made eye contact, Nick abruptly picked up his books and headed toward their table. Brooklyn watched him leave, apparently mid-sentence, then shot Amanda a questioning look before angrily scribbling in her notebook.

"Hey, guys."

Nick nudged aside the books across from Amanda and took a seat. Drew pulled his history book over his notebook and flashed Nick a relaxed smile.

"Hey, man! How's it going?"

"Trina said you guys saw a good movie," Amanda added brightly. "That one with all the love stories."

"I guess…" Nick shrugged and rolled his eyes at Drew. "Trina's choice. I was surprised you guys weren't there."

"Oh, uh…" Amanda felt her face freeze as she turned to Drew for help. She'd been having a telepathic conversation with a creature on another planet while their friends were at the movies.

"Valentine's Day weekend," Drew answered smoothly. "We had plans on our own."

"Oh, gotcha!" Nick winked and Drew shrugged, letting the insinuation go.

Amanda fidgeted with her hands, remembering how Drew had surprised her at her locker on Thursday morning with a heart-shaped box of chocolates and a tiny stuffed koala. She'd completely forgotten about the holiday, then tried to make up for it with a hand-drawn card and a candy bar from the vending machine.

"It's not a big deal though," Drew said lightly. "Just a made-up holiday to sell cards and stuff."

He kissed Amanda's hand, then laughed when the teacher shot them a scolding look.

"Anyway," Nick said brusquely. "I've been rewatching all the videos from the play."

Amanda was still looking at Drew as he squeezed her hand and gently let it go.

"Oh, yeah? Find anything interesting?"

"Just that bit where Amanda stood up. What were you going to do? Storm the stage?"

Amanda rolled her eyes. They'd been over this before.

"I told you. I don't know what I was thinking. Trina was on stage. Weird men showed up. I guess I panicked."

"Right," Nick nodded slowly. "Kinda strange to jump up like that. When everyone else thought they were part of the show."

"I'd been running lines with Trina, so I knew it wasn't."

Nick shrugged with one shoulder, then studied Amanda with narrowed eyes.

"Something you wanna say, man?" Drew challenged with an edge in his voice.

"Nah." Nick shook his head, then patted the table with one palm before coming clean. "All right, yeah. It just seems like we might have a mutual interest here."

Amanda inhaled swiftly but kept her face blank, despite the flip in her stomach.

"See, my cousin's got me on this chat site. A place for safe talk about what's really going on with these things. These travelers."

His disgust sickened Amanda, but she recognized the moment as her chance to get some inside information for Cameron.

"What do you know?" She lowered her voice and leaned in, as if afraid of being overheard. Nick's solemn nod showed respect for her caution. He glanced at Drew, who hunched in slightly as well.

"They're alien, for sure, but they look human. Probably from a planet with very similar conditions to Earth. Because then they'd evolve like us. Some guys think the disappearing thing is done with tech, like they have a cloaked ship in orbit phasing them up."

He paused, gauging their reactions. Amanda pressed her lips together to hide her happiness at how wrong they had it. Drew laughed outright and said they watched too many movies.

"Yeah, I don't buy that one." Nick sounded defensive. "More of us think it's biological. Probably an evolved survival skill. We're working out ways to test them. To see who might be hiding among us."

"Test them how?" Amanda gripped Drew's leg under the table, and Nick shrugged.

"Throw water on them, stuff like that. No one's come up with a solid test yet."

Amanda remembered how Nick had spilled a huge bottle of water down the table at lunch one day, splashing nearly everyone before grabbing a stack of napkins he happened to have on his tray.

"You need a special login to access the site, but I could get you in."

"I don't know, man," Drew said with a skeptical shrug. "But I'd check it out."

Nick tightened his jaw, and Amanda guessed he was about to take back his offer. The site wasn't a joke to him or some casual thing to check out. After a deep breath, she placed her free hand on the table next to his, steadily met his gaze, and said, "I'm in."

Nick nodded once and slapped the table lightly before getting to his feet.

"I'll send you the deets."

He sauntered back to his table, and Amanda watched Brooklyn pepper him with questions. As he half-smiled at whatever she was saying, Amanda doubted that Brooklyn would ever be invited to his secret club. She did wonder if Trina knew about it though. And, if so, why she had never mentioned it.

§

Psychic engineers exhibited more abilities than typical travelers, but less than psychic architects. Instead of building mindspace houses and connecting doors to new worlds, they maintained those psychic structures using their own special skills.

For over six months, Amanda had been shadowing the society's leading engineers in the hopes that their skills would help her develop her own unique abilities. Gerald, Dorothy, and Elaine had taught Amanda about the pure mindspace—a layer of energetic space that existed beneath the developed mindspace—and had become mentors in other ways as well.

Today, they met in the manor, a mindspace house that was officially named the Thomas House, after Alice Thomas who had been the architect before Edmund. It was built with the opulence of an English country manor with high ceilings, sweeping staircases, and rich furnishings. It also featured a terraced garden they could see from the drawing room windows.

"Is this architect's journey a tradition?" Gerald asked. "Or something Edmund made up himself?"

Dorothy frowned at the question. "Does it matter? There are no records of it. But engineers don't keep records of our mysteries either."

"True," Gerald agreed. "But we know Edmund had some kind of training with Alice, just like she was trained by the architect before her. If it's a tradition for architects to involve off-world allies in their training, our researchers should be looking into the historical records of our past architects' closest off-world allies. Not our own."

"I'm sure they've thought of that," Dorothy countered. "There's a whole team looking into this."

Elaine had been quiet throughout the discussion. Now, she sat taller and cleared her throat.

"I'm not sure any of us should be looking into any of this." She faced their surprise with defiant confidence. "We don't reveal our mysteries to travelers who aren't psychic engineers… Well, except for Amanda, who will become an architect. Should any of us know the mysteries of psychic architects?"

Gerald and Dorothy eyed each other uncomfortably.

Elaine sighed, as if sorry to be the voice of reason.

"Why *don't* we tell other travelers about the pure mind-space?" Amanda asked suddenly, turning away from her view of the garden. "I've kept it secret like you asked, but… It doesn't make sense."

"It's a mystery," Elaine reminded gently. "It's only to be shared with those who can appreciate it."

Amanda put her hands on the back of an upholstered chair, feeling the thick brocade under her palms as if her body was physically there instead of waiting for her back in her bedroom.

"Don't we want travelers to know everything about how psychic travel works? Especially the scientists, who are missing a big piece of information by keeping the pure mindspace a secret. It's like if no one was ever told about gravity just because they can't see it."

"It is not like that at all." Dorothy waved away the comparison. "No one can *see* gravity, but we are all affected by it in the same way."

"The pure mindspace could only be taught in theory," Gerald explained. "Travelers who do not have engineer or architect abilities will never be able to access that level of consciousness for themselves. They would have to *believe* what we say about it. That leaves too much room for wild speculation and social unrest. It's better we shroud our work and the pure mindspace in mystery."

"But they already believe in the mysteries," Amanda reminded. "They know you can do things they can't, they just don't know what."

"It's easier for people to believe in the unknown when they know nothing about it. Give them specifics and they'll tear it apart. Give them nothing and they'll accept that it's an unknowable mystery."

"If they know about the pure mindspace, they'll want to experience it," Dorothy insisted. "But they can't."

"It's why we don't tell normals about psychic travel," Elaine joined in. "Normals could never experience it for themselves. Knowing that some of us are different—in ways that give us access to things they can never have—would only create division and mistrust."

"Jealousy, too," Dorothy added. "And fear. It's dangerous for people to feel inferior. Or superior. It's better when those of us with extraordinary gifts are taught to humbly keep them to ourselves."

"But that's…" Amanda sputtered to a stop. She wasn't sure what she thought of that outlook, but she didn't like it. After a moment to reflect, she said, "It's like you're the billionaires of the world saying poor people just don't understand how to spend money, so you'd better keep it to yourselves."

"Wealth disparity," Gerald said ruefully. "Now that's a problem people should care about!"

Dorothy scowled at his distraction, then corrected Amanda again.

"It's not like that either. Money can be shared if those who have it choose to share it. We do not control who does or doesn't have psychic travel abilities. And we don't choose which travelers will have additional engineer or architect skills either. Not yet at least."

Amanda considered that. The previous High Council had been pushing traveler scientists to discover how to enable or disable traveler genes in people who had them. Arcadians already had that technology. In time, scientists could learn how to give traveler genes to those who weren't born with them or take them away from people they didn't want to be travelers.

"Secrecy may soon be a moot point," Gerald reminded. "These stunts from the Vertex are raising questions among normals. Talk among travelers is shifting, too. More than ever are saying it may not be worth the effort to stay in the shadows anymore."

"If that curtain falls, we'll all be under a microscope," Dorothy predicted sadly. "Especially those of us with a deeper understanding."

They were only a handful of engineers these days. The younger ones had all sided with Lucas during his rebellion and overthrow of the previous High Council. Some were now publicly aligned with the Vertex.

"As far as I know, they've kept our mysteries sacred," Dorothy said, "but I doubt that will last long. Especially if the outside world finds out about us."

"News interviews, talk shows, tell-all books," Elaine added with a shudder.

Amanda's stomach churned as she imagined sitting in a newsroom with reporters badgering her about what it meant to be the next psychic architect.

"Amanda? Are you okay?" Elaine's concerned voice cut through her fears. Amanda glanced at each of their faces and felt the room closing in around her.

"Yeah, I'm fine. It's just… I forgot an appointment. Can we pick up the training next week?"

When Amanda faded from the manor house, she wasn't surprised to find herself standing in the first-floor den of the birdhouse. She didn't have an appointment in Arcadia, but she needed some time away from her own world so she stepped through the familiar door.

The gatehouse was a large structure that had been built around a proximal field connecting Arcadia to the mindspace. Travelers could conjure doors anywhere in that field as they passed in and out of the world. Yet the Arcadians had also thoughtfully included private rooms along the back wall, understanding that travelers might want time to converse in the mindspace before physically moving their bodies through a door in the house.

Security and customs areas were set up at the front of the gatehouse. Scanners checked for tech being brought in or out of the world, while both Arcadians and PTS-assigned travelers manned tables to physically inspect items carried by hand or in bags. The sight of those tables brought uneasy memories of the banned books Amanda had once smuggled in for Mitra.

Just past security, travelers could pick up translator discs to be worn during their stay and returned before leaving. The small discs affixed to a spot just above and behind the left ear, providing instant translation of foreign languages in the wearer's mind.

Walking to the science lab where she usually worked, Amanda smiled politely as she passed both Arcadians and alien visitors. She often wondered how the Arcadians had first adjusted to finding populated worlds through space travel. Mitra had said it was a smooth transition, but it had happened long before he was born. Decades before Edmund had created a door to Arcadia.

Amanda didn't expect people on Earth to accept extra-terrestrial life as easily, especially since their planet's only current connection was through psychic travel abilities the vast majority of them would never have.

"Amanda!" Mitra happily invited her into his lab and offered to put on a pot of hot cranberry juice. "What brings you to brighten my day?"

His eyes peered into her soul and Amanda felt a frizzle of energy snake through her body. She perched on a stool near his favorite workspace and accepted a warm glass mug.

"Change of scenery," she answered vaguely.

Amanda's support team was planning an official visit to deliver the relic to Dr. Webb and learn about the training Edmund had left in their care. Today, she wanted to talk about anything but the architect's journey.

"Then let's change your scenery," Mitra suggested. He fished out two lids for their mugs and said it was a beautiful day for a walk through the city.

"Don't you have work to do?" Amanda protested. But Mitra gallantly dismissed her concern by saying he was due for a break and couldn't think of a better way to spend his free time.

Stepping from the building onto the wide sidewalk, Amanda paused to take in the glittering glass city. Hover carts quietly sped by. Small aircraft threaded between the city's upper stories. Delicate trees and sculptures dotted the sidewalks, while the city was bathed in a gentle wash of birdsong.

When she glanced to her left, Amanda was startled to see Lucas Flynn heading straight toward them. He wore his typical black pants and sweater, but his carefree expression seemed lighter than usual. Genuinely relaxed.

"Are you here to see Dr. Webb?" Mitra asked after a polite greeting.

"Yes." Lucas grinned slyly, adding that he hadn't expected to see Amanda today.

"Neither did I," Mitra replied, "but it's a very happy surprise."

"I'm sure." Lucas raised an eyebrow Amanda's way and she tried to ignore the heat in her cheeks.

"We're taking a walk," she told him sharply. "That's all."

Lucas dropped the sly grin.

"Lovely day for it," he offered, expressing a kindness that was more disarming than his usual flippancy.

Lucas entered the building, and they began their walk. Mitra pointed out some colorful birds on a nearby bench. Amanda looked their way and sipped thoughtfully at her hot cranberry drink.

It is a lovely day for a walk, she told herself reassuringly. *And I needed a change of scenery.*

She couldn't find a flaw in that logic, yet her mood had dimmed since running into Lucas and there was a twist in her gut she couldn't explain. Looking up at Mitra's sunlit face, she pushed the feeling away and followed him into the city.

Chapter 6

The First Relic

Long purple grass clung to their boots as Amanda and Rory moved toward the heart of the Vherahna Forest. The proximal door they'd just stepped through was the first psychic door Amanda had ever opened. It faded from sight as they moved into the clearing, leaving them to face the same sunset view that had been Amanda's first glimpse of this now-familiar world.

The tuntum trees stretched around them. Their slender branches reached toward the sky even as their twin trunks began to slowly twist down for the night. There was a rhythmic humming in the air. *Tuntum. Tuntum.* Amanda now knew it came from the coiling motion of the trees. If they were close enough to touch one of those purple trunks, there would be a warmth under the bark. A pulsing of the sap that flowed within.

"Any trial in Terra-V can't be that bad, right?" As she asked, Amanda pictured Alira's serene face and the quick flashes of joy that were Caeph's bright smiles. She had friends in this world. People she'd grown to love and trust.

"Are you worried?" Rory asked as they neared the humming tree line. *Tuntum. Tuntum.*

Amanda shrugged. "It's the Vherahna. They're kind and supportive. Plus, Mitra reminded me that I'm a pretty big deal here. I mean, I did find their lost tribe, overthrow the Churukh royalty, and basically restore balance to their whole world."

"Wow, you're basically a hero." Rory's wry amusement pricked Amanda's ego.

"I'm not saying I did it alone," she quickly defended. "But, come on, I did fulfill their prophecy. Won't that count for something?"

They crossed the wooden bridge at the edge of the clearing, passing under gradually lowering branches.

"We don't know anything about these trials yet. Maybe you should think of them as less of a test and more as a chance to—" Rory stopped talking as a flash of movement darted behind a nearby tree.

"Hello?" They edged closer, stepping off the worn path.

Dusty indigo bushes beside the tall tree rustled lightly. A moment later, a small oval face peered out from behind the pale purple trunk. Deep blue hair framed the shining face and violet eyes gleamed warily as they darted from Rory to Amanda.

"It's a child," Rory noted, relaxing her hand away from the knife at her belt.

A whistling melody cut through the trees, interspersed with chirps and short rippling hums. Amanda recognized it as the Vherahna native language, though the tones were impossible for humans to imitate correctly. They turned to see a Vherahna Elder approaching with the loping gait that appeared effortless for their long limbs. It was Tras, one of Alira's trusted companions.

"Good day," he offered before turning to the child with a beckoning gesture. "This child is from our reunited tribe. She has not yet learned English or been given an English name, but she does know about our waking dreamer."

Amanda beamed, ignoring the amused shake of Rory's head. She was proud to be called their waking dreamer.

"I'm happy to meet her."

The girl was nearly Amanda's height, which was small compared to the slender stature of a Vherahna adult. She cautiously crept out from behind the lowering tuntum tree, letting her thin fingers trail against its bark as long as possible. There was an edge in her expression. A hardness that Amanda had never seen in a Vherahna before, despite the difficult times they'd endured.

"How is she adjusting?" Rory asked carefully, and a shadow passed over Tras' face.

"Relatively well." Amanda felt a sinking sensation in her chest as he added, "Transitions can be challenging."

The trees whispered around them. *Tuntum. Tuntum.* Amanda studied the child's face. Her eyes never rested anywhere for more than a moment before shifting to gauge her surroundings.

"Can I help?"

Tras thanked her for the kind offer. As he spoke, Amanda noticed that she was no longer disconcerted by the double blink of the Vherahnas' eyes. It was another rhythm in Terra-V, like the thrum of the sacred trees. *Tuntum. Tuntum. Blink-blink. Blink-blink.*

Farther up the path, a traveler wearing a blue tunic over light chain mail trotted toward them. He raised a hand in greeting and Amanda saw that it was Dimitri, one of the knights who had accompanied her first journey through Terra-V. As he approached, the young girl darted behind Tras and peered warily around his torso.

"You found her!" Dimitri smiled, crouching a bit to catch the girl's eye before she quickly looked away. "All's quiet at the edge now."

"Was there trouble?" Rory tensed, snapping into her previous role as a knight stationed in Terra-V.

"Nothing to worry about," Dimitri said, though his bright tone did nothing to ease Rory's stance. She and Amanda both knew Dimitri would put on a sunny face even when heading straight into danger. In response to Rory's intent stare, he explained, "We ran off some loyalists close to the forest. The skirmish startled our young friend here, but no harm was done."

"We were within the forest's protection," Tras clarified. "Though our hunt for herbs had led us close to the tree line."

"Loyalists?" Amanda seemed to be the only one who didn't know what that meant.

Rory and Dimitri exchanged a heavy look before he said, "Churukh still loyal to the old royalty. They pop up from time to time. It happens when regimes change."

Amanda thought about that on their walk to Alira's small house. For her, the fall of the Churukh royalty was in the past. Yet those who lived here were still navigating a new way of life.

After a warm greeting, Alira ushered them to her table where she poured three cups of aromatic tea. She hadn't changed since the day of their first meeting. Her lithe body moved with grace. Her opalescent skin shimmered with pastel hues, and her purple eyes brimmed with life.

Waiting for the tea to cool, Amanda pulled a Pyura fossil from her pocket. It was the smallest of the four relics and had a distinctive slash of purple running across one side of its rounded body. Amanda had known this relic was meant for Terra-V the moment she saw it. Just as she had sensed which relic was right for each of the other worlds.

"It is beautiful," Alira complimented, turning the fossil over several times before handing it back.

Amanda looked at Rory questioningly.

"Edmund wanted you to have it," Rory clarified, though an advance team had already explained the situation.

"I understand the relic's purpose in Amanda's training," Alira said. "Though I won't be the one to accept it."

"Why not?" Amanda watched Alira sip gently from her cup. "You're the leader of the Vherahna."

Alira set her cup on the table with a soft smile.

"I am the highest elder of the Vherahna," she agreed, "and I have read Edmund's instructions. Yet I have nothing more to teach you at this time."

"You mean I've passed this trial?"

"Do you feel you have passed a trial?" Alira's voice was kind but curious. "Do you know how to see what cannot be seen?"

Amanda shifted in her seat, recalling that line from Edmund's message. In a flash of memory, she saw the fiery glow of Alira's eyes anchoring her to the cold stone of the fortress courtyard. It was night. Torches burned from the surrounding walls and Amanda desperately fought to send a message for help without fully slipping into the mindspace. That effort to stay in two places had led to the creation of a new doorway between their worlds. Yet Amanda still had no idea how she'd done it.

She looked down at her hands and shook her head.

"Mhevek and I have discussed Edmund's instructions. He is in a better position to help you."

"Mhevek?" The name brought a memory of silk robes and pineapples, floral tea, and a city walled in deep gray slate. "But Mhevek is in Sage Village. That's a two-day ride from here."

They had planned to deliver the relic this morning, then do the same with Dr. Webb in Arcadia in the afternoon. Between her school schedule and organizing a new trip, meeting with Mhevek would delay their progress by at least a week. Rory had another suggestion.

"Not if we use a door."

Amanda shook her head, not understanding. When she saw Alira's steady gaze, the truth washed over her.

"You aren't coming with me? What about Caeph?"

"Caeph is needed in the new Vherahna forest. I am needed here."

Amanda sat speechless. It had never occurred to her that the trial on Terra-V could be held without the Vherahna. Alira was the first being she'd met in another world, back when she knew nothing about psychic travel and thought she was having a vivid dream.

"Why did you agree to have us here today if you knew you weren't going to help me?"

Rory frowned at the accusation in Amanda's tone, but Alira responded to the hurt.

"I wanted to see you and wish you well." Her eyes regarded Amanda softly through two rounds of double blinks. "You are growing quickly," she added. "You will do well with the challenges to come."

After finishing their tea, Alira walked them out of her home and into the village center.

Across the river, Amanda could see Vherahna moving between the communal kitchen and washrooms. In the distance, she could see a glimpse of the building where they created their vhe-infused products to share with distant Churukh. Alira also looked that way, gesturing to a passerby and calling out in the lilting song of their native language. Amanda realized it was Tras leading the girl they'd met earlier down a path to the far end of the village. She waved awkwardly, reminded that most Churukh didn't speak English. She hoped Rory remembered enough of their language to get by in Sage Village.

"Be happy, Amanda," Alira said, taking both her hands. "You are in our hearts, even when we are apart."

A surge of energy rippled up Amanda's arms as Alira closed her eyes and emitted a low, gentle hum. A healing warmth washed over Amanda, lightening her spirits. When she looked again, Alira was watching her with a kind shimmer in her violet eyes. *Blink-blink. Blink-blink.*

"You have made a good start here." Her whisper carried on the wind and wrapped around Amanda's torso like a plate of armor against the coming trial. Yet there was sadness in her words, knowing she would not be by Amanda's side for this part of her journey.

§

They arrived at Sage Village a short time later, entering through a proximal door in guest chambers attached to the renowned library. It was the same guest room they'd stayed in during Amanda's first journey through Terra-V. On the balcony looking over the pineapple fields, Amanda remembered her late-night talk with Caeph. It felt both like yesterday and long ago.

Mhevek was not surprised when they found him in the library's main hall.

"How you've grown," he said in greeting, his rough voice at odds with the trailing silk robes that draped his stocky form. Unlike the willowy Vherahna, the Churukh were stout people with jet-black hair and thick skin in swirling shades of gray. Their eyes were an emerald green that varied in brightness depending on the amount of vhe in their bodies.

"Do you know why we're here?" Rory asked, getting right to the point.

"Yes," Mhevek said gravely, "Alira and I have discussed the matter in full."

Amanda reached into her pocket for the relic, but Mhevek quickly stopped her. "No, child, wait! If that's the sacred relic, you must not give it to me here."

"Okay?" Amanda agreed uncertainly, and Mhevek explained that a moment such as this required the ritual of a tea ceremony.

"Go refresh yourselves and tea will be laid shortly."

Amanda wanted to tell him that they'd just had tea with Alira, but she knew this ritual was about more than tea. Her previous adventure in Terra-V had begun with a visit to the Library at Sage Village where she, Alira, Caeph, and Mhevek had shared a tea ceremony designed to show Amanda the next step of their journey. She didn't think it had worked at the time, but the vision she'd had during the ceremony had ultimately led to finding the Churukh royals' hidden fortress.

"It's part of the process," Rory said as they left the library to wander within the walled limits of Sage Village. "We knew he wouldn't just hand over Edmund's instructions."

Did we? Amanda thought but didn't say.

Instead, she turned her attention to the colorful village center. On their last visit, Amanda had arrived by horse through the walled city's massive gates. She'd seen a bit of the cobbled streets on their way to the library and guest chambers, but she'd spent most of her free time visiting her feathered horse, Iveryn, out in the stables.

The market stalls around the library were similar to those she'd seen in the square outside of the Churukh castle. Here they had a more festive styling. Colorful silks hung from tent posts and baskets of flowers adorned the wares.

At the first stall, the vendor beckoned them with a friendly wave. Rory exchanged a few syllables that sounded more like grunts than words, then looked at the vendor's display more carefully. Cards painted with various colors were propped on small stands beside polished rocks of a matching hue.

"Are the cards for sale or the rocks?" Amanda asked, seeing the beauty in both.

"Neither," Rory answered. "She isn't selling anything. She says she trades in ideas and the displays are to channel them."

"How do you trade ideas?" Amanda studied the nearest card. Its cobalt blue center gradually shifted to aquamarine at the edges. The rock had similar qualities, appearing cobalt wherever Amanda focused her gaze and fading away to aquamarine. It reminded Amanda of the mood rings she and Trina had once bought at a summer fair.

After a few more grunts, Rory said, "You stare at a display and tell her what you see. In return, she tells you something about yourself."

"Like an inkblot?" Amanda wasn't sure if psychologists really used inkblots, but she'd seen them on TV shows.

"I guess." Rory shrugged. "It's like reading tea leaves or tarot cards. Which you can probably do at other booths here."

Amanda didn't have to ask Rory's opinion of these mystical arts. She was too sensible, too science-minded to accept any of it, and Amanda was inclined to agree with her. But they had time to waste, and she was curious about the displays.

"Let's do it!"

Rory sighed, tipping her head back to face the sky.

"Fine, you do it. I'll translate. But only because it's free."

Skimming the table, Amanda searched for a display that stood out to her. One featured the same rose hues as Iveryn's feathers. Another reminded her of the lilac and violet foliage found in the Vherahna forest. Finally, her eyes were drawn to an inky black display. The rock was smooth obsidian, while the card seemed to have been painted with layers of black that deepened the longer Amanda stared. It was like looking into a void.

To see what cannot be seen.

The words floated through Amanda's mind as she stared into the blackest black paint she'd ever seen. There was nothing there. There was something there. She couldn't see it, but she could sense it. A *something* in the layers of black. Her gaze went out of focus as she scanned for hazy lines. Edges. A curve. Anything. Beneath the card, the obsidian gleamed, nearly reflecting a shadow of the something hidden within the paint. Amanda's eyes shifted between the paint and stone, hoping to catch a glimpse of the something if she caught it off guard.

After some time, Rory nudged Amanda, saying the vendor wanted to know Amanda's ideas after studying the display.

"I don't know," Amanda stammered. "It's so… There's something… I can't see it but there's something…"

"Yes," the vendor agreed in a raspy voice that startled Amanda until she remembered that many Churukh knew a few words of English.

Her English *yes* was followed by a series of excited grunts and yaps that Rory puzzled over before attempting to translate.

"She thanks you for sharing your idea and has a message in return. She says you are the cricket. You are the sea."

Still entranced by the blackness of the stone and card, Amanda had to force her mind to process the words. She looked from the vendor to Rory helplessly.

"What? I'm a cricket? And the sea?"

Rory shrugged.

"What did you expect? It's always some vague gibberish with this stuff. Lots of room for you to take it however you want."

She thanked the vendor just as a page from the library came to say Mhevek was ready for them.

Entering the library, Amanda looked up at its ribbed canopy of pale stone and the pastel murals painted between each arch. The abstract murals mirrored the stained-glass windows high on the library's walls. One panel drew her eyes with its rippling blues, like the sea. But there was no cricket in sight.

Rory and Amanda joined Mhevek at a low table in the library's central hall. Several Churukh monks stood in silent witness. The tea ceremony was like the one Amanda had attended before. Mhevek led a series of chants before pouring a pale blue liquid into each of the cups. They were each given a waxy flower to place in their herbal tea. Amanda watched her blossom unfurl in the hot liquid. This time, its petals were a vibrant orange and gold surrounding a heart of Kelly green.

During their last tea ceremony, Mhevek had made a plea for Amanda to awaken an inner wisdom that would guide their prophesied journey. Now, he simply asked her to present the Pyura relic. Mhevek held the fossil before him, murmuring grumbled sounds as the monks around them bowed reverently. He handed the relic to an aide and placed his hands in his lap.

"Our ceremony has concluded."

"That's it?" Amanda questioned without thought, earning a disapproving nudge from Rory's knee.

"Yes," Mhevek smiled, unbothered by her blunt question. "There is no more for us to do today."

"No more?" This time the question came from Rory. "I thought we might review the instructions Edmund left with you."

"Oh, no." Mhevek shook his head, still smiling. "Edmund's instructions clearly state that they are not to be shared with you until the trial is complete. We are to teach you in our own way, in balance with the guidance left for us by Edmund."

"When?" Amanda had forgotten her tea until Mhevek took a thoughtful sip from his own cup.

"When will we begin?" Mhevek considered carefully. "We have already begun."

"With this tea ceremony?" Rory asked, sensing Amanda's growing frustration.

"No, no," Mhevek laughed lightly. "Long before that. We are well on our way."

"On our way?" Amanda clenched her hands beneath the table. "On our way to what? The trial?"

"Oh, the trial." Mhevek frowned softly as if he'd bitten into a sour fruit. "I do not like the idea of that word. Though I suppose, yes, the trial has begun."

"Can you tell us the rules of the trial? The guidelines? Or the goal?" A vein in Rory's jaw twitched, the only sign that she was bothered by this turn of events.

Mhevek considered while slowly sipping tea.

"We will travel to the art colony in the mountains," he decided, gesturing for another monk to step forward. "Once we have arranged our journey, you may meet us there. I believe you have the means of doing so."

"Yes," Rory agreed. "We have a door to your mountain region and a small outpost of knights in the area."

"You will not need them." Mhevek waved the idea away. "The art colony is peaceful."

"I insist on it."

Mhevek graciously assented, saying, "There is no need for insistence. All are welcome."

Amanda and Rory stayed to finish their tea, and talk turned to lighter topics. Amanda told Mhevek of their visit to the vendor in the village center. He was intrigued by the display Amanda had chosen and delighted by the vendor's pronouncement.

"The cricket and the sea! What a divine omen. Both feature in our sacred stories. I will tell you about them when the time is right, but not today."

"Thank you," Amanda said uneasily, biting back her impatience.

Not today was beginning to feel like the theme of her journey.

Chapter 7

Lunch with a Friend

Opening her eyes, Amanda threw up her hands and said, "That was a waste of time!"

She and Rory were sitting in her bedroom, their usual home base for planned travel. Amanda would sit on her bed, her back against the headboard, while Rory took the chair across the room. It was an out-of-the-way space where they could come and go without bothering her mom.

"No, it wasn't," Rory disagreed. "It got the ball rolling."

"Did it?" Amanda reached to pick up her phone from the nightstand. "It didn't roll very far."

Rory chose not to answer. Instead, she opened the door and stepped out into the living room. A moment later she returned and asked if Patty had gone out.

"Probably with Cameron," Amanda muttered. Rory watched her from the doorway, noticing how she frowned at her phone.

"What's up?"

"Nothing." Amanda stood, leaving her phone face down on the bed. "Trina wants to get lunch. You know, we're back way early, do you want to see if we can move up our meeting with Dr. Webb?"

Amanda opened a drawer as she spoke, pulling out jeans and a sweater. She had dressed for the morning in the clothes she wore for planned visits to Terra-V: a lightweight protective suit covered by a linen tunic and matching pants. In Arcadia, they could wear their everyday clothes. For Rory that usually meant black tactical pants and a fitted black sweater. Amanda wore whatever was comfortable.

"Why don't you get lunch with Trina? We have time."

Amanda shrugged, exchanging her green sweater for one with blue stripes.

"Aren't we having lunch? Mom left pizza money."

"Use it with Trina," Rory said casually, but something in her tone tickled Amanda's curiosity.

"You don't want to get lunch? Is there somewhere else you'd rather be?"

"Uh, no." Rory screwed her face into a look of confused denial, though the hint of a smile crept in. "I'll just get a jump on the mission notes while you're gone."

"Mission notes?" Amanda wasn't buying it. "You aren't going to make me help with them?"

Rory rolled her eyes and sighed, dropping into a more familiar look of exasperation. "I think I can handle the mission notes myself, since nothing happened."

Amanda winced at her sarcasm, then laughed lightly and sat on the edge of her bed to unlace her boots. When she finished, she glanced at her face-down phone.

"Yeah, well, we could talk about what we'll say to Dr. Webb. Or go over our plans for next week?"

"Amanda." Rory used her *level with me* voice. "Why don't you want to get lunch with Trina?"

After a long look at the ceiling, Amanda kicked off her boots and sighed.

"I don't know. It's an off-world day. My mind is on more important things than Trina's latest crush or whether she'll get a part in the spring musical."

Rory stood her ground by the door, studying Amanda carefully.

"Go to lunch with Trina," she decided. "I wouldn't mind some time on my own, and you could use a break from all this, too. Trust me."

Amanda raised an eyebrow. Usually, Rory was all about work, but lately, she'd been slipping away for mysterious breaks and *time on her own.*

A surge of water from the washing machine in the hall closet cut into Amanda's thoughts. She wondered when her mom had left home and where she had gone. She'd said something about errands over breakfast, and Amanda had assumed that was code for spending the day with Cameron. They'd been together most weekends, which was nice in a way. And weird in others.

"Fine," Amanda agreed reluctantly. She sent Trina a quick text, then dropped her phone and asked, "Can I get changed now?"

"The room's yours," Rory laughed. "Be back by 3."

She raised both hands in the air, elbows tight at her waist, and faded into thin air.

Trina's sister dropped them at the pizza place on her way to the Pilates studio three doors down. They'd have about 90 minutes before Izzy's class ended, giving them time to grab a slice and browse the bookstore next door.

"Pilates?" Amanda asked as they brought their trays from the counter to a table by the front window.

"It's Izzy's latest obsession." Trina rolled her eyes and reached for her soda. "Every Saturday from now to eternity. Or until she gets bored."

"And switches to roller skating," Amanda suggested.

"Or kickboxing," Trina laughed.

"Or pottery," Amanda added, but Trina shook her head.

"Pottery was last fall. For about a week."

"Oh, right." Amanda remembered the lopsided bowl on a ledge in Trina's kitchen.

"So, when are you dumping Drew?"

Amanda choked on her pizza and coughed until her eyes watered.

"Why would I dump Drew?" she asked, after a long gulp of water.

"When you didn't text back, I tried him." Trina chewed slowly. "He didn't know where you were and didn't seem all that happy about it."

"Oh." Amanda picked a slice of black olive off her pizza. Drew knew exactly where she was that morning, but she guessed he was tired of making up excuses for her.

"It's another guy, right?" Trina leaned forward, her eyes glinting with excitement. "Drew seemed to think it's another guy."

"What? No." Amanda flushed. "Did he say that?"

"Not exactly." Trina shrugged. "But he didn't deny it when I suggested it."

"Why would you suggest that?" Amanda stared in horror as her cheeks continued to burn.

"Well, he said he doesn't keep tabs on you and doesn't know what you do when you aren't together. Like, it's really common for you to go off and not tell him where. Another guy is *trés* obvious."

"There's no other guy."

"A girl then?" Trina raised an eyebrow questioningly. "You can tell me anything, I swear!"

"No, not a girl either!" Amanda stared into the distance, gathering her patience. "I mean, not like *that*, but in a way. I was just with Rory."

"Your cousin?" Trina sounded skeptical. She'd met Rory once last spring and they'd claimed she was Amanda's cousin. "Isn't she, like, *old* to be hanging out with."

"Not really," Amanda shrugged, forgetting the times she'd called Rory old. "She's cool."

"Okay, well, whatever. But I still say there's something off with you and Drew."

"You're just bored and looking for drama."

"Not true." Trina smiled slyly. "If you were around more, you'd know I've been busy hooking up with Nick."

"With Nick?" Amanda recoiled, remembering how Nick had questioned her in the library. Nick was a senior and he obviously had a thing for Trina, but she'd sworn they were just friends. She said she kept him around because he had a car, which embarrassed Amanda, even when Nick laughed like he was in on the joke.

"Well, not like *hooking up*," Trina clarified, "but we've been messing around."

Trina and the other kids at school were always dropping vague phrases like that. Amanda was never sure what they meant but always felt too awkward to ask.

"So, you are dating Nick now?"

Trina sighed dramatically. She scanned the half-empty restaurant as if looking for someone to sympathize with her over Amanda's cluelessness.

"Not everyone needs to define everything." She paused, giving time for Amanda to respond. When she didn't, Trina rolled her eyes. "You can be such a child."

Amanda sat straighter. "I'm older than you!"

Trina shrugged, taking a bite of her pizza.

"If you acted like it, maybe Drew wouldn't seem so frustrated all the time."

For the second time, Amanda's face flamed. She squeezed her mouth shut, wanting to shout that there was more to dating than *hooking up*. Or whatever Trina meant. But a creeping worry snuck in. She and Drew kissed and held hands, but she'd rather talk to him than anything else. Did that make her a bad girlfriend?

"Maybe it's because you were friends for so long before dating," Trina suggested, watching the doubt play across Amanda's face. "You still have him in the friend zone."

"That's not a thing," Amanda answered automatically. She hated the whole idea of the *friend zone*. As if friendship was just a lower rung on a ladder toward dating.

"Sure, it is," Trina countered, then sipped at her soda. "I'm not saying it's a bad thing. Some people are just better as friends than with *l'amour*. But dating means more than holding hands."

Amanda picked at her pizza, trying not to let Trina get to her. What she did or didn't do with Drew was none of Trina's business.

"Come on, do you even think Drew is sexy?" Trina pushed, leaning closer to catch Amanda's eye.

"He's my boyfriend," Amanda snapped.

"That's not an answer."

"Yeah, he's sexy, okay?" Amanda looked out the window and caught a faint glimpse of her own reflection. Her lips were pressed into a tight line and her eyes were glaring.

"Okay, okay!" Trina half-laughed and tore off a piece of her pizza crust. "I just hope you tell him that. Guys need to know you're into them for more than conversation."

"Enough!" Amanda smacked her hand on the table. "My relationship is between me and Drew. And we're good."

Trina stared, her mouth hanging open in surprise.

Amanda took another bite of her pizza, chewing and swallowing mechanically.

After a long silence, Trina hesitantly said, "I'm not saying you should rush into doing stuff or like *se coucher avec lui*. It's just… Well, you don't seem all that gaga over him. I mean, picture kissing him. Right now. Does that, like, excite you?"

Amanda rolled her eyes, but an image instantly came to mind. Deep, soulful eyes. Soft lips. A melting in her belly as he leaned closer and closer…

"Okay!" Trina laughed, seeing Amanda's face soften. "Maybe you're hot for Drew after all!"

Laughing shakily, Amanda told Trina to shut up. The conversation shifted back to Trina and Nick, and Amanda tried to listen. If she was careful, she might have a chance to suss out more about Nick's suspicions.

But she couldn't focus. She was too distracted by the face that had appeared when she imagined being kissed. The face that wasn't Drew.

§

Later that afternoon, Amanda and Rory met Dr. Webb to deliver the Pyura relic Amanda had chosen for Arcadia. It was a sloped, lightweight fossil that vaguely reminded her of a bird in flight. Dr. Webb accepted the relic graciously, turning it to catch the light before placing it on the center of the desk.

"I'm inclined to simply hand over all of Edmund's instructions," she admitted. "Now that you've brought me the item that's supposed to show you're ready to begin. But I'm not sure they would be all that helpful."

Dr. Webb explained that Edmund's instructions seemed to reference information from missing sources.

"I suspect your training here builds on what you'll learn in other worlds, though Edmund implies your training will be in tandem. There are only two goals he lists that are specific to Arcadia. He says by exploring creativity and truth, you will learn to *build what already exists*. He also says it will help if you *reveal what was once lost*."

Her words settled heavily. After a brief pause, Amanda voiced the question they were all thinking. "Is he talking about connecting our mindspaces?"

Beyond the glass walls of Dr. Webb's office, they could see towering buildings and cars flying through midday traffic. The city's ever-present birdsong was muted by the quiet zone Dr. Webb had activated. It was a courtesy to ensure private discussion, and Amanda fleetingly wondered who was being kept from overhearing them.

"In Edmund's time," Dr. Webb began slowly, "Arcadians had long forgotten psychic travel. The story that we are all descendants of travelers from another world was mere folklore. Only fringe mystics claimed to have an ability for psychic communication."

"And no one knows how that ability was lost?" Amanda tried to picture Arcadia in the late 1800s. Even then, their society's technology was far more advanced than anything on Earth.

"There are theories, nothing more," Dr. Webb said dismissively. "Space travel was relatively new to us when Edmund appeared. Our scientists and diplomats were focused on those explorations. Though Edmund's appearance lent credence to the mystics who had been largely driven out of civilized society."

Her emphasis on *civilized society* sent a chill down Amanda's spine.

"Did Edmund visit those mystics?" Rory asked, not missing a beat.

"He did," Dr. Webb confirmed. "His explanation of psychic travel fit with the stories they claimed to have inherited from our ancestors. Those claims had been embellished over the years, of course, but there was enough evidence for our scientists to explore the possibilities."

"And then you believed the mystics who had psychic abilities?" Rory asked.

"In part," Dr. Webb tentatively agreed. "Early in our space program, scientists had developed technology that responded to certain psychic energy. Amanda, you've used similar tools in your work with Mitra. After meeting Edmund, our scientists expanded that research, eventually isolating genes that could be reactivated to enhance psychic communication."

"The mystics were involved in that research?" Rory's wary tone said something in this story bothered her.

"To a point." Dr. Webb lightly stroked the Pyura relic, then clasped her hands in her lap. "The mystics have their own beliefs, which include some distrust of our scientific processes. The collaboration was not easy, and we soon parted ways."

Rory fixed Dr. Webb with a steely gaze.

"Your scientists experimented on the mystics, learned everything they could from them, then tossed them back out of your civilized society."

"Not exactly." Dr. Webb frowned. "But that's one way to see it."

Silence stretched between them as Amanda puzzled through the story. After several tense moments, she ventured her own question.

"By the time Edmund left these instructions, you'd already gotten some psychic abilities back? And he knew about your mindspace?"

"No," Dr. Webb corrected. "That did not happen during his lifetime. Edmund made visits to Arcadia for about 10 years and spent most of that time creating new gateways between our worlds. At that time, his visits to mystics were considered… *unconventional*. It was decades later when our scientists discovered genetic differences among mystics and learned how to reactivate those latent genes in more of the population."

"Your civilized society hadn't accepted the mindspace," Rory confirmed. "But your mystics had and likely shared that information with Edmund."

"That is possible," Dr. Webb agreed with a tight nod.

Amanda's eyes rested on the Pyura relic in the center of Dr. Webb's desk. It glinted lightly in the overhead light but couldn't tell her anything more about Edmund's plans for her training. She set aside the history lesson, bringing their discussion back to the present.

"If Edmund's instructions don't tell you about a trial, what kind of training am I supposed to do here?"

"He allows space for us to create your trial," Dr. Webb explained. "One that embodies creativity and truth to build what already exists…"

"And reveal what was once lost," Rory finished grimly.

"Do you think I need to connect our mindspaces?"

Rory tensed at Amanda's question, but Dr. Webb sadly shook her head.

"I don't know what it means," she said. Then added, "I do think that's a possibility."

"I don't," Rory cut in firmly. "Edmund expected the next psychic architect to emerge at any moment, if not before he died then soon after. He wanted *civilized* Arcadians to accept what the mystics knew and rediscover their own psychic abilities. He wanted Amanda to help them think creatively to find the truth. He didn't know anything about genetics or expect your scientists would work that out before the next architect emerged."

"That's a possibility as well," Dr. Webb conceded. "Though if he *had* known about the separation of our mindspaces, we can extrapolate that he would want Amanda's creativity to bring us back to the true mindspace and reveal the psychic travel that was once lost to us."

Rory sighed.

Dr. Webb softened her gaze and said she understood Rory's concerns.

"Connecting the mindspaces is a big ask," Rory told her. "It seems better suited to a psychic architect with her full powers, not one in the initiation phase of her training. Don't you think?"

"Perhaps," Dr. Webb agreed, "but there's no timeline on the trial." She took a deep breath before adding, "I also suspect that Edmund's instructions are not complete."

"You said that before," Amanda reminded. "Are there still mystics around? What if he left part of his instructions with them?"

Rory's eyes shifted to Amanda with pride.

"That is what I suspect," Dr. Webb admitted reluctantly. "There are religious orders that trace back to our early mystics. They keep their own historic records, separate from our national archives. We could request that information."

"Can we meet them ourselves?" Amanda brightened at the idea, wondering if the mystics were the Arcadian allies Edmund had referenced in his message.

"Eventually," Dr. Webb said in a clipped tone. "But we should go through proper channels. I will contact the mystics first and see what I can find out."

Rory accepted that, saying it was best to know more before any decisions were made. Amanda knew she was right but hated the idea of another setback. Even her closest relationships were turning out to be more complicated than she had thought.

After their meeting with Dr. Webb, Rory suggested they stop by Mitra's lab on the way out.

"He may have more to say about the mystics."

"No," Amanda quickly disagreed. "Let's not bring him into it yet."

Rory said there was time for a quick hello anyway, but Amanda ignored her and pressed the elevator button for the ground floor.

There were no numbers to watch in an Arcadian elevator. Instead, the buttons for each floor briefly flashed as they passed by. Amanda kept her eyes on the blinking lights, knowing it was impossible to get anything past Rory. As the moments passed, she could feel Rory studying her face, watching every twitch of expression to figure out why she had refused to visit Mitra.

When they neared the lobby, Amanda finally dared a glance and was surprised to see Rory gazing at the elevator doors. Her shoulders were casually relaxed, her thoughts a million miles away.

The elevator doors opened.

Rory stepped back for Amanda to lead the way, then frowned when she hesitated.

"What's up? Change your mind about Mitra? We can go back up."

"No," Amanda snapped, stepping out of the elevator, and hastily leaving the building.

Rory caught up easily and matched Amanda's pace for half a block, before inquiring, "Do you want me to ask or leave it alone?"

"Leave what alone?" Amanda balled her hands into fists as she marched down the wide sidewalk.

"Whatever is bothering you," Rory suggested as they neared one of the city's many pocket parks. The green space tucked between two buildings had trees, flower beds, and benches. There was also a metal sculpture tall enough for a few people to stand inside.

"We could use a quiet zone." Rory gestured toward the sculpture.

"I don't need that." Amanda sped up as they passed the park. The gatehouse was in sight when she finally said, "I'm just annoyed at Trina."

"Ah." Rory nodded. "What did she do now?"

"She just—" Amanda broke off, embarrassed to repeat Trina's suspicions. "She's just annoying this year. Being a diva about theater and throwing around French words when she knows I take Spanish. It's bad enough when she and Brooklyn do it, but it's really stupid when no one there knows what she's saying."

"That sounds annoying," Rory sympathized. "Kinda pretentious."

"Totally pretentious!" Amanda agreed, liking that description. "I think she likes that most of us don't speak

French. Like, she wants to know something we don't. She and Brooklyn both."

"She's spending a lot of time with Brooklyn?"

They crossed the parking lot at the gatehouse. Amanda stopped near a railing where she could look out across the empty field that separated the city from the forest. The birdsong that lightly filtered through the city streets was even louder here.

Amanda shrugged. It wasn't about Brooklyn.

"It annoys her parents, too," she said with a sigh. "The French stuff. They were glad she was finally taking Spanish last year because they hate that she can't speak it better, especially when her abuela visits. But she had to switch to French to take theater, because of the schedule."

"Maybe she wants to be different from her family." Rory leaned both forearms on the top railing and watched a flock of birds sweep over the field. "Did her siblings all take Spanish?"

"I think." Amanda shrugged again. "Trina always has to stand out. Get all the attention."

"And you don't." It wasn't a question. Rory knew how Amanda badly wanted to blend in, but she often didn't have that choice. "Must be hard to understand why Trina would want that."

"I guess." Amanda crossed her arms. She had only brought this up to put off telling Rory what Trina had said about Drew, but it was becoming clear she was upset about more than that.

CHAPTER 8

OPTIMAE VIRIDI

For her trip to Optimae Viridi, the third world in the architect's journey, Amanda had been given lightweight khaki pants, a linen button-down shirt to wear over a cotton tank top, and sturdy, tan climbing boots. When she came out of her room dressed for the trip, with her hair plaited in two neat braids, Patty frowned.

"I don't like the sound of this world."

They'd had this conversation before, and Amanda was sure they would have it again. Patty's support would never include being entirely comfortable with her teenage daughter visiting new worlds and meeting alien creatures. Secretly, Amanda liked her concern.

"Rory will be with me the whole time," she reassured. "And Cameron. And Lucas."

It was rare for all three of them to chaperone Amanda on a trip, but this was her first visit to Optimae Viridi—more commonly known to travelers as Opt-V.

The world was relatively safe for travelers who had permission to be there, but not a place to visit casually without running into trouble with at least one of the three tribes that lived there. This trip had been prearranged to allow a meeting with the Tribal Council to discuss Edmund's plans for Amanda's architect training.

Cameron had carefully described the world to Patty, trying to find a balance between honesty and reassuring her of Amanda's safety. After seeing pictures of the native tribes, Patty had to work at referring to them as people instead of creatures.

"The *people* there sound like they could be dangerous."

"People here can be dangerous," Amanda reminded before biting into a peach from the bowl on the kitchen counter. "You're afraid of the people on Opt-V because they aren't human."

Patty poured herself a cup of tea.

"This was easier when Judy was here. You don't know what it's like to sit at home without any contact while you're off on some other world."

"Aunt Judy knows we're going. She can still call or text you if we send her any messages. But this should be a fairly short trip. Five or six hours at most."

"You'll be in a jungle?" Patty eyed Amanda's travel outfit as if skeptical of its ability to protect her.

"Kind of. They say Opt-V is more like Hawaii. Lots of microclimates."

Amanda finished the peach and filled a glass of water.

Patty dunked her tea bag a few times, then looked up sharply.

"Have you been to Hawaii?" It was the kind of question most mothers would not have to ask their daughters. But most daughters couldn't travel around the world in the blink of an eye.

"No," Amanda confirmed, "but there is a door to Hawaii. Funny story: it was the first door Edmund made, way back before he built his own mindspace house. He was trying to connect to a remote place in Opt-V and that's where the first travelers who went through thought they were. Until they met up with some missionary who told them they were in Hawaii."

Patty smiled uneasily as Amanda laughed.

"Gerald thinks maybe that's why Edmund brought pineapples to the worlds he discovered later."

Finishing her water, Amanda checked the time.

Patty saw the dart of her eyes and rushed to ask, "Are you sure there's nothing important happening at school today? No tests?"

Amanda's off-world travel was usually planned around her school schedule. Sometimes, like today, it was too hard to coordinate, given the time differences between worlds and the need to convene Opt-V's Tribal Council.

"I'll make up any work I miss." Amanda took the teacup from Patty's hand, set it on the counter, and gave her mom a hug. "I'll be home before you know it."

Before Patty could reply, Amanda faded from sight, stepping through the door to PTS headquarters.

The traveler atrium was relatively quiet for a Thursday morning. A few doors shimmered into existence from spots across the expansive white marble floor, then disappeared as soon as the travelers they transported stepped through. The atrium's high ceiling rose above semi-opaque windows that let softly filtered sunlight glint across its white and gold walls. Small trees dotted the space, growing in huge ceramic planters.

With a wave at the guards, Amanda passed from the hidden atrium into the much smaller public lobby. She looked through glass doors at the busy Chicago street while waiting for the elevator, then hummed to herself on her ride up to Lucas' office. She was meeting the others there and had shown up early to prove how reliable she could be, even without Rory by her side.

When the elevator opened outside of Lucas' office, Amanda was surprised to find him talking with a woman she'd never met. She was dressed in black cargo pants and combat boots. Just below the sleeve of her black t-shirt, Amanda saw a familiar V-shaped tattoo. The Vertex.

"Amanda," Lucas greeted smoothly. "You're right on time."

"So, this is Amanda." The woman smiled, offering her hand. "I'm pleased to meet you."

Amanda shook her hand, looking to Lucas for help. He smirked behind the woman's back, then warmly introduced her as Elma Anthony.

"Elma is our primary liaison with the Vertex."

"Oh." Amanda crossed her arms over her chest, unsure of anyone who represented a group that had threatened her.

"I had hoped to meet you sometime," Elma said warmly, noting Amanda's discomfort. "And I would like to apologize for any concern raised by the protest at your school. It is unfortunate you were caught in the crossfire of a larger political issue."

Amanda silently stared at her, trying to sort through the apology that didn't feel like an apology.

"I've explained to Elma how much better it would be if your architect training were completed before a large shift in our operation." Lucas spoke to Amanda, though the message seemed to be more for Elma's benefit.

"And I've explained to Lucas how difficult it can be to negotiate over an indefinite goal," Elma added with a brittle smile. "Though, I'm told you are making good progress on your training?"

Amanda was saved by the ding of the elevator behind her. She turned to see Cameron and Rory wearing twin looks of concern.

"You're early," Cameron said to Amanda, stepping past her to confront Elma head-on.

"A little," Amanda stammered, until Rory shot her a look to stay quiet.

"We were wrapping up a meeting," Lucas explained with a gesture toward Elma.

"And now I'm leaving," Elma assured airily before flashing Amanda another cool smile. "It was lovely meeting you, Amanda. I do look forward to talking with you again sometime."

Cameron stepped aside, letting Elma enter the elevator, which Rory had held open with one arm. As soon as she was gone, Cameron glowered at Lucas.

"We'll talk about this later. Amanda, we have a few points to go over and then we'll be off. Are you ready to go?"

Amanda nodded, then followed his open-arm gesture into Lucas' office. As Cameron and Rory were taking their seats, Lucas hung back to offer Amanda a reassuring shrug. His grin seemed to say *Don't worry about them. I know what I'm doing.*

Amanda looked away.

§

Traversing Opt-V was like walking through soup. Steamy soup with vining tendrils floating all around and spiky ferns reaching into their dirt-trodden path. Beyond the heat and humidity, the world's slightly stronger gravity made each step feel heavy, like wearing ankle weights in mud. Amanda wanted to take off her outer shirt but settled for unbuttoning it to let a breeze cool the sweat gathering on her tank top.

The house door had brought them to the yard of a wooden outpost nicknamed the Travelers Embassy. There, Amanda was surprised to learn that psychic travelers on Opt-V were simply called travelers. Unlike on Terra-V where they were called the English or on Arcadia where they were referred to as the Maiorum.

"Whatever works for our hosts," Thorvald, their guide in Opt-V, had told Amanda lightly.

Travelers in Opt-V had a relatively good relationship with the three races who lived there: the Erlopes, Leotria, and Nicules. While travelers in Terra-V had taken on the roles of mediator and police to broker a truce between the Churukh and Vherahna, here, the tribes got along well enough on their own.

They also allowed travelers to maintain an outpost and explore the world for their scientific and cultural interests. As long as they kept a respectful distance.

After walking for about 45 minutes, the traveler party reached the edge of the rainforest. Amanda gasped as the trees gave way to a mountain vista with a crystal blue sea glistening in the distance. Snow-capped peaks rose to their left, far beyond a clearing that held a cluster of stone and wood buildings. Beside the settlement, a rocky path wound down to the ocean shore, leading past shallow ledges dotted with steaming hot springs.

"The Tribal Council meets in the central hall," Thorvald explained. He was a traveler from the outpost who had spent nearly 15 years living on Opt-V. In that time, he'd become a trusted friend of the tribal leaders and spoke a bit of each of their languages. He was also fluent in the neutral tongue they used for intertribal communication.

Amanda studied the large building at the center of the settlement. It had a stone foundation topped by weathered boards of dark wood. There were deep insets for windows, though they did not appear to be filled with glass. Instead, taut gossamer panels rippled lightly between wooden frames.

Two smaller structures sat on either side of the main building. One made of stone, the other of wood. As Amanda scanned the towering trees that scattered throughout the clearing, she saw slatted wooden structures built high into the canopy.

They all paused to drink water and rest after the long walk. Though she had learned about Opt-V before the trip, and would never admit it to her mom, Amanda was nervous to meet the natives of this new world in person. She looked around the clearing for signs of life but only saw trees and plants swaying in warm breezes.

"This will be a private meeting," Thorvald clarified. "The camp is neutral ground, a place for the tribal leaders to meet near the edges of the rainforest, mountains, and sea. You'd have to travel into each territory to interact with the tribes."

Entering the central hall, Amanda tried to hide her excited curiosity. The leaders of the Erlopes, Leotria, and Nicules were suddenly there in front of her, as if they'd stepped from the pages of her study guide.

Each elder had their own place on a designated wall of the large room, excluding the wall that held the arched entryway. Their seats and decorative surroundings echoed their personal tribes, reminding Amanda of a series of displays in a museum.

To the left, Elder Cordrowr sat on a high-backed chair built from driftwood and decorated with seaweed and shells. The design continued to the sand-coated wall behind him. Like all Erlopes, Cordrowr had a blend of amphibian and reptilian features. A face like a frog and a body similar to a crocodile. Erlopes walked on two legs and had two short but functional arms, as well as a spiny tail that nearly reached the ground. Seated, it was hard to gauge Cordrowr's height, though it was easy to see he would tower over the others.

Though Cordrowr was intimidating, the depth of his gaze was reassuring. He held his head high, studying Amanda and the others carefully. Something about his cautious demeanor appealed to Amanda. She knew the Erlopes were introspective and wise. They lived long lives and spent much of their time in isolation, contemplating their world. She'd been told they were the philosophers of the three tribes.

Directly across from the entryway, an elaborate spray of carved wood created an elegant perch for Elder Ilta, leader of the Leotria. Branches with fragile sprays of pale blue flowers clustered on either side of the filmy white bunting that backed her perch. The Leotria's bird-like race had both powerful wings and delicate arms sprouting from a lithe, feathered torso atop two spindly legs. Ilta's hooked beak gleamed white gold and her feathers shifted from pale pink and fuchsia to deep purple and midnight blue. Her bright black eyes were framed by long lavender lashes and her gaze was as sharp as the claws on her hands and feet.

Amanda was fascinated by the idea of a human-bird hybrid and wished she could know how it felt to soar through the sky. The coloring of Ilta's feathers reminded her of some of the feathered horses on Terra-V. Yet the horse's feathers were short and sleek, except for lush plumes of their peacock-like crowns and tails. The feathers on Ilta's body looked softer and longer, ready to fluff up for warmth in their mountain home. The Leotria had a reputation for being both clever and tricky. Amanda thought she could see that in the glint of Ilta's bright eyes.

Off to the right, leafy branches framed a vine-woven seat, then extended to cover the wall and a large portion of the floor. Elder Keah, who led the Nicules, crouched eagerly on the woven seat, setting it swinging lightly with every fidget. Her compact body was covered in soft, coffee-colored fur. Her long arms reminded Amanda of an orangutan, though her face more closely resembled a sloth. She was clearly eager to meet their visitors and flashed them each a wide, toothy smile.

There was a childlike energy in Keah's movements, and Amanda couldn't help smiling in return. The Nicules were considered the most human-like of the three tribes, though Amanda found it hard to think of Keah that way. She looked so much like an animal on a nature show that Amanda began to wonder why the animals in their own world weren't treated with the same respect as the tribes on Opt-V.

"May I present our esteemed visitors and introduce them to your wise council?" Thorvald greeted the elders with a graceful gesture toward Amanda and the others. He then repeated his question in a language that sounded more like animal calls than a series of words. Amanda knew it was the blended language of the tribes.

Cordrowr rumbled a short reply followed by a flick of his tongue, and Keah quickly followed suit with her own lilting chatter. An undulating shiver rippled down Ilta's wings as she quietly tilted her head toward each of the newcomers in turn.

Thorvald laughed.

When he turned back to the traveler party, he said, "Cordrowr says I should drop the formal act, but Keah thinks a little ceremony would be a nice change."

Cameron's smile was tight as he asked Thorvald to introduce everyone. Amanda hung back, standing close to Rory's side as she watched each member of their team be presented in turn. From Thorvald's introductions, she could tell the tribal elders had been briefed on who they would be meeting, just as their team knew all about the elders. The introductions were a formality.

"And last but not least, our future architect, the reason for this meeting, our own Amanda Jones."

Thorvald rattled off the words smoothly, effortlessly switching between English and Opt-V's neutral language as if to prove he was saying the same words in each tongue. Amanda still wished she had an Arcadian translator disc so she could hear from the elders herself.

The tribal elders seemed particularly interested in Amanda. Knowing she was young for a traveler, they asked many questions about her age, size, and place in society. Once their curiosity was satisfied, they spoke fondly of Edmund, patiently waiting for Thorvald to translate.

Cordrowr and Ilta had known Edmund personally, as their lifespans were much longer than that of a human. Cordrowr had been fifth in line for his throne at the time of Edmund's frequent visits, while Ilta had been a young girl. Keah had only heard stories of Edmund, as Nicules typically lived about 65 years, though she was quite impressed by the stories he'd left behind.

This soon led to the purpose of their visit, and the room quieted in anticipation.

After a brief exchange, Thorvald translated somberly.

"Edmund has charged the Tribal Council with teaching the next architect courage and restraint so that she can, in his words, live with bravery and boundaries."

He paused, giving weight to those words.

Amanda remembered what she had learned about the tribes of Opt-V. Their races had many differences and largely lived in separate areas. Yet, they also admired their neighbors and helped each other through trade and cultural exchange.

Thorvald continued. "To live in harmony, each tribe teaches their young about differences in their neighboring tribes. That includes a rite of passage at a certain age. Simple trials designed by each tribe for their neighbors to highlight some valued element of their culture. The council believes Edmund would want Amanda to complete each tribe's rite of passage."

Cameron, Lucas, and Rory all turned to Amanda. Thorvald resumed his conversation with the elders, which became a buzzing background against the dizziness that swarmed Amanda's mind.

"You okay?" Rory whispered, and the room came back into focus.

"Yes," Amanda muttered weakly, distracted by what it might mean to complete a tribal rite of passage—no, *three* rites of passage—in a strange world.

Thorvald then pointed toward crude wooden stools of various heights that were lined up on either side of the arched doorway. They were invited to bring over chairs and get comfortable as he explained more about each of the tribe's rites.

"The Erlopes live several hundred years. They have a longer view of the world and temperaments that are as deep as the sea and as still as the sheltered lagoons. They are few in number and live solitary lives outside of set social rituals.

For their rite of passage, Amanda will spend one night alone in a chosen lagoon."

Rory quickly protested.

"Amanda doesn't go anywhere without me."

Thorvald glanced over his shoulder at Cordrowr before saying, "The terms are not negotiable. If Amanda is not ready, she is welcome to wait until she is older."

"I'm ready," Amanda blurted hastily, ignoring Rory's apprehension.

"They are *her* trials," Lucas reminded lightly. Rory scowled and Cameron sighed.

"Let's hear about all of the rites of passage before we make any decisions." Cameron settled the matter, gesturing for Thorvald to continue.

"After her night in the lagoon, Amanda will meet the Leotria higher in the mountains. They are a social tribe, migrating from place to place with the seasons. Leotria are also very active and spend much of their lives in a cycle of metabolizing and replenishing energy. Their rite will be a timed race."

"A race against who?" Amanda asked.

"Whom," Lucas muttered, then shook away his own correction with an apologetic shrug. There was something off about him, something brittle and hard as he slouched to one side with his arms crossed and his boots casually perched on the lowest rung of his stool. *He's worried,* Amanda realized, though she wasn't sure if the worry was related to her safety or her ability.

"Yourself," Thorvald answered plainly. "It will be a short race. I believe around 100 meters."

"At high altitude," Rory added pointedly. "On a world with higher gravity."

Ilta twittered to catch Thorvald's attention, then carried on a brief discussion with him.

"The race will be modified for Amanda's human form," Thorvald reassured them, "and further adapted after Amanda's ability is assessed. That's all I can tell you. Not knowing the details in advance is part of the test."

Amanda didn't like the uncertainty of the race, but she did enjoy running and a 100-meter timed race sounded easy. Even if it was higher up in the mountains.

"The Nicules' rite will take place the following day, giving time for Amanda to rest," Thorvald went on, after a quick consultation with Keah. "Nicules live throughout the rainforests, forming family groups within their larger tribe. These close relationships are a key aspect of their culture. They rely on each other to develop tools and structures that make the forest more habitable. For their trial, Amanda will lead two teammates through obstacles spread throughout the forest."

Before she could ask, Thorvald conferred with Keah and told Amanda, "After meeting you all today, Keah has chosen Rory and Lucas as your teammates."

"That's it?" Rory asked, surprised to be included so easily.

"What kind of obstacles?" Lucas raised an eyebrow, but Thorvald assured them that there would be nothing excessively dangerous in the course.

"Keah has brought travelers through some parts of their forest. We haven't seen all of it, but there are various structures that they've built—bridges, platforms, that sort of thing—which have puzzles or hidden elements that need to be solved to access certain parts of the forest. Keah says you will be sent through a route that other travelers have not used, and she says an important element is that Amanda is meant to lead."

"She can do that," Rory answered easily. "I trained her myself."

Amanda smiled faintly at the praise. She was glad Rory and Lucas would be with her in the forest, but getting them to follow her lead might be the hardest challenge of all.

Chapter 9

Making Plans

Sitting in the void of the pure mindspace, Amanda mulled Edmund's first two goals: *to see what cannot be seen* and *to build what already exists*. The first could be a reference to accessing the pure mindspace since it was an empty place beneath the psychic houses that only psychic engineers and architects could access.

But what did it mean *to build what already exists*? Did Edmund want her to connect the Arcadians' separated mindspace? Or was he referencing the connections between worlds? Did they already exist in some cosmic sense, just waiting for an architect to add doors?

"Do you want to help with the next door?"

Elaine appeared beside Amanda, followed by Dorothy, Gerald, and a wooden door banded in iron. They appeared to float in the dark emptiness.

"This one's a bit thready. Want to give it a boost?"

"I don't know. I should probably get to the gym…"

Gerald scoffed. "Training your body isn't half as important as training your mind."

"Now, Gerald," Elaine scolded, "you're not the one facing those trials on Opt-V. I would be worried about them, too!"

"At our age, so would I," Dorothy cut in, eyeing Elaine's fluffy, sweater-clad body and orthopedic shoes. "But Amanda is ready for the physical stuff. We need to help with her other skills. And we still don't know what Stellaria will bring."

"Ah, Stellaria," Gerald said wistfully. "I haven't been to Stellaria in ages."

"We should plan a trip!" Elaine clapped her hands in excitement.

As they talked, they shifted out of the pure mindspace. The room became visible around them. They were in the great hall of the castle, formally known as the Martio House. Stone walls and stone floors. A few muted tapestries hung between the thin windows. It was the same room where they had first met, though now Amanda relaxed in their company in a way she rarely could with others. Even in the chill of the gray castle, she felt at home.

During their first meeting, Amanda hadn't known where the doors in the castle's great hall led. Now the doors loomed large, pulling her focus even as she tried to listen to the engineers' chatter. These were the doors to Opt-V, though that hadn't been the world's official name when it was discovered in the 13th century. It had been renamed Optimae Viridi in the 1800s when travelers established a more permanent presence.

Three original doors led to the heart of the Erlopes, Leotria, and Nicules' territories. The fourth, created by Alice Thomas in the 1800s, led to the traveler's outpost. The fifth was Edmund's accidental door to Hawaii.

Amanda forced her attention to the engineers' talk of vacation plans.

"You've all been to Stellaria?"

"Oh, yes," Elaine answered happily. "It's one of the most popular getaways for travelers."

"Of course, you can't just show up or the place would be overrun," Dorothy told her. "You need to book in advance and be approved or you won't get past the secure gateways at each door."

"What if a traveler skipped the doors and set their origin point in Stellaria?"

Amanda often wondered about that possibility in any of the worlds where PTS tried to control access. A traveler could easily go through official channels to get there, reset their origin point by traveling back through the house directly, and then travel in and out of the world as often as they liked.

"It happens," Dorothy admitted uneasily. They all knew that was a loophole Lucas and his band of rebels had often used when they were living in exile. "But travelers who do that are usually caught quickly."

"You'll love Stellaria," Gerald said, changing the subject. "Its small villages are kind of like Colonial Williamsburg, but they have no use for money, or class systems, or wars. The villagers just live together in harmony. Amazingly, we haven't managed to screw that up for them yet."

"They love having travelers visit," Elaine gushed, clasping her hands happily. "Some travelers even fall in love and marry native Stellarians. Of course, there's a lot of red tape, but it's worth it for those in love."

"It's shocking more travelers haven't tried to exploit that." Dorothy's cynicism cut through Elaine's romantic reverie. "I bet there will be a clamor for marriage visas before the end of summer."

Gerald and Elaine looked grim. Seeing their faces, Dorothy brushed off her own prediction and turned back to the door that needed maintenance.

"Why before the end of summer?" Amanda asked, picking up the tension in the room.

"It's nothing," Gerald told her.

"A silly rumor," Elaine agreed.

But Amanda was insistent.

"The Vertex claims to be planning something big by the end of summer. Something that will end the secrecy once and for all."

"This summer?"

Amanda looked at the doors leading to Opt-V and shivered. It was already mid-March. She'd barely begun training for the trials she'd have to pass there. Worse, Mhevek and Dr. Webb hadn't laid out any concrete goals for their worlds, and she hadn't even been to Stellaria yet.

Panic bubbled up from her stomach, but Amanda was getting good at pushing her fear back down. *There's still time,* she told herself. *Stay focused.* Slapping both hands to her thighs, Amanda looked at the engineers gathered around her and got down to business.

"All right, step one: I need to see what cannot be seen. Alira says she has nothing more to teach me. Mhevek says we've already begun training—whatever that means—and that Churukh woman in the market said I'm a cricket and the sea. How does any of that help me see what cannot be seen?"

Elaine hesitated, eyeing the others. She was still unsure if Amanda should be telling them anything about her sacred training, but that hadn't stopped her from listening in on these discussions. Dorothy pressed her lips together and squinted into the distance, showing she was deep in thought. Only Gerald was ready with an answer.

"I've been thinking about that whole cricket and sea thing. I even talked to one of my historian buddies who spent some time in Terra-V about 20 years ago. He said a lot of Churukh folklore involves crickets. Though they aren't crickets like our crickets."

"Yeah, they're bigger," Amanda confirmed. Her support team had said the same thing at a recent meeting. "More like really big beetles, but they chirp like our crickets."

"Right!" Gerald pointed at her with a nod, then went on. "They're also great at surviving extreme temperatures, storms, and all that. But in folklore, they're more magical. They show up at just the right moment, and they bring exactly what's needed in every story. As if they can see the future. Something no one else can see."

"Okay…?" Amanda wasn't sure where he was going with that thought. She couldn't see the future and had never heard of that being part of a psychic architect's special powers.

"Now the sea, or ocean, also shows up in Churukh folklore. It represents knowledge, more precisely, all of the knowledge there is to know about everything. If someone were to *be the sea,* they would be all-knowing."

"So, the Churukh think Amanda is an all-knowing creature who can predict the future?" Dorothy sounded skeptical.

"No, that's too literal!" Elaine broke in, then bit her lip, still torn on how involved she should be. After a brief internal struggle, she sighed and said, "There's a bigger picture here. The sea is a symbol of knowledge, and the cricket is an example of *applied* knowledge. Mhevek plans to take Amanda to their art colony, a place where creation takes place.

"Think about it," she urged, with an excited shake of her hands. "An architect creates structures that connect worlds. There's an underlying sea of knowledge that the architect has to tap into at the right moment. It's like what Michelangelo said about carving stone!"

Dorothy and Gerald brightened with understanding, while Amanda looked at them all in frustration. She knew Michelangelo was an artist from way back in history, but she had no idea what he'd said about carving stone.

"He said the sculpture was already in the marble," Gerald explained slowly, still pondering the idea himself. "Just waiting for him to carve away the extra stone to set it free."

"An architect doesn't have to be all-knowing," Dorothy added. "She just needs to see something under the surface, waiting to come out."

"Yes!" Elaine clapped loudly, bouncing in her seat. Dorothy matched her wide smile. Gerald's slow nod became surer with each bob of his head. But Amanda continued to frown.

"Uh, guys?" All eyes turned to her, almost as if they'd forgotten she was there. "We kinda already know that. Not the sculpting stuff, but the creating what's already there. It's the next step of Edmund's trials, remember? First, it's *see what cannot be seen.* Then, it's *build what already exists.* But how? What does that actually mean?"

Elaine's hands had frozen mid-clap. She settled them in her lap and fidgeted while saying, "Oh, yes, well…"

Amanda stood up and walked around the large stone room, stretching her arms overhead one by one. Talking about this wasn't going to solve anything. She needed to go to the art colony with Mhevek, complete the trials on Opt-V, and learn more about the mystics on Arcadia.

She stopped walking and spoke into the empty room.

"Reveal the value in what was once lost."

All eyes studied her intently.

"Dr. Webb said that was an extra clue for their trial. What does *revealing something lost* have to do with building something that already exists?" An idea was pulling at the edge of her mind, not quite formed but coming together with her words. "The Arcadians lost more than their psychic travel abilities. They lost the original connection between our worlds. The one their ancestors used to get to Arcadia in the first place."

"No one knows how they destroyed that door," Dorothy added with a frown. "The council at the time was so intent on preventing more unauthorized colonization that they buried or destroyed all records of it."

"Except for the place of the door!"

Gerald shot across the great hall, moving down a narrow passageway that led into the castle's great chamber. The others followed without question and stared as he pointed at a blank space framed in a stone outline on one of the walls.

Looking around the large bedroom with its canopied bed and stone hearth, Amanda saw the same stone frame around the remaining wooden doors. The detail was easy to miss among the scattered wall hangings and upright cabinets.

"This was the original connection Martio made to Arcadia. When the door was destroyed from the other side, the frame around it remained, and no architect was able to make a new door in its place."

Amanda stepped to the wall and hovered her hand over the smooth space where the door had been. Faint energy flickered. Her heart leaped as she closed her eyes and felt for its rhythm, but it was gone without a trace. Even when she slipped into the pure mindspace and focused on the same area, she couldn't feel a thing. Blinking back to the visible room, Amanda dropped her arm and sighed.

"Nothing?" Dorothy asked.

"We don't feel anything either," Elaine confirmed.

"But there could be something there," Gerald persisted. "Something leftover that could be built again. Once Amanda learns how to see what can't be seen and build what already exists."

Without answering, Amanda studied the empty place on the wall again. It looked like a decorative arch. As if nothing had ever been there. She almost told them about that fleeting glimpse of energy, but it had disappeared so fully, she doubted it was ever there at all.

$

"**O**ff belay!"

Amanda heard Rory's call as she reached for a handhold and eased her way to the anchor at the top of the crag. She and Rory were rock climbing on a beginner route in Kalymnos, Greece.

"You made it!" Rory cheered, then watched with approval as Amanda clipped into the anchor and called down that she was also off-belay. Once secure, she turned to see the deep blue sky blending seamlessly into the soft ripples of the Aegean Sea.

"Wow, it's beautiful!"

Rory smiled softly. This was their first outdoor sport climb, after weeks of practicing on indoor training walls at PTS facilities, and she wanted it to be special.

From the ground, their belayers squinted up at Amanda with pride. They were some of Rory's traveler friends who knew the crags at Kalymnos well. They'd chosen one of the easiest routes, where they could use the top roping setup Amanda already knew. Like Rory, they were sure climbing would get Amanda in shape for whatever came up during her trials in Opt-V.

"I wasn't too sure about this," Amanda admitted, still mesmerized by the rich blues of sky and water against the golden brown of the sloping crags. "But look at that view! This is so much better than the climbing wall."

"Next, we'll switch it up with bouldering in France," Rory promised. "You'll love Fontainebleau!"

As Amanda's gaze swept over the wide blue sea, the architect's journey crept in. They were visiting Stellaria in a week and plans were coming together for her trials in Opt-V. This climbing trip was part of her training, but it felt like being on vacation when she should be working.

"Rest a few minutes before we go down?" Rory asked, then shot a message to the belayers below.

Worry etched Amanda's face as she considered her theory about the original door to Arcadia being part of Edmund's training.

"Should I tell the support team?" she asked Rory, after explaining where her thoughts had gone.

"That's up to you." Rory shook her arms, releasing tension from the climb.

"But I'm supposed to keep them in the loop, right?"

Rory looked over Amanda's gear, preparing to set her up for their descent. A salty breeze ruffled her hair.

"Not necessarily." She glanced at Amanda and saw her confusion. "The support team is there to *support* you. They're a resource, not a group you need to report to."

Amanda thought about that as she watched Rory pull up a length of rope.

"Think of how Mitra treats the scientists on his team," Rory suggested as she worked. "He values their input but he's clearly in charge and gives them specific tasks. He doesn't run every idea by them."

Amanda wasn't prepared for the sudden mention of Mitra. She felt shaky despite her feet being braced on a relatively wide ledge.

"That's different," she said quickly, not wanting to think about him—or Trina's suspicions—while she was 30 meters above solid ground.

"Not really," Rory corrected casually, pausing in her reach to the anchor line. "Mitra would probably have good advice about working with a support team. Ask him the next time you hang out."

"I don't hang out with Mitra!" The anger in Amanda's voice surprised them both. She shook her head, adding, "We just work together."

"Okay," Rory answered uneasily. "Did something happen with Mitra?"

"No, it's fine. Can we lower down now?"

"Sure." Rory let it go, knowing they weren't in the best place for a tense discussion. "Let's get you back on belay."

The focus on technique chased away Amanda's sudden bad mood. By the time they were safely on the ground, she fist-bumped their belayers and laughed about the few scary slip-ups she'd had both going up and down the crag. The travelers launched into tales of their own climbing adventures, and Rory hung back, watching Amanda carefully. When their stories were told, Rory's friends went off to climb on their own. Rory and Amanda caught a ride back to the nearest proximal zone.

"I had a great time," Amanda reassured, wanting to make up for her earlier outburst.

"I'm glad." Rory waited for more.

"I'm just a little edgy. A lot going on with the trials, and Stellaria." Amanda nearly went on to include Trina and Mitra, but Rory spoke into the pause.

"I need to talk to you about that. About Stellaria."

"Yeah?" Amanda held her breath, fearing the trip was postponed.

"Judy is going to take you on this one." Rory rushed on before Amanda could react. "We thought it would be nice for you to spend some time together. Since she's been gone. Plus, I have some personal business next weekend."

"Oh." Amanda bit back her initial questions and asked why Lucas wasn't taking her instead.

"He's busy, too." Rory looked out the car window, then back at Amanda. "I was hoping you'd understand."

"Yeah, sure." Amanda didn't mind Rory not going with her, but she did wonder about Rory's *personal business.* Especially when Lucas happened to be too busy to travel at the same time.

She studied the back of their driver's head, then quietly turned to stare out the window. They were headed away from the sea and toward the chapel that secretly doubled as a PTS gateway. Riding past densely packed buildings, Amanda thought about the chapel's secret proximal door and wondered what else in her world was hidden in plain sight.

§

Amanda's spirits picked up as the trip to Stellaria drew closer. She was eager to finally see its celebrated charm for herself. Its quaint villages with stucco buildings gathered around town squares. Its farmlands and orchards, black-smiths and weavers, glass makers, carpenters, and more.

Most of all, Amanda wanted to see the plant that had given Stellaria its English name.

In her off-world training, Amanda had heard all about the vining plant with tiny flowers that covered the ground and climbed trees, spilled from decorative planters, and was even woven into thatched roofs. On Earth, there was a similar plant called chickweed or *Stellaria media*. The off-world version had been named *Stellaria niger* due to its difference in coloring. Instead of bearing tiny white flowers with yellow centers, *Stellaria niger* boasted jet-black petals with hearts of gold and cobalt blue.

There was another striking difference. In Stellaria, the shiny flowers reflected light, giving off a rainbow-hued gleam, like a drop of oil on wet pavement. Their centers also glowed brightly from within, like strings of tiny holiday lights. At night, clusters of the tiny blooms were enough to light up a room.

Amanda was so taken with the pictures she had seen of villages blanketed in fairy lights, she broke her own rule about discussing psychic travel at school.

"We're going to just miss Vasar. That's a festival for their first day of summer. Or as close to what we call summer since there are like five seasons on Stellaria. But we're going during the day, which is such a waste! I don't know why they couldn't plan it at sunset."

Amanda and Drew were sitting in a hallway with their backs against a row of lockers. They'd skipped lunch and wandered off to talk before the bell sent them back to class.

Drew nodded. "Yeah, you said that yesterday."

"Oh, sorry." Amanda hugged her knees, realizing she had been dominating the conversation.

"It's okay." Drew reached to tuck her hair behind her ear. There was a soft smile on his face as he leaned in close. "I like when you tell me things."

His lips brushed hers and Amanda quickly pulled away.

"We're in school!" She scanned the hallway, checking the windows on the classroom doors for anyone who might be watching.

"No one's here," Drew promised, inching closer. He kissed her again, this time threading his fingers through the back of her hair. Amanda's heart raced as she pictured a teacher storming into the hall and having to explain her behavior when the school called her mom at work.

"Not here!" She pushed Drew away and instinctively wiped her mouth.

"Not here," Drew echoed bitterly. "Not at school. Not on the bus. I barely see you anywhere else."

He leaned into the lockers, letting his head bang against the metal.

"You know how busy I've been." Amanda crossed her arms over her chest. "I go straight from school to off-world briefings, or climbing, or meeting my research team."

"Yeah, I know." Drew pressed his lips together. His hands clenched into fists, knocking lightly against his bent legs. "You're very busy."

Amanda bit her lip, trying to remember the last time they'd been to a movie or even hung out in the apartment's party room. There had been that day Judy came to say she was moving, but that was over a month ago. It was also the day her architect's journey had officially begun, along with extra training and off-world missions that had taken up nearly all of her evenings and weekends.

"I have Stellaria on Sunday, but I can get some free time on Saturday… Except, I might have to go to Arcadia. Dr. Webb is stalling on this meeting with the mystics, and Lucas thinks it would help if I work with them on this other idea…"

"Right, Arcadia." Drew sounded bitter.

"Yeah. What's wrong with Arcadia?"

"Nothing," Drew scoffed, then took a deep breath and relaxed his hands.

"You know how important this is," Amanda reminded, and Drew closed his eyes. When he turned to face her, there was sadness in his smile.

"I know it's important," he agreed. "I just don't know if I'm important."

Amanda stared at him, not sure what she could say. Of course, he was important. But what did that mean? He had said he would support her training, and now he was complaining about it?

"You're important," she said, but her delay in answering hung between them.

Drew stared grimly at the lockers across the hall.

"Hey," Amanda said, grabbing his arm. "You said you'd support me through this, and now you're mad that I'm not spending enough time with you?"

Drew looked at the ceiling and said, "That's not it. I mean, I don't know. Maybe that's it."

Amanda let go of his arm and shook her head.

"You knew I'd be spending more time in training," she reminded him. "More time off-world."

"I know, but…" Drew stopped himself, clenching his fists again.

"But what?"

"But there's a guy off-world."

The words seemed to echo in the quiet hallway. Amanda's mouth dropped open, then snapped shut when he turned to her with fear in his eyes.

"I hear the way you talk about him. You light up. It's always, *Mitra says this,* or *Mitra says that.* You're so impressed with him."

"He's really smart," Amanda argued weakly. "Am I not allowed to like working with him?"

"If that's all you're doing with him."

Drew refused to look at her, and Amanda's anger spilled over.

"You think I'm messing around with Mitra? Behind your back?"

"I don't know," Drew snapped. "It's not like you're messing around with me."

Amanda's face flamed. She heard Trina's voice saying, *dating means more than holding hands.* She remembered how she sometimes felt when Mitra looked deep into her eyes, then pushed that thought away, knowing she'd done nothing wrong.

"So, what? I won't make out with you in a school hallway, so I must be cheating on you?" Tears stung her eyes and Drew's anger deflated.

"Well, no… I didn't mean that. I just… I don't know where I stand."

"You're my boyfriend," Amanda said. As if that cleared everything up.

Drew grabbed her hand again, searching for the right words. Amanda glanced at the clock on the wall, knowing their time was running out.

"You have a whole other world out there. *Worlds.* That's what's important to you, and I'm not a part of that."

"Not directly…" Amanda hesitated, then switched gears. "But once I get through this architect training—"

"You'll have even more to do," Drew finished.

Amanda looked at their clasped hands. He didn't move but she could feel him slipping away. Drew also seemed to feel the moment passing.

"Look, I can get on board with waiting at home while you go off and do important things. But I'm not sure you want that. You have a big future, and I don't know if I'm in that picture."

"In the picture?" Amanda tightened her grip on his hand, desperate to hold on.

"In your future," Drew clarified. "Am I part of this big life you're always dreaming about?"

The bell rang, and Amanda jumped. There would be a stampede of kids in a moment and her mind was already crowded with Drew's fears.

"We are sixteen," she reminded him. "That's way too young to be thinking about, like, our whole adult lives."

"Is it?" Drew clenched his jaw and dropped her hand. "You think about being an architect and sitting on the High

Council someday. You talk about your future all the time. What you don't talk about is *our* future."

Two doors opened and kids poured out of classrooms on their way to the second lunch period. Farther down the hall, Amanda could hear shouts from kids leaving the cafeteria and heading their way. She hastily stood up, brushing off the back of her jeans.

"So, do you?" Drew was on his feet, clutching one of Amanda's arms and ignoring everyone around them. "Do you think about our future at all? Creating a life together? A family together?"

"A family?" Amanda stammered. "I mean, I've never pictured you *not* being in my life, but…"

"But I'm not part of your *other* life. The one where normals don't belong."

"Drew, I…" The words caught in Amanda's throat. She didn't ask to have psychic abilities when he didn't. "Look, I know you want to be part of that, but…"

"I do want to be part of it!" Drew's voice rose and some passing students glanced their way. "I want you to need my help with it."

"Well, I don't *need* your help."

The words slipped out and Amanda was surprised by the hurt on Drew's face. She tried to explain, saying she had other people for that. Drew held up one hand, cutting her off.

"Yeah, that's the problem."

He started to walk away, and Amanda hurried after, reaching out for him.

"Drew, wait!"

Kids in the hall turned to stare. Trey was among them, leaning against a locker with a smirk on his face, but Amanda didn't care. She twisted her fingers together and said the first thing that came to mind.

"I want you in *this* part of my life. And in the future, I… I just don't know what will happen." Her voice dropped to a near whisper, and Drew stepped close enough to hear. "I can't think about that now."

She watched conflicting emotions play across Drew's face. Someone jostled into her back, sending her stumbling against Drew's chest. He caught her easily, a hand on each arm, and quickly kissed her lips before letting his forehead rest against hers.

"That's not enough," he said hoarsely. "I want to be with you. Forever. Part of your life isn't enough."

Letting go, he took several long strides before Amanda called out, "Drew, stop!"

This time he kept his back turned as the kids around them fell silent.

"Are you still my boyfriend?" Amanda's voice shook. She ignored the murmurs from the crowd and studied the droop of Drew's shoulders. After a long silence, he shook his head.

Amanda barely heard him say, "Not anymore," before a rush of noise and movement flooded the hall, blocking her view as he walked away.

CHAPTER 10
STELLARIA

Amanda turned off her alarm and pulled the covers over her head. She was deep in a dream of flower-draped lockers and jewel-eyed birds when her mom shook her shoulder, saying, "Amanda! Wake up! Aunt Judy is waiting for you!"

"Where's Rory?" Amanda mumbled, still caught in her search for the bird that was laughing from a distance.

"Judy's taking you to Stellaria. Remember?" Patty sounded exasperated as she snapped on Amanda's bedside lamp.

"Ow!" Squinting in the harsh light, Amanda looked for the clock on her cluttered nightstand, then startled at the time. "I'm late!"

"Yes." Patty sighed, stepping aside as Amanda hurried to the bathroom across the hall.

Ten minutes later, Amanda was dressed and saying goodbye.

"Hold on!" Patty stopped her. "You need to eat something first."

"No time!"

"It will take five minutes." Patty held out an apple and a granola bar.

Amanda pocketed them both, promising to eat as soon as she got there.

Rushing, her flustered mind brought her to the birdhouse instead of the temple's elegant red and orange room. She stood in the main hallway of the Victorian house, looking into the den with its white doors to Arcadia, and tried not to think about her last conversation with Drew. She had more important things to do today.

Looking down, Amanda watched the hardwood floor dissolve into an intricate tile design. When she lifted her head, she was surrounded by silk wall hangings and lush furnishings in warm red, orange, and gold hues. A buzzy, scattered feeling fizzled through her. She fixed her eyes on the gleam of a gold statue to keep from fading back into her apartment.

"Where have you been?"

Judy stood with crossed arms and pursed lips. She was dressed simply in dark canvas pants with a beige sweater and low-top hiking boots. The strap of a sling bag stretched across her chest, and the blue streaks in her dark hair peeked from braids that led to a messy bun at the back of her head. Her dark-rimmed glasses flashed in the glow of a crystal chandelier.

"Overslept," Amanda muttered, turning gingerly to the door that would lead them to Stellaria's main village square.

Like the other doors in the room, it was carved teak with raised images of vining leaves and small flowers. The rich sheen of the dark wood beckoned for Amanda to reach out and touch it. She slid one hand over the surface and felt the energy pulsing within. The sensation grounded her in the mindspace and her breathing steadied. With a slow exhale, Amanda smoothed back her hair and straightened her pale pink sweatshirt, aware of the apple bulging in its center pocket.

"I thought you were going to wear a sweater." Judy frowned at the crooked hood bunched at the back of Amanda's neck, then glanced at her ripped jeans and blue sneakers. Before Amanda could respond, Judy said, "Never mind, it's fine."

They stepped through the carved door into an old building whose interior plaster had chipped away in several places, showing red brick below. Instead of looking shabby, Amanda thought the exposed brick gave the space an artistic charm, especially with vines of Stellaria spilling out of planters hung at intervals along each wall. Her heart skipped at the sight of the famous flowers, confirming she was finally in the last world of Edmund's initiation.

Though the brick building was large, there weren't many people inside. There were no scanners to walk through, like those on Arcadia, but a traveler guard was busy sweeping a handheld scanner over a couple who had arrived ahead of them. Judy and Amanda passed through a similar screening and answered a series of standard questions.

While the guards who spoke to them were friendly, Amanda found it hard to relax under the gaze of the armed soldiers who lined the walls. They stood in relative ease, dressed in Kevlar uniforms and helmets. They also cradled large guns and appeared ready to act at a moment's notice. Amanda spotted gas masks, shields, and other riot gear stashed in easy reach on a low shelf behind them.

When Amanda and Judy were cleared to leave the building, Amanda saw the gatehouse was surrounded by a 15-foot metal fence topped with sharp spikes. A three-story brick building towered on one side of the gatehouse, outside of the fence. On the other side, a metal structure that looked like an airplane hangar glinted in the sunlight.

"Those are the barracks," Judy explained, nodding toward the three-story building. "It's where the travelers who are stationed here as guards live. They rotate in shifts, so the proximal zone is covered 24 hours a day. We could visit sometime, but not today. There's not much to see anyway. Some guards are asleep, but most are waiting in the barracks on backup."

"Backup for what?" Amanda looked at the brick building, noticing its flat roof with a ledge where she imagined snipers could perch their guns. It was the kind of detail Rory liked to point out on their travels.

"Potential threats," Judy answered lightly before walking down the short path to the manned gate in the center of the fence. Amanda hurried after her.

"I thought Stellaria was a peaceful place."

"It is." Judy looked grim. "The guards are here to keep it that way."

Once they'd cleared the barrier and heard the metal gate roll closed with a decisive *clank,* Amanda gazed around her new surroundings. The area reminded her of the region just west of home where there were farmlands and wineries. They were in the foothills of mountains with larger peaks hazy in the distance. In one direction she saw far-off trees. In another, fields with crops climbing wooden stakes. Wild Stellaria grew in patches alongside the road and up the side of a nearby wooden stable.

Stepping closer to the nearest plant, Amanda saw the flowers were even prettier in person. From a distance, the jet-black flowers were an eerie sheen against the pale green leaves. Up close, the blue disc within the dark petals showed a ring of azure with a circle of gold at the center. The surface of the disc was a faceted crystal that reflected light in several directions. Amanda longed to visit at night and see the strings of flowers light the village.

Straight ahead, a cobblestone road wound its way past scattered buildings, some with barns and animal pens. A small cart traveled along the road at a quick clip, carrying the visitors that had arrived ahead of them into the village. Within moments, a similar wooden cart rolled out of the adjacent stable, pulled by a creature that looked very similar to a donkey but with smaller ears and piebald spotting in shades of tan and burnt orange.

The woman driving the cart appeared to be human. She wore a long green skirt and lace-up boots with a woolly white sweater and a blue ribbon tied to the end of her dark braid. Climbing into their seats, Amanda saw that the woman's eyes had blue rings similar to the center of a Stellaria flower. Her skin was covered in ash-gray hair, so fine that it was barely visible.

"Avu yai!" she called happily, showing straight white teeth that sparkled faintly.

After they repeated the woman's greeting, she switched to English to offer them a ride. Judy thanked her for picking them up and chatted about the lovely weather, a topic that Amanda had learned was literally universal.

Watching the foreign countryside roll by made it easier to leave memories of Drew back in her own world. Here, she could focus on what really mattered. But the moment Amanda had that thought, the pain she'd seen in Drew's eyes flashed through her mind.

"Are you feeling all right?" Judy asked quietly. "Do you need some Vhelox?"

Amanda shook her head. She wasn't travel sick and hadn't needed Vhelox to steady her body since her first few months of psychic travel. Yet there was a buzzing behind her eyes and the sway of the cart sent her stomach lightly pitching. At Judy's urging, she accepted a whiff of Vhelox. The synthesized mist wasn't as effective as a vhe transfusion from the Vherahna, but it calmed Amanda's body and cleared her mind.

Riding into town was like falling back in time to a pre-industrial era that never existed on Earth. There were no motor vehicles. No power lines. No electric lights. Wide roads offered plenty of space for both pedestrians and donkey carts. Brick, stone, and clapboard buildings sat far from the roads allowing room for fruit trees and wooden benches. Raised garden beds lined building fronts, brimming with vegetables instead of blooms, while herbs flourished in many window boxes.

"It's beautiful," Amanda said as the homes and gardens became closer together.

"First visit, young one?" the driver called back with a smile in her voice. "Wish we had taken the road by the orchards. A longer path but lovely with the trees in flower. Maybe for your road back? Apple flowers are my favorite! And apple flowers mean apples will follow soon!"

Feeling the apple through her sweatshirt, Amanda remembered that villagers here would only have access to fruits and vegetables in season. There were no grocery stores with shipments from other parts of the world. She nudged Judy, asking if it was safe to share, then pulled the fruit from her pocket.

"I brought an apple from home," she told the driver, reaching it up toward her elevated seat. "Would you like it?"

"An Earth apple! For me?" With a wide smile, the driver accepted the shiny fruit.

"Is it very different than your apples here?"

"Perhaps." The driver held the apple up to the light. "We've heard it said you have many apple types on your world. We have two. One that is a little red and tastes sweet. The other is a strong yellow and has a bite!" She laughed, appreciating the English expression, then looked back at the apple in her hand. "Never seen an apple this red. Does it have a name?"

"Yes, but I don't know it." Amanda looked to Judy for help, and she said, "I think it's called a Red Delicious."

"Red Delicious!" the driver echoed happily. "Avu yai! My family will share this apple with a wish for your happy health."

She polished the apple lightly on her shirtfront and nestled it carefully in a wide pocket.

Judy gazed at her niece with a pleased smile, then leaned in to whisper, "Well done. Was that your breakfast?" Amanda shrugged and pulled out the granola bar.

By the time they neared the village square, Amanda felt more confident about their visit. She was eager to meet the town elders and learn about Edmund's plans for her in this new world. The place where she would learn *knowledge and wisdom to wield power sparingly.*

§

The cart came to a stop in front of a white clapboard building with red double doors. An older woman stood outside wearing pale blue linen pants and a white shawl over a white tunic. There was a basket hooked over one arm and a polished stone hanging from a woven string around her neck. She had short silver hair and bright blue eyes. The eyes of a Stellarian.

"Avu yai!" Judy greeted the woman brightly before introducing her to Amanda as Niane, one of the village elders.

"The others will meet you soon," Niane promised. "First, we will tour our village center."

As they strolled the cobblestone streets, Amanda enjoyed the sweet, crisp air and the distant sounds of happy people talking and laughing throughout the village. The buildings sat relatively close together in the heart of the village, yet lush gardens created space for tranquility and privacy.

Niane brought them into several businesses to greet the artisans who ran them and anyone else they happened to see. Amanda met tailors, cobblers, carpenters, glassmakers, and metalworkers. The village provided for itself, creating clothes, furniture, and sundries of daily living. Amanda particularly enjoyed the mercantile, which was a general store, and the printing press where books and newspapers were created by hand. There was also a post office, where Amanda was surprised to see carrier pigeons waiting to quickly send messages to the farther edges of town or even to villages in other parts of Stellaria.

When the tour ended, Niane brought Amanda and Judy back to the white building with the red doors. It was a large hall where village meetings were held, as well as seasonal dances, flower shows, art exhibits, and other community events. Three village elders were there to meet them.

"Avu yai," Anra greeted, offering firm handshakes and an efficient smile. She was a small, athletic woman with shoulder-length salt-and-pepper hair and an energy that seemed barely contained in her khaki pantsuit and gray laced boots.

"Avu yai." Kasper drew the customary phrase out, seeming to ooze toward them with gliding steps. His hand gently enveloped each of theirs, coupled with a slow bow that gradually returned his thin frame to its full height. His copper hair glinted with silver and was brushed back in stylish waves, which were echoed by the curved ends of his thin mustache.

"Avu yai!" Mardin greeted with more spirit. Like Kasper, he wore pale slacks tucked into calf-high canvas boots and a pastel sweater. Mardin was the oldest of the group by far, yet he moved with surprising fluidity as he shook hands and ushered Amanda and Judy toward comfortable seats clustered in a circle at one end of the long hall.

"Our village tour was enjoyable?" Kasper asked slowly, tasting each word as Amanda imagined their driver would savor her Earth apple. She tried not to smirk at the thought as Judy chatted for a few minutes about the shops they had visited.

"Yes, the village is lovely," Anra broke in with an impatient wave. "Amanda wants to talk of more important things."

Focus turned to Amanda as she startled to attention, hoping her secret amusement hadn't been obvious to everyone.

"Well, yes," she agreed uneasily. "I mean, I am curious about the information Edmund left with you. But I enjoyed the village tour, too."

"Our village enjoyed a great friendship with Edmund," Niane said fondly. "We did not know him ourselves, but our grandparents spoke of him well and his stories are now woven into our own."

"We are honored to assist Edmund's wishes for your future, Amanda," Mardin added grandly. "With hope and charity, we will offer goodwill as you carve a destiny worthy of your predecessor."

Amanda looked at Judy hopefully, flustered by the expectation in his voice.

"How do you plan to train Amanda?" Judy asked, following Anra's lead by getting directly to the point.

The elders grew quiet. Niane looked at Kasper. Anra and Mardin looked at each other. Amanda felt her stomach sink. Something wasn't right.

"You do have instructions that will help train Amanda?" Judy tried again.

"Perhaps," Niane responded for the group. "Edmund's letters describe his successor's journey. Our role is to present Amanda with a quest."

"A trial," Anra corrected emphatically. "The *fourth trial* were Edmund's words."

"Yes," Kasper agreed, refusing to quibble over words. "A task to be completed."

"What task?" Amanda thought of the trials she would face on Opt-V. The race, the team obstacle course, the night alone in a lagoon. She couldn't imagine what challenge she would have to pass in a peaceful village.

Mardin cleared his throat.

"Edmund asks you to consider how you can improve our way of life."

Amanda blinked in the silence.

"Your way of life?" Judy asked. "In Stellaria?"

"Yes." Mardin nodded firmly.

"Edmund wants me to improve your way of life?" Amanda repeated slowly.

"Edmund asks you to consider how you can improve our way of life," Anra confirmed, echoing Mardin's exact wording.

"Is there a right answer?"

"Yes," Niane answered. "Guidance on the correct answer has been provided."

"One answer?" Amanda imagined the improvements she could bring to the village. Electricity. Indoor plumbing. Cell phones. Computers. Beyond their own technology, she could skip ahead to advanced developments in Arcadia. Solar panels. Hover carts.

"Edmund describes an answer which will show you are ready to become your world's next architect."

To wield power sparingly. Amanda remembered the overall goal of her task in Stellaria. How did that tie in with finding a way to improve the villagers' way of life?

Having nothing more to share with Amanda about Edmund's instructions, the village elders invited Amanda to return for their upcoming apple blossom festival. Amanda smiled at the idea but couldn't think beyond the puzzle they'd given her.

After a pleasant conversation about the history of their village, including several stories about Edmund's adventures, Judy said it was time for them to go home.

"Come back often," Niane offered as she walked them toward the street and waved over a passing donkey cart. "Edmund's answer cannot be given to you, but we are able to discuss your ideas and perhaps offer gentle guidance. Avu yai."

Amanda thanked her and they climbed into the cart.

As the donkey pulled them slowly out of the village center, Judy sunk into her seat and nudged Amanda's shoulder lightly.

"We'll figure it out."

"Yeah, I know." Amanda nodded without a smile. "I just hoped it would be something more…"

"Instructive?" Judy suggested.

"I guess. It's like I'm still learning, but everyone expects me to already have the answers. Or just magically figure it out. Like with—"

She stopped talking and crossed her arms.

"Like with?" Judy prodded gently.

"Nothing, just…" Amanda hesitated, feeling a lump growing in her throat. Looking away, she quickly said, "Drew broke up with me."

She couldn't see Judy, but she could sense her surprise.

"Your mom didn't tell me."

"She doesn't know."

"When?"

"Three days ago. At school."

Judy waited. The cart rocked over cobblestones as they passed fruit trees laden with peaches and nectarines. Amanda summed up the story, starting with Trina's meddling and ending with Drew's talk of their future together.

"You're only sixteen!" Judy exclaimed, earning a raw laugh from Amanda.

"That's what I said!"

"Look," Judy began, reaching for Amanda's hand. "I like Drew. He's a decent guy. He's also scared of losing you, and he's not handling it well."

"He can't be that scared, since he dumped me."

"That's why he dumped you," Judy corrected. "He's so afraid that you'll leave him someday—that he can't measure up to your fabulousness—that he'd rather dump you now than wait to be hurt."

Amanda thought about that.

"Should I talk to him? Try to reassure him or something?"

"No," Judy answered decisively. "He's a good guy, but he's got some growing up to do. He has to figure out who he is on his own. Build up his own confidence."

"Right, but…" Amanda hesitated. "What if he was right? About Mitra?"

"Did something happen with Mitra?"

"No." Amanda shook off the question, noticing that Rory had worded it the same way. "I mean, nothing *romantic* or whatever. We're friends. But… he is… attractive. Is it cheating to have a friend who I sometimes think is, um…"

"Hot?" Judy suggested. "Sexy?"

Amanda squirmed and blushed.

"Amanda," Judy began gently. "You are allowed to find people attractive. That's not cheating. That's just being human with eyes and hormones. Cheating is more complicated. It can be physical or emotional. But an emotional affair is more than occasionally noticing a friend is attractive."

The gatehouse fence came into view and Amanda sighed, still confused.

"Look, this is part of being sixteen," Judy reassured her. "You're just starting to figure this dating stuff out. So are Trina and Drew and all your other friends. Instead of only talking to them, keep talking to me. And your mom and Rory. We don't always get it right either, but at least our brains are fully formed, and we have experience that might help you skip some hard lessons along the way."

"My brain is still cooking," Amanda laughed, repeating what her Biology teacher often said about teenagers.

"Until you're about 25," Judy agreed. "But it works pretty well already. You just need a little guidance."

Amanda squeezed Judy's hand.

"I wish you could come home for dinner. Mom misses you, too."

"I wish I could, too." Judy leaned over to kiss Amanda's temple. "But my origin is set in Phoenix now. The nearest door to you is New York, and that's still hours away. I'd have to fly like a normal."

"I know." Amanda sighed. "I wish there was a door closer to me."

"You can make one someday," Judy suggested, and Amanda smiled at the idea.

They reached the gatehouse fence and thanked their driver for the ride, exchanging the customary *avu yai* and friendly waves.

After the guard let them through the fence, Amanda asked Judy about the meaning of avu yai.

"I mean, I know it's for hello and goodbye, but what does it actually mean?"

"It's hard to translate." Judy considered her answer. "I've been told it's like a wish to live your best life."

Avu yai. Amanda considered that as they passed the final security checkpoint and prepared to open a door back to the mindspace. *Live your best life.*

"Oh!" Judy interrupted her thoughts with a sharp clap. "I have the best idea! Let's go to Paris!"

"What?" With anyone else, Amanda would have assumed the suggestion was a joke, but she recognized the gleam in her aunt's eyes.

"Come on!" Judy nudged. "We have time before you need to get home. Let's catch up. Girl talk over a café au lait at one of those charming little bistros."

"Ugh, not Paris!" Amanda groaned, thinking of Trina and Brooklyn. Though the idea was tempting.

"What's wrong with Paris?" Judy threw up her hand before tossing out other ideas. "You pick then. London? Madrid? Hawaii? San Francisco? Pick a door, any door! You're sixteen and a psychic traveler, let's get out and live our best lives! Avu yai!"

Looking at the door Judy had conjured, open to the temple's lush red and gold room, Amanda gave Paris a second thought. She'd never been, and it would kill Trina if she knew.

"You know what, let's go to Paris! We'll hit a café and I'll catch you up on all the crazy in my life."

"A perfect afternoon!" Judy beamed. "Avu yai!"

"Avu yai!" Amanda repeated, and all her problems felt a little bit smaller.

CHAPTER 11

THE PARTY

"I didn't mean for you to break up."

They were in Patty's car—Amanda driving and Trina in the passenger seat—on their first solo outing since Amanda had become an officially licensed driver. In the two weeks since their breakup, an uneasy politeness had settled in between Amanda and Drew. The tension between Amanda and Trina had been harder to crack.

"I know you didn't," Amanda answered absently as she crept up the street in search of a space to easily park.

In one week, she would be spending her Spring Break completing trials in Opt-V. She didn't need any added stress, so she'd agreed when Trina suggested they celebrate her new driver's license by going to this party together.

"His loss," Trina said, getting out of the car and waving at some friends Amanda barely recognized in the fading light. Trina pulled out a mirror to check her lipstick before adding, *"Quelle damage."*

Amanda smirked, recalling the bread and cheese, followed by delicious pastries, at the sidewalk café in Paris. Judy had cackled at her description of Trina's constant French phrases and they had gotten silly with their own exaggerated accents.

Once inside, Amanda leaned against a kitchen counter, sipping soda as Trina accepted a red cup filled from a keg. She was glad to have the excuse of driving so Trina wouldn't nag her to at least have one drink. The taste of beer made her gag, and it embarrassed her to see friends act stupid and get sick after drinking it.

The party was at Nick's house. His parents were out of town and the crowd was steadily growing. Drew was there. Amanda had seen him out in the living room with a red cup of his own. She didn't know if it was beer or soda but decided it was none of her business. That didn't stop her from stealing glances, only to quickly look away when she caught him checking up on her, too.

Amanda!

Lucas' voice echoed through her mind. She let part of her focus drift into the mindspace while the rest of it kept sight of the kids laughing around her. The temple's blue and gold room appeared like a hazy overlay on the cheery yellow and white kitchen. Lucas grinned from beside a carved door. A column set with blue and gold stones was to his left and mosaic tile swirled beneath his feet. The vibrant setting made her shared attention even more jarring.

"I need you to pop over to Mumbai with me." Lucas held out a hand as if ready to help her step fully into the mindspace.

"Now? I'm at a party." The words she said in the temple came from her thoughts and wouldn't be heard by anyone in Nick's kitchen.

"Sneak away," Lucas urged. "Twenty minutes tops."

Amanda agreed and the image from the mindspace disappeared, leaving her fully present in the suburban kitchen. Lucas knew she would need a few minutes to find a safe place to travel. She thought of locking herself in the bathroom, but someone was sure to need it while she was gone. A sliding door in the kitchen led to a patio where some kids were hanging out and into the dark backyard beyond. She could slip outside and disappear in the shadows if she was careful about it.

"Where are you going?"

Trina was at Amanda's side the moment her hand touched the door.

"Just getting some air."

"I'll come with."

Amanda froze. Scanning the kitchen for a distraction, she caught Nick watching them intently.

"I think someone wants you to stay here," Amanda suggested, tilting her head toward Nick.

Trina shot him a smile and bit her lip, then pulled her gaze away with a frown.

"No, you're here alone," she told Amanda dutifully. "I'll stay with you."

Amanda laughed at Trina's sudden loyalty and insisted she would be fine on her own.

Outside, there were more kids than Amanda expected. The patio chairs were full. A few kids sat on the cold stone floor while small groups spilled out into the shadowed yard. Amanda wandered between them, awkwardly steering clear of the couples making out, before finally heading around the house toward the street. She decided to slip into the dark backseat of her car and travel to the house from there, giving herself a private place to return.

In her hurry to slip away, Amanda didn't notice Trina following quietly behind.

§

Amanda had been to India for meditation and yoga training, but this would be her first trip to Mumbai. Lucas was waiting for her in the temple when she arrived, her body in the backseat of her car and her conscious self standing beside him.

In the grandeur of the temple's blue and gold room, silk tapestries hung from gilded walls, ornately tiled archways framed a series of carved doors, and an abstract mural filled the domed ceiling. At one end of the room, a low, mahogany table was surrounded by plush red cushions.

"Look, I know you're pressed for time," Lucas said as soon as she appeared. "I won't keep you long, but I've been negotiating with some international leaders from the Vertex, and they want to meet you before we go further."

"On a Saturday night?"

"It's Sunday morning there."

"Oh, right. But why do they want to meet me?" Amanda eyed the door warily, and Lucas raised an eyebrow. "Yeah, okay, I know. Next architect. But why now?"

Lucas let his hand drop away from the door.

"The short answer: I'm buying you time to get through your training and tap into those fancy architect skills before our world cracks apart. The rest I can explain later."

He opened the door to Mumbai and Amanda found herself staring across the threshold into what appeared to be a shabby hotel. The stone floor was laid out in earth-tone tiles, the walls were a dingy taupe, and there were clusters of upholstered furniture that had seen better days.

Lucas stepped through the doorway and Amanda followed, her body instantly transported from the backseat of her car to solid ground on the other side of the planet. Turning, she saw daylight filtering in through arched, opaque windows. At one end of the room, a tall reception desk stood before a peeling mural. At the other, a line of latticed wood screens obscured her view of the front door. Behind her, the proximal door was already fading from sight.

"Welcome to Mumbai," Lucas said with a sweep of one arm. This timeworn hotel looked nothing like the sleek PTS training center Amanda had visited in Mysuru.

"Why is it so…?" Amanda trailed off, wrinkling her nose at the fetid scent of dust and mildew. She could hear a truck backing up and people shouting at each other outside. Peering past the latticed dividers, she noticed men in dark uniforms posted just inside the front door, likely put there to stop normals from entering the fake hotel.

"Dated?" Lucas suggested with his usual smirk. "We're in a prime location of old Mumbai, near the Gateway of India. The perfect place for a psychic door in 1775. But times change."

Lucas started toward the open staircase that ran along one wall, leaving Amanda hurrying to catch up. On the second floor, he turned down a central hallway with doors along either side. Several doors on the right were open, showing a long office space with scattered desks and a large conference table.

Eight people were gathered in the room. Some sat at the table while others selected coffee and doughnuts from a table on the far wall. One woman stared pensively out a window and didn't turn when Lucas and Amanda entered the room. They were all strangers to Amanda, though she recognized the Vertex insignia on some of their clothes or tattooed on exposed arms.

"Here she is," Lucas announced in his understated way, as if offering a paper clip rummaged from a desk drawer.

Amanda nodded uncertainly and twisted her fingers together until she caught herself and straightened her spine. When she'd faced situations like this in the past, Rory had always told her to hold her head up and believe that she mattered as much as anyone else in the room.

"She's so young," a man at the table said bluntly.

"She's sixteen," a woman responded while putting a doughnut on her plate. "What did you expect?"

"You're pitching a deal that rests entirely on this child?" Another man asked Lucas angrily.

Amanda felt a rush as her face flushed and her eyes narrowed in on the man's condescending sneer. She imagined Rory's voice telling her to get angry. Anger was better than feeling intimidated, and their rudeness deserved her anger.

"This *girl*," she said, "has already created one psychic door and has begun to master mysteries of psychic design that are beyond your limited understanding. She's also standing right in front of you, so you can stop talking as if I'm not in the room."

The woman with the doughnut, put down her plate to clap lightly, saying, "You tell him!"

Lucas grinned and stepped closer to Amanda.

"I told you she has fire. Amanda is young, but she's determined. She's made amazing progress in a short time and is on track to develop her full architect potential in no time. If we don't send this entire society into chaos while she's trying to learn."

The room broke into heated conversation. Amanda tried to follow the debate, but she felt weak as the adrenaline she had used to defend herself rapidly washed away. She concentrated on the jittering under her ribcage and the shaking in her legs, taking slow breaths to keep the room in focus. When she felt steady enough to listen again, Lucas seemed to be rehashing an earlier point.

"How many times has this land been redeveloped in the last 240-some years? How long can we keep up the hotel front? There's a growing push to redevelop the chawls all around here and hanging on to a fake hotel isn't helping anyone. We have space for a new door in the U.S. Consulate, and we're close to having an architect who can make one. If you just hold off a little longer, we can move to the BKC and convert this building to much-needed apartments."

Amanda tried to process what he was saying, making note of the unfamiliar words so she could look them up later. Or ask Gerald. She did grasp that Lucas wanted her to create a new door in another part of Mumbai, and her heart raced at the idea of having to deliver on the promises he was making.

"It's not just here where we have this problem," Lucas went on, oblivious to Amanda's growing anxiety. "How many proximal zones are in dangerous or inconvenient areas? How many new cities have become important destinations since we last had an architect? There's no proximal zone in Delhi, Ottawa, Mexico City, Washington, or Kyiv."

"There we go!" One of the men slapped his hand on the table. Amanda noticed the familiar V-shaped tattoo just below his shirt sleeve. "More political maneuvering. You say creating more proximal zones is to add convenience and help build community, but adding doors to strategic places also makes it easier for governments to send in their mercenaries. That's another reason you want secrecy!"

Lucas' eyes flashed but his lips pressed into a white line, containing whatever retort he had ready.

Beyond his tense profile, Amanda saw the woman at the window finally turn to face the group. It was Elma Anthony, the Vertex liaison she had met outside of Lucas' office. She offered Amanda a soft smile before turning her stern attention to Lucas.

"You used to be with us." Her clear voice carried through the room, silencing any murmuring, and pulling all the attention her way. "You used to see the harm in a shadow government hiding our abilities and advantages from the primitives. Before you became one of them."

Lucas nodded at Elma in easy agreement.

"I did see the harm, and I still want transparency. For our society and for everyone in our world. I am questioning the timing and the process, not the end goal."

"Isn't that what dictators always say?" Elma asked coldly. "They're working toward democracy *someday*. When they decide their people are ready. Yet they never seem to be ready."

No one moved in the room. All eyes shifted between Elma and Lucas, watching their argument play out. Amanda watched them as well, but her mind was tripping over what she'd already heard. She wildly wondered what Elma had meant when she said Lucas used to be with them.

Had Lucas once been a member of the Vertex? And who were the *primitives*? Was that the term the Vertex used for normals?

Amanda watched Lucas' shoulders rise and fall as he took a deep breath. He then turned to her with his usual charm and said, "Amanda, go on back to your friends. You don't need to be here for this."

Though his tone was light, the steely set of his features left no room to argue. After quickly scanning the room, Amanda hurried downstairs and hastily conjured a door. It was a relief to step through and open her eyes in the dark backseat. Until she saw a shadowy figure leaning against her car.

§

Amanda eased out of the backseat and stared at Trina across the car roof. Trina was clearly angry. Her arms crossed and mouth set in a hard frown. But it wasn't clear how long she had been standing there. Or whether she would believe that Amanda had been in the dark backseat the whole time.

"Hey," Amanda said softly, testing the waters.

Trina's mouth twitched to one side.

"I just needed a break," Amanda offered weakly. "From all the people."

"And?" Trina asked stiffly.

"And I didn't want to bother you, or make you leave, so I came out here to clear my head. I thought I could head back in before you noticed I was gone."

"That I believe," Trina laughed dryly. "The last part."

Amanda wrapped her arms around her ribcage and glanced toward Nick's house.

"Look, Drew and I just broke up. It's not easy to go out and act like everything's okay. Especially when he's in there and I don't know what to—"

"So, you've been here?" Trina interrupted. "Hiding out in your car?"

"Uh, yeah…" Amanda made a show of being confused. "You just saw me get out."

"But I didn't see you get in, did I?"

Their eyes met and Amanda saw Trina's suspicions. She had been trained on how to misdirect a situation like this. Encourage a normal to question what they might have seen. Respond with anger to throw gas on the fire, then shift the focus of the fight, showing disbelief at the person's wild claims.

"How should I know what you saw?" Amanda's voice rose, even as she kept the confusion on her face. "I don't follow you around. Keeping tabs on you. Why are you tracking every move I make?"

"I followed you because I was worried," Trina snapped. "I saw you get in the car, and I saw when you weren't in the car. Now, you're back."

She finished with a shaky breath. Her eyes glittered in the faint moonlight.

Amanda calculated quickly. She could say she got out of the car to walk around and then got back in, hoping Trina hadn't been watching the whole time. Or she could insist she had never left.

"What are you talking about?" Amanda decided to play up her disbelief. "I've been right here."

"No, you weren't." Trina's anger fled and her voice cracked. She hugged her chest and said, "You curled up on the backseat like you were going to sleep, and then you disappeared. I saw it. I saw your body just… fade away. And now you're back."

Amanda noticed shiny lines where tears had run down Trina's face. She pictured her screaming and banging on the car door, panicking at what she had seen. Likely terrified and remembering Nick's conspiracy theories about aliens who could disappear.

Hating what she was about to do, Amanda forced a strangled laugh of disbelief.

"How much did you drink tonight?" she asked, then ran a hand over her face. "I mean, wow! You've been spending way too much time with Nick."

Trina didn't say anything, but tears pooled as she gripped her arms tighter.

"So what? I'm an alien now?" Amanda rolled her eyes, then tried to laugh the whole thing off. "Look, it was a trick of the light or something. And, fine, I'll admit it. I heard you out here, but I didn't want to talk to anyone, so I pretended to be asleep. I thought you'd give up and go inside. I didn't think that you would…"

"She knows." A voice interrupted from the shadows of a nearby tree.

Drew stepped into the dim light.

"You're lucky she texted me instead of Nick."

Amanda's arms dropped by her sides. Her heart raced and fog filled her mind.

"What are you talking about?" She wanted to give him a chance to explain, to catch her up on whatever cover story he had used with Trina. But if he had covered, why stand back, waiting for Trina to walk her into a trap?

"She knows," Drew repeated, this time with disappointment dripping from each word.

Amanda's eyes skipped between them, still making sense of the situation. Trina had watched her disappear. She had panicked and texted Drew. And then what? Instead of covering, Drew had just told Trina her secret?

"You're one of them," Trina said. The accusation came without anger, but Amanda stepped back as if she'd been slapped. *One of them.* "You're one of them, and you didn't even tell me. You've been lying to me."

Staring at the ground, Amanda felt the world collapsing around her.

"It's not like that…" She spoke softly then trailed off, knowing it was exactly like that.

"I can't talk to you. Not telling me was bad enough, but then to lie to me?" Trina threw up her hands and stomped toward Nick's house.

"Trina, wait! Please!" Amanda hurried after her, ready to beg forgiveness or promise anything to keep Trina from talking.

"Don't!" Trina spit angrily. She turned just long enough to give Amanda a withering glare. "I'm not going to say anything. I'm a better friend than that."

As Trina stormed up the street, Amanda shook her hands and bounced her weight from foot to foot. She couldn't process anything beyond thinking, *This is bad. This is really bad.*

"Hey."

Drew sounded worried, but Amanda spun on him, yelling, "How could you? You couldn't have come up with something? Anything?"

Drew's expression hardened. "She knew. She saw you disappear and was freaking out."

"That's why she shouldn't know!" Amanda stomped her foot. "Knowing is dangerous."

Drew looked sharply away. Amanda didn't know what he was thinking, but when he turned back, she recoiled from the scorn in his glare.

"So, you were protecting her by lying? By making her think she was crazy?"

In a flash, Amanda remembered how she had thought she was losing her mind before Judy showed up to explain psychic travel. The fear tasted like metal at the back of her tongue.

"This isn't my fault," Drew said coldly. "And you don't need me to watch out for you, remember?"

"That's not fair!"

"Exactly," Drew agreed, his voice husky and his jaw tight. "You don't get to pick when you need me and when you don't. And you don't decide how I take care of my friends."

"I thought I was your friend." The words ripped like glass through Amanda's tight throat.

Drew pressed his lips together and looked at the sky before meeting her gaze with a film of tears in his eyes.

"I thought you were, too. But what you just did? That wasn't the friend I know."

CHAPTER 12
MHEVEK'S LESSON

The Churukh art colony nestled in the mountains, far from the Vherahna forest. In Edmund's time, when danger to the Vherahna was at its worst and Churukh were sick and dying for lack of vhe, travelers had tried to use proximal doors to transport vhe-infused products from the Vherahna Forest to those in the mountain region. Yet vhe could not survive the trip through the mindspace. Later traveler scientists developed their synthetic Vhelox, which helped a little but was not a replacement for true vhe.

Amanda thought about that when she and Rory met Mhevek at the art colony. Now that the corrupt Churukh royalty had been overthrown, the Vherahna could travel more freely throughout Terra-V, providing life-giving vhe through direct contact and leaving infused items to store between visits. Yet Amanda was finding out that the transition hadn't been as smooth as she had hoped. Distances were great and Vherahna missionaries were few. Scattered

Churukh loyalists hadn't accepted the new regime. Some were eager to step into the roles of the deposed royals.

As they toured one of the colony's many galleries, Mhevek told them Churukh artists had been greatly affected during the years of limited vhe and had translated their suffering into profound works of art.

"You can see the change in their work now," Mhevek said, turning a corner to show the paintings and sculptures created after a recent visit from the Vherahna. Where pieces from the past had shown subdued palettes and sorrowful subjects, the art in this display was awash in vibrant colors and filled with abundant joy.

The artists themselves were excited to meet Amanda and Rory. So excited that Amanda was embarrassed by their attention and begged Mhevek to tell them she hadn't done that much. After a few words in Churukh, the artists shared a gentle laugh and smiled shyly at her. Amanda didn't know what Mhevek had said to them, but she was glad they seemed more relaxed around her.

"How do you make something like this?" Amanda asked, admiring a delicate sculpture that reminded her of spun sugar. She had expected a practical answer about how it was formed, but the answer Mhevek translated from the artist spoke to its creative start.

"She closes her eyes, and the warmed floss echoes the emotions in her heart."

Studying the shifting pinks and purples in the airy sculpture, Amanda saw how the general shape expanded and lightly twisted back on itself at the edges. It formed a loosely woven spheroid that shimmered in the light, like a soap bubble if it were filled with fine spider webs. The piece hung from a clear glass hook, giving the impression that it floated on air.

"It's beautiful." Amanda studied the piece, wondering if the practice of sculpting without sight was related to Edmund's lesson to *see what cannot be seen*. She was on the edge of asking when a commotion outside the gallery drew everyone's attention.

The two traveler knights who had accompanied them from the mountain outpost exchanged hand signals with Rory before stepping outside.

Several artists rushed to the window and Rory called out to them in rough Churukh, echoed by Mhevek who ushered them behind an interior wall. Amanda dropped her hand to the small knife belted at her waist, her self-defense training kicking in.

One of the knights flashed a hand gesture through the wide window, but Amanda didn't recognize its meaning.

"Move!" Rory yelled, hustling Amanda through a door at the far side of the gallery.

Two artists huddled behind easels in the next room. Rory barked a warning as she pulled Amanda down a short hallway and into a narrow space that had one door and no windows, except for a small round opening on the door. It was the room where they had first entered the gallery. Amanda stumbled to a stop, worrying about Mhevek and the others they'd left behind.

Rory peered out the door's small window, assessing whether they should chance reaching the nearby proximal zone or return to the mindspace from here. She paused, listening to the quiet around them. Whatever was happening seemed to be contained on the far side of the gallery.

"Loyalists," Rory told Amanda softly. "I don't know how many."

"What do they want?"

Amanda still lightly gripped the knife at her belt. She saw that Rory's blade was in her hand.

Before Rory could answer, she lunged toward Amanda, pushing her roughly as a Churukh loyalist lunged into the room. Amanda hit the floor on her hands and knees, then instinctively rolled out of the way. She'd seen Rory spar with other travelers but never fight an actual enemy. She and the Churukh circled each other, thrusting blades forward and spinning out of reach.

In her dazed state, it took a moment for Amanda to realize they were both armed with knives. She unfastened her own small blade from her belt and held it in a shaking hand, even as she backed against a wall and scanned the doorway for more danger. Her eyes were turned away when the Churukh fighter dropped to the ground with a strangled cry. A pool of dark blood spread on the stone floor.

Rory spun toward Amanda with a look of concern and relief, then dropped to one knee. Blood splattered across her face and a wider stain spread high on her shoulder, right in the spot where her protective vest ended.

Dropping her knife, Amanda rushed to catch Rory before she slipped to the floor.

"Lucky hit," Rory said with a smirk before her half-smile disappeared in a wince. "Pressure," she mumbled, fighting to stay conscious.

Boots thundered down the hall. When two knights burst through the doorway, they found Rory on the ground and Amanda pressing her own sweater hard against Rory's chest. Tears rolled down Amanda's cheeks, but she didn't feel them. All she could see was Rory's pale face.

§

"She's going to be okay."

Cameron sat beside Amanda on the lilac grass and gazed across the mountain vista. A strike team had been called in and the area had been cleared of any remaining loyalists. They were sitting outside the traveler outpost where Rory had been taken for immediate care.

"Her vitals need to stabilize before she can travel, but excellent doctors have come to her."

Amanda nodded. She had washed up in the outpost and someone had given her a sweater to shield against the mountain chill. It was too big. The sleeves hung over her hands, but it was clean, unlike her own sweater which was stained with Rory's blood.

"They were after me, weren't they?"

Amanda remembered how Rory had pushed her out of the way.

"Possibly," Cameron agreed. "Mhevek says they kept the plans of your visit here quiet, but people talk. It could have gotten to the loyalists."

Amanda nodded solemnly. She didn't have to ask why the loyalists would be after her. She was the waking dreamer. Her quest to fulfill the Vherahna prophecy had led to the overthrow of the Churukh royalty. That had been good for the Vherahna, and nearly all of the Churukh, but those who had profited in the corrupt system hated her and the travelers for destroying it.

"Should I bother asking if you'll come home before Rory can travel?" Cameron waved off her protest. "It's okay. I promised your mom I would ask."

Thinking of her mom home alone, worrying, almost made Amanda reconsider. But she couldn't leave Rory.

"It's okay," Cameron repeated. "I told her you're fine, and I'll stay with you."

Amanda thanked him, noticing how casually he had said *come home* as if they lived in the same place. Like Rory, Cameron had relocated to Amanda's town. Rory had moved when she was assigned to be Amanda's training agent, and Cameron had followed around the time Patty learned about psychic travel. Amanda had been to Rory's apartment but not to Cameron's home.

The shrubs behind them rustled as Mhevek made his way over and took a seat near Amanda.

"It's time I told you about the cricket and the sea," he said plainly, pulling Amanda's thoughts from her mom and Cameron's relationship. Cameron shifted, watching Amanda carefully. Her gaze rested on distant fields and villages far below the mountain as Mhevek's story began.

"The cricket was full of energy with many plans for all he wanted to do. But he was a small creature in a large world and impatient with the time it took to travel from place to place. One day, hopping beside the river, the cricket saw a branch floating by and realized he could ride that branch more swiftly than he could fly or hop.

"He landed on the branch and sang as the current quickly carried him along. Yet the cricket had never been to this part of the river and did not know that just around the next bend, the river widened and reached its destination. Before the cricket realized what had happened, the swift current had washed him straight out to the sea."

Amanda turned to Mhevek, studying his encouraging expression with confusion.

"And I'm the cricket?" she asked, remembering the fortune teller's claim.

"You are," Mhevek confirmed. "The cricket took an action that helped in the moment, without knowing what would come around the bend. We are all the cricket in that way, never knowing what the future may hold."

"I don't understand," Amanda admitted. She glanced at Cameron who sat quietly, mulling Mhevek's story.

"There are consequences to all actions," Mhevek explained. "Good and bad. You discovered the royal's Vherahna captives, which led to the good consequence of restoring balance for many in our world.

"There is also the bad consequence of royal loyalists who are no longer restrained by the old treaties. They feel free to acquire what they want by force, as the knights used force to depose their royal leaders."

"Now, wait a minute," Cameron said sharply. "King Otmurkh and Queen Enghrid invalidated the treaty by keeping Vherahna captives, and by imprisoning our travel party. We were well within our rights to step in, even with the use of force. And you, Mhevek, have been part of the council rebuilding order here."

"Yes, yes," Mhevek agreed quickly. "You have not done anything wrong. One does not have to do wrong for there to be bad consequences. Good and bad ripple from every decision."

"But I'm the cricket," Amanda persisted, feeling a prickling anger in her chest. "I'm the one making choices without knowing what will happen later. Like Rory being hurt."

"Amanda." Cameron reached for her arm, insisting, "That is not your fault."

"Exactly!" Mhevek clapped his hands, drawing both of their attention. "Amanda, you are the cricket, and you are the sea. The sea is not good or bad. The sea simply exists. It sustains life and can take it away. Not through its own actions but by forces beyond its control. The wind, the tide, storms, and the folly of those who do not see its vast unknowns."

"I don't—" Amanda broke off, her head spinning. "What does any of that mean?"

"For you to come into your powers, you must *see what cannot be seen*. Know that there are things you will never know or even know that you should try to see."

"Unknown unknowns," Cameron muttered, his brow furrowing as his lips pursed.

Amanda looked from Cameron to Mhevek, trying to understand but still stuck on the idea that she had made this happen. By helping the Vherahna, she had also set in motion a faction of Churukh loyalists who would go on to injure Rory.

"This is not how I would want you to learn this lesson," Mhevek told Amanda gravely. "I had only hoped to show you the effects of royal politics on the artists in this distant mountain. Yet, I believe the actions today have given you an example that you will draw on throughout your life."

Mhevek pulled the Pyura relic from his robe and offered it to Amanda in his upturned palms.

"Your trial in our world is complete."

§

When Amanda returned home, Patty swept her into a tight embrace. Over her shoulder, Amanda saw a tossed salad in the center of the table, a large pot simmering on the stove, and a fresh pan of brownies on the counter. Her stomach rumbled, and the darkening sky told her it was long past dinner.

"Go clean up and we'll eat," Patty told her, after one final squeeze.

Amanda could only nod, still worried about Rory but glad to be home.

Fifteen minutes later, after a quick shower, Amanda pulled on her pajamas and left her bedroom. Across the dim living room, her mom was still standing near the dining room table. Now, though, she was held in Cameron's arms as he swayed her lightly from side to side.

Amanda hesitated. Before she could decide whether to interrupt, her mom looked up at Cameron and he bowed his head to kiss her full on the lips.

Ducking back around the hall corner, Amanda felt her chest tightening. *This isn't news,* she told herself firmly. She had suspected they were dating for a long time. Patty had practically admitted it whenever Amanda teased her but seeing them together *like that* was more shocking than she had expected.

Amanda slipped into the birdhouse, ready to call out for Rory when she remembered Rory was recovering in a hospital bed. Because of her. She thought of Judy but her aunt was working with a new traveler, and she didn't want to interrupt her for every little thing.

Coming back to full focus in her bedroom, Amanda eyed her phone. Her fingers itched to text Drew, but they hadn't spoken since Nick's party. Same with Trina, who had asked for space to think about their friendship.

After waiting a few minutes, Amanda peered around the corner. Her mom was setting the table while Cameron cut the brownies. She straightened her hoodie and thought about Mhevek's lesson.

If she had never connected with Cameron in the attic, he wouldn't be dating her mom. Her first trip to Terra-V may not have been approved, and the lost tribe of the Vherahna would still be captive. Rory wouldn't have become her training agent or be in a hospital now.

On the other hand, that connection had rescued the captive Vherahna, toppled the corrupt royalty, and saved many Vherahna and Churukh lives.

Beyond Terra-V, her actions had helped Lucas and the rebels overthrow their own corrupt High Council. Of course, they had also emboldened the Vertex, threatening the secrecy of the entire Psychic Traveler Society.

Amanda puzzled over the ripples spreading from every action she had taken so far. As a traveler and in every part of her life. She hoped her choices were leading to more good consequences than bad but tallying them up wasn't easy. Especially as the ripples continued to spread.

Heading toward the kitchen, Amanda smiled at the warm greeting from her mom and Cameron. She still wasn't sure if she should put their relationship in the good or bad consequence column. She wanted them both to be happy. She just hadn't originally seen this coming. Like she hadn't been ready for the loyalist attack today. And then something clicked in the back of Amanda's mind.

Unknown unknowns.

There were things she could worry about, like the way she had watched her mom and Cameron getting closer over the last few months. And there were things she could never begin to imagine happening. Like developing psychic travel abilities.

She wasn't sure what unknown unknowns had to do with being a psychic architect, but the idea felt like a piece of a puzzle fitting into place.

CHAPTER 13
SPRING BREAK

S tretched out on a couch in the manor house library, Amanda relayed the recent events to the engineers. She rushed through the part about Rory's injury and focused on Mhevek's story about the cricket and the sea.

"He gave me a letter from Edmund, too," Amanda told them. "Something he left for after the trial was done. The research team has it now, but the gist was that everything we do has a ripple effect we can't always predict."

"Isn't that true for everyone?" Gerald asked from his place by a bookcase.

"Yes." Amanda yawned. "But he says architects need to be more aware of what they can't know. Because their ripples can have bigger, world-changing consequences."

She was still tired from traveling and hadn't slept well since Rory was injured.

Gerald scoffed. "So what? You aren't responsible for what other people do after your actions."

"I don't think that's what he was saying," Dorothy jumped in. She and Elaine were sitting on the couch across from Amanda.

"Victorian nonsense," Gerald said as he resolutely crossed his arms. "Edmund and his wealthy friends may have preached austerity and personal responsibility, but their lifestyle didn't reflect that."

"Edmund left his society friends to live out his later years off-world," Dorothy reminded.

"Exactly! Worrying about a ripple effect didn't stop him from connecting to new worlds!"

"That's what he said," Amanda cut in. She sat up and rubbed her eyes with both hands before going on. "His message said architects need to be aware of the ripples we cannot see, but not afraid to make them. Or else we'd never have the courage to make new connections."

"Oh, well, yes," Gerald grudgingly conceded. "That is a fair point."

Amanda shrugged. Her mind flashed back to the blood flowing from Rory's shoulder and the lifeless Churukh on the floor beside them.

"You're only responsible for your own actions," Elaine said gently but firmly, seeming to suspect the direction of Amanda's thoughts.

"I know," Amanda agreed uncertainly. "But if my travel abilities hadn't kicked in… If I hadn't gone to Terra-V, or helped Lucas, or…"

Dorothy stopped her.

"You are doing exactly what Edmund doesn't want you to do. You play a part in the world, like everyone else, but you aren't responsible for what anyone else does. You can only do your best with what you know in any given moment."

Nodding, Amanda felt a lump form in her throat. She wanted to say that doing her best wasn't enough when it led to Rory being stabbed while defending her, but she kept that observation to herself.

"Why don't we try something without ripples today?" Elaine suggested brightly. She opened her arms, drawing attention to the beautifully decorated library, as she said, "Being a psychic architect is more than connecting locations with doors. Someday, you will build a house of your own with all its furnishings and décor. Let's try making something! Right here in this room!"

Amanda eyed the room skeptically, but Dorothy quickly agreed and even Gerald seemed intrigued by the idea.

"What? Like, make a vase or something?"

The room was already decorated with small statues on the mantle, large paintings on the walls, and glass knick-knacks on the end tables. Amanda had never given much thought to the many objects spread throughout the mind-space houses. They simply existed, giving each room an added touch of reality.

"Here, can you copy this?" Gerald held out a silver snuff box. It fit easily in his palm and had decorative scrollwork etched across the lid. Amanda took the box and felt its slight weight, reminding herself that none of this physically existed. Her body was back in her bedroom and this whole library, the whole manor house, only existed in a shared mindspace.

"I don't know what to do," Amanda admitted nervously. "It's not like Edmund's lessons have been giving me any actual instructions."

"Sure, but you can try." Gerald sat beside Elaine, patting her knee to show he liked her idea.

"No pressure," Elaine added. "Think of it as a game."

"Try dropping into the pure mindspace," Dorothy suggested.

Amanda nodded and let the rest of the room fade into darkness. A moment later, Dorothy, Elaine, and Gerald appeared across from her, floating effortlessly above the invisible couch. Looking at her open palm, Amanda brought the silver box into view. It glinted softly, despite there being no visible source of light. Amanda opened her other hand, trying to imagine a second silver box.

There was complete silence as she focused on her empty palm. She remembered how it felt to draw an existing object from a room into the pure mindspace, and she tried to do the same thing. But she knew there was not a second silver box in the library.

Studying the details of the existing box, Amanda began to form a picture of it in her own private mind. She closed her eyes and pictured a copy sitting in her empty hand. She could feel its weight and texture. She could imagine each of her hands cradling its own delicate box.

With her eyes still closed, Amanda questioned what she was doing. The new silver box only existed in her own mind. But wasn't the mindspace—pure or otherwise—all in her mind? Where did her mind separate from the shared mindspace? Did she have a mind of her own?

A slashing pain shot through her head. Amanda's eyes flew open, and she found herself sitting upright in bed. Her back was against her headboard and her arms rested by her side. Blinking, she let her gaze drift around her bedroom, then willed herself back into the manor library.

The engineers were anxiously waiting for her, still sitting on the couch.

"What happened?"

"Are you okay?"

They all spoke at once, and Amanda assured them that she was fine, just a little shaky from the effort and confused about what had happened.

"You nearly did it!" Elaine told her happily. "The new box was in your hand for just a moment."

"Then it disappeared," Dorothy added.

"Then you disappeared," Gerald added.

After Amanda described her experience, they marveled at how close she had come and discussed theories on how the process might work.

"Do you want to try again?" Elaine eventually asked, but Dorothy shut that down saying Amanda should rest.

"You don't want to wear yourself out before your trials in Opt-V," Gerald agreed.

"Is that still on?"

Dorothy's question quieted the room.

It was Amanda's spring break and the trials in Opt-V had been planned for Thursday, giving her two days to complete them and two days to rest before going back to school. Now that Rory was injured, the High Council was considering whether to reschedule.

"I don't know. Lucas and Cameron said they can take me, but Rory was supposed to be part of Keah's trial."

"And I will be!"

Amanda jumped at the sound of Rory's voice. In the mindspace, no one could see each other unless they wanted to be seen, and Amanda had wanted to see Rory very much. As she hurried to Rory's side, the engineers greeted Rory as well, happy to see that she looked strong and healthy.

"You're out of the hospital!" Amanda hesitated before hugging her, afraid to cause pain.

"It's just a scratch," Rory laughed. Though she didn't lift her left arm when pulling Amanda into a quick embrace.

$

As expected, Patty had grown increasingly nervous about the trials in Opt-V. Now that the trip was only a day away, Cameron had left work to spend time with her and Amanda. He wanted to go somewhere fun, but Amanda was dragging her feet and Patty didn't want to push. She made a pot of coffee instead, giving Amanda time to decide what she wanted to do with the day.

Twenty minutes later, Amanda was still scrolling through her phone. Not looking for things to do but browsing the traveler news network. There were no new reports of Vertex stunts, and Amanda wondered if Lucas' negotiations were keeping them at bay.

Thinking of the promises he had made in Mumbai set her stomach quaking, especially since their plans to meet with the Arcadian mystics had stalled. After negotiating terms for several weeks, they ran into scheduling issues with her training and trips to other worlds. A meeting had finally been set for early May, allowing time to rest after—hopefully—completing the trials in Opt-V.

Amanda looked up from her screen to where her mom and Cameron were drinking coffee at the dining table. They were talking quietly, heads close together. As she watched, Cameron placed his hand over Patty's and smiled softly.

Her phone vibrated and Amanda was surprised to see a text from Drew.

"Any big plans this week?"

She read the text twice.

The date for her trial in Opt-V had been set after their breakup. Amanda had thought about telling him when she was going, but she never did. Before, Drew would have had all the details. They would have met in the party room to reassure each other that she would be fine and the mission would go well. But that was before.

Amanda hesitated. She could ignore the text, let him wonder if she was off-world and out of reach. But she knew he could see that she had read the message.

"Opt-V," she texted back. Then watched dots dance at the bottom of her screen as he typed a response. She assumed he would know what she meant. That this was the big trial with each of the tribes. That it might be dangerous. She wondered if he would worry about her and what it meant if he did. Her phone vibrated.

"When?"

"Tomorrow." Amanda's hand shook as she hit send.

Did he want to know more? Would he ask her to meet in the party room? She thought about suggesting it herself, knowing she could convince her mom and Cameron to wait on the outing while she went to see him.

The dots disappeared without a new text arriving. Amanda bit her lip, trying not to chew the spot that was already raw from her restless night of biting.

"What's the plan?" Cameron called over as Patty brought their coffee mugs to the sink.

Amanda blinked at him, momentarily forgetting what he was talking about. When she looked at her phone, there was still no new text.

"I don't know," she said with a frown. "Do we have to do something?"

"It's spring break!" Patty reminded, stepping near the table to casually rest a hand on Cameron's shoulder. They had been doing more of that lately. Standing close and touching each other.

"So what?" Amanda didn't mean to sound annoyed, but her irritation was loud and clear.

"So, it's spring break," Patty repeated. "We should do something fun before…" She trailed off awkwardly.

Cameron came to the rescue, saying, "Before work takes over the whole break."

Amanda shrugged.

"We can head into the District," Cameron suggested. "Walk around the Mall. Visit some of the Smithsonian?"

Amanda's phone vibrated. The text was from Drew, but it wasn't a suggestion to meet up or even a question about her trip. It just said, "Good luck."

Those two small words swam in front of Amanda's eyes. She waited, but the dots didn't reappear.

"Thanks," she typed back shortly and put her phone face down on the cushion beside her.

"Is everything okay?" Patty asked, eyeing Amanda's phone and crossed arms.

"Yep," Amanda said, then turned to look out the sliding glass doors.

"If you'd rather do something with your friends today…?" Patty asked vaguely, leaving space for Amanda to share. When she didn't, Patty rushed on, "With Trina, I mean. You haven't done anything with her all week, and it is your spring break."

Amanda knew she was avoiding bringing up Drew—because of the breakup—but the mention of Trina was even worse. It had been over a week since Nick's party, and Amanda still hadn't warned anyone at PTS about Trina's discovery. She was hoping it wouldn't be a problem. Trina had avoided her at school last week, and Amanda had kept her distance, too.

"No, we can spend the day together," Amanda said, making the decision as she spoke. "We could go to the Tidal Basin. Walk around the FDR. Unless it's too crowded with the cherry blossom crowds."

The Franklin D. Roosevelt monument was one of Amanda's favorite places in Washington. Instead of being a single statue, the monument was a series of four outdoor areas, paved in stone and divided by red granite walls that featured engraved quotes and flowing waterfalls.

"I love that idea," Patty happily agreed. "We can bring a picnic to Hains Point and eat by the river. We can manage some crowds, right?"

"I've never been to the FDR memorial," Cameron admitted, reminding them that he hadn't lived near the nation's capital very long.

"Oh, then we have to go!" Patty clapped her hands together. "I think the cherry blossoms peaked a few weeks ago, but it will still be pretty."

She pulled out her own phone to look up information about the annual festival, and Amanda smiled at her enthusiasm. They usually avoided the District during popular tourist times, but she kind of liked the idea of showing Cameron something he had never seen before.

Ten minutes later, as they waited for Patty to change her clothes, Cameron sat beside Amanda on the couch and joined her in staring out the terrace doors.

"A different kind of adventure for us," he said, referencing their off-world trips.

Amanda remembered their first journey through Terra-V. Asking Cameron endless questions during every rest break. Spending time together in the stables with their feathered horses, Iveryn and Ynhara. Cameron had been the first to tell her about psychic architects.

"Remember when I knocked you flat?" Amanda asked with a barely contained smirk.

Cameron laughed freely.

"Outside that barn, on our way to Sage Village," he recalled. They'd been practicing her self-defense techniques while waiting to get back on the road.

"You told me not to hold back," Amanda reminded.

"And you didn't," he said, chuckling again. "I was so proud of you then. I still am."

Amanda kept her eyes trained on the balcony beyond the glass doors, though she was very aware of Cameron sitting beside her. She remembered the stories Cameron had told her about her dad. From back when they worked together. Before she was born and when she was too young to have remembered Cameron as a family friend. Before her dad died and long before she and her mom knew anything about psychic travel.

"Are you okay with this?" Cameron asked tentatively. "With me being here with you?"

"Yeah," Amanda answered carefully, changing the meaning of his question. "It will be good to have you in Opt-V. Especially with Rory still recovering."

"Right, but I meant—" Cameron began but was cut off when Patty breezed into the living room.

"Ready?" she asked, picking up the cooler they would fill with sandwiches and chips from the nearby deli.

"Yep!" Amanda jumped off the couch and joined her at the apartment door.

When Cameron stood up, he paused, trying to catch Amanda's eye. She briefly made eye contact and smiled unsteadily, saying, "Come on! This is, like, my favorite place in D.C."

"Thanks for sharing it with me."

Amanda shared the warmth in his gaze, then quickly looked away, embarrassed but happy.

CHAPTER 14

SERENITY AND SURRENDER

Through careful planning, the High Council had timed the evening of Amanda's first trial on Opt-V to align with morning in her own time zone. Her night alone in Cordrowr's chosen lagoon would then last about six and a half hours, which hadn't sounded that bad to Amanda. Yet, stepping through the door from morning into twilight was always unsettling.

The lagoon itself was eerily beautiful. Its blue-green water was almost fully enclosed by large rocks and jungle trees, both dripping with dark, thick vines. The tall trees cast deep shadows in the fading light, yet the lagoon was softly lit from within by glowing strands of seaweed and circling schools of bioluminescent fish. A stream on one side of the lagoon snaked through a break in the trees and out to the distant sea. On the far side of the pool, a thin waterfall brought a steady stream of water through the rainforest and down from the mountaintops.

Rory, Lucas, and Cameron would be with Amanda throughout the two-day trial, aside from her time alone in the lagoon. Speaking through Thorvald, Cordrowr welcomed them to his domain. He introduced two Erlopes who would be patrolling the perimeter of the lagoon in case of emergency, though he did not elaborate on the kind of emergencies that could come up.

Amanda wanted to be cool and take the Erlopes' strangeness in stride. But that was hard when they towered over her with their scaly bodies shining in the fading light. She couldn't help but notice their similarity to upright crocodiles. Except instead of having elongated, tooth-filled snouts, they had softer faces that sat above pouchy necks, with wide mouths, and frog-like eyes.

Thorvald told them that the lagoons were relatively safe. This trial would focus more on facing solitude and Amanda's inner self, not on wilderness survival.

"You've got this," Rory reassured.

Then it was time for them to go.

The ground surrounding the lagoon was covered by a soft blue moss that glinted under the reflected light of two rising moons. A formation of flat rocks stepped down one side of the waterfall, offering an ideal place for Amanda to unfold a thin blanket and sit with her soft pack wedged between her back and the next higher rock.

Amanda was prepared for the darkness of the lagoon but not for its various sounds. The waterfall's once-soothing gurgles and splashes soon had her on edge. She couldn't tell if the irregular trickles and plops were from the falling water or from creatures beneath its murky surface.

Loud shifts in the surrounding trees also sent Amanda's imagination into overdrive. She knew there were no large predators, like rhinoceroses, tigers, or lions in the area, but there were many other animals. She'd been briefed about mischievous sloth-like creatures, shy rodents with furry ears and tails, and cunning sharp-billed birds.

With her body and mind on high alert, Amanda resisted the urge to talk to Rory through the mindspace. She wanted to prove that she could be alone with her thoughts and face whatever challenges Cordrowr expected that to bring. Besides, they had agreed to limit messages so she could stay alert to her strange surroundings.

The waiting reminded Amanda of the medical tests PTS doctors had run on her after she'd accidentally created her proximal door to Terra-V. For one, she'd had to lie still in an MRI machine while vibrating sounds echoed around her. She'd passed the time with a calming meditation she'd learned from her yoga teacher. One that linked her breath with a series of mantras.

Alone in the dark lagoon, Amanda tried the meditation again. *I breathe in love. I breathe out compassion. I breathe in compassion. I breathe out peace. I breathe in peace. I breathe out love.* She repeated several rounds, losing her place whenever a sudden sound pulled her attention.

As she settled into the meditation Amanda did feel calmer, but her peace soon gave way to boredom. Tucking her blanket back in her pack, she decided to explore the lagoon. She walked slowly to fill the time, stopping at every rustle in the tree line, and peering into the dark jungle until her galloping heart slowed.

Once, as she stood still as a statue, a trio of rodents scurried from the trees to the water's edge. Amanda tried to remember the name of the animal. *Jojovari,* or something like that. They scampered close to a shallow spot and deftly lapped at the water. As they drank, a glowing fish splashed through the surface and sent the animals scurrying back to the trees. Amanda laughed at the interaction and continued her exploration.

By the time she'd made it back to her perch on the flat rock, Amanda decided to check in with Rory. She kept half her attention fixed on a glowing patch of algae while another part of her mind wandered into the castle's great room, which housed the doors to Opt-V.

Rory quickly joined her.

"How long has it been?" Amanda asked, hoping she was at least halfway through the night.

"About an hour," Rory admitted reluctantly.

"That's it?" Amanda could see Rory as a hazy image hovering over the glowing lagoon. "I still have, like, five-and-a-half hours to go?"

"Yeah. Well, more like five hours and 20 minutes or so."

"Oh, well, that's much better." Amanda's sarcasm made them both laugh.

After a brief chat, Amanda stood up and scanned the lagoon. She considered how fast time passed when she was taking a test at school or when she and Drew slouched on the party room couch, playing games on their phones. The casual memory of Drew caught in her chest as she pushed it away.

Studying the starry sky, the minutes felt endless.

Though she didn't have her yoga mat, Amanda found a relatively flat area in the grass and moved through a series of standing yoga poses. The familiar sequence made it easy to tune out her thoughts and focus on the shapes her body was making.

As she bowed and reached, stepping her foot back to Warrior I and opening her arms to Warrior II, Amanda remembered learning this practice at the training center in Mysuru. They'd often practiced in an enclosed courtyard or in a large, sparsely furnished room near the top of the building. Amanda had never left the center and hardly believed she was in India unless she was looking out one of the building's wide windows.

Now, Lucas wanted her to go back to India and create an updated proximal door in a different section of Mumbai. As well as a door in Delhi and several other cities. Beyond India, he seemed to be making plans for her to create proximal doors in countries all around the world. Making promises she couldn't yet deliver. The idea broke her calm and sent her heart racing.

Pacing the edge of the lagoon, Amanda checked in on the night sky. Two moons were still visible in the clearing between the trees. She noted their position and tried to calculate how far they'd moved since night began. It was hard to tell from her changed vantage point, so she went back to her pack and blanket and settled in on the flat rock by the water's edge.

Whenever she was in a rural area, sitting under a blanket of stars, Amanda felt sad for people who lived in areas like her town. Places where there was too much light pollution to appreciate the wonder of a star-filled sky. She had heard some people felt small when they thought about the vastness of the universe, but she felt excited by an expanse of stars, wondering which were surrounded by planets with life and if any of them were the worlds she had already visited.

Amanda knew it was Earth's distance from other inhabited planets that had kept their world isolated, unlike Arcadia's position in a more populated galaxy. It was strange to know intelligent life existed throughout the universe when normals could only guess at it. Especially when some of her friends thought travelers like her were aliens.

Eventually, Amanda set her wandering thoughts aside and sent another message to Rory. She was surprised to hear over half the night had passed and felt proud of how easy it had been. Despite a little boredom, there was nothing difficult about being alone with herself.

They talked until a rustling in the trees brought Amanda's full attention back to the lagoon. Just as the mindspace faded from sight, a bird the size of a small cat swooped through the trees and landed on the rock in front of Amanda.

The bird had dark, shiny eyes, a long, pointed beak, and wings that unfolded to twice their size. In a thin shaft of moonlight, Amanda could see it also had sharp talons that clicked against the rock as it jittered from side to side. Her heart sped up and her palms felt damp.

For a wild moment, she wondered if she had brought this on herself by thinking the trial was too easy, then she pushed that thought away. Rory would call that superstitious nonsense. The thought of Rory reminded Amanda of an acronym from her survival training: STOP. Slow down, think, observe, plan.

Cautiously easing her pack in front of her, Amanda pressed her back against the rough stone and pulled her knees tight against her chest. It wasn't much of a shield, but it would help if the bird attacked. Shifting the pack also made it easier to unsnap its side pocket with a trembling hand, keeping her eyes trained on the strange bird.

Despite its sharp beak and claws, the bird seemed equally wary of Amanda. It flinched when she slipped her hand into her pack and flapped its wings when her slight movement sent some loose pebbles scattering down the rock ledge. Amanda froze. Her heart pulsed in her throat. When she dared to move again, she quickly pulled a small knife from her bag, hoping she wouldn't need to use it.

The bird stared at Amanda, scratching its claws on the rock. Amanda stared at the bird, gripping her weapon.

She didn't know how long they stayed locked in those positions. Eventually, the bird shifted farther back on the rock and crouched its body as if settling into a nest. Its feathers plumped lightly. Its neck retracted. A bright eye stayed fixed on her every movement.

Gradually, Amanda convinced her body to relax. She loosened her grasp on the knife but kept it in hand. She desperately wanted to stand and stretch her legs, but she was too afraid to startle the bird.

"I guess you're my company for a while," she said softly, grinning as the bird cocked its head in response. "Do you want to hear a story?"

Amanda spoke softly to the bird, rambling over the events of her life since finding out she had psychic travel abilities. She described the other worlds she had visited and relayed a shortened version of her journey to fulfill the prophecy of the waking dreamer.

Lulled by the waterfall and a cricket-like chirping that had begun in the trees, Amanda found herself telling the bird about Drew. She murmured the story of their friendship and their first kiss. By the time she got to their breakup, there were tears on her face and an ache in her heart. She missed Drew. Whether he was her boyfriend or her friend, she had been happier with him in her life.

Whenever she thought of him now, she could only see his disgust at the way she had treated Trina.

What you just did? That wasn't the friend I know.

"Trina isn't speaking to me either," she told the bird.

With that admission, her ribcage seemed to crack apart. Her stomach shook and the thoughts she'd been pushing down for over a week came tumbling out.

"I complain about her being a bad friend, but I'm the one who's been lying to her. I mean, yeah, I could say it was for her protection, but it was more than that. I liked having something that was just mine. Something special."

Tears welled as she remembered fighting with Trina at the back-to-school dance. There were so many times she had looked down on Trina for wanting attention, without ever accepting that she wanted to feel special, too.

"Having a secret made me feel better than her."

Hearing the words out loud, Amanda knew it was a truth she hadn't wanted to admit.

"But it's also so hard," she went on, blinking back her emotions. "I have to learn crazy hard skills that no one else can do, and everyone acts like I'm the key to stopping this major world crisis. Because I have potential that they don't. But what if I don't reach that potential?"

Her voice cracked and her teeth chattered.

"Then when Trina found out, I lied to her. I tried to make her think she imagined it. I know I was trained to do that, but I thought I was better than that. That I wouldn't put a friend through that to protect myself. Because it wasn't about protecting psychic travelers. I was afraid of how her knowing would screw up my training. And I didn't want her to know. I wanted it to stay my secret."

Amanda wanted to stop talking, push all her thoughts and fears back down, but it was too late for that.

"And I haven't told anyone about Trina finding out," she admitted with shame. "I'm so caught up in my stuff, I haven't even cared how Trina is handling it. And I know how dangerous it is to find out. How people crack up over it. I saw my mom go through that."

Amanda stopped talking as memories rushed back. The days when her mom stayed on the couch, staring into space, and trying to make sense of a world where there was a whole hidden society of people who could psychically travel to other worlds. Where her daughter was one of those people, and her husband had been, too, without ever telling her.

Wrapping her arms around her bent legs, Amanda let tears flow until her thoughts ran dry.

"Okay." She nodded at the bird. "Maybe it's not that easy to be alone with myself."

The bird stood up and stared at her, then cocked its head to one side. With a deliberate shake of its feathers, it promptly flew away.

"Well, all right then," Amanda laughed dryly. "I guess you listened as long as you could!"

She watched the bird soar up through the space above the lagoon and noticed a faint light creeping over the trees. Her chest ached and her body trembled in emotional exhaustion. But she'd made it through the night.

§

By the time the sun had risen, Amanda had dried her tears. She hadn't handled Trina's discovery well, but it wasn't too late to do something about it. She would tell Rory and accept the consequences. Then she would find a way to connect with Trina. Help her through the shock the way Cameron had helped her mom.

After she made it through her trials.

When Cordrowr spoke to Amanda, with Thorvald translating, he asked if she had discovered anything during her night of solitude. Amanda nodded solemnly and said she had. He didn't ask what but studied her face intently, content with whatever he saw.

Amanda wanted to talk to Rory then, but Ilta was waiting for them high in the mountains. They had only been given an hour to rest and prepare to meet her. Rory and Lucas returned to their own homes during the break. Cameron accompanied Amanda home where there was just enough time to clean up, eat a quick meal, and assure Patty she was okay before they were due back in Opt-V.

The door to the Leotria's home opened onto a rocky, windswept expanse. The mountain continued to rise above this open area, though the view from their perch was already enough to make Amanda squeamish whenever she stepped too close to the edge. The mountain setting also brought Amanda's thoughts back to the art colony in Terra-V. The day Rory was stabbed.

"How are you feeling?" Rory asked as Ilta and Thorvald had a quiet conference at the race site.

Amanda watched Ilta gesture at one marker and then another. She appeared to be explaining the rules to Thorvald so he could translate. Her pink and purple wings were folded close, feathers trailing like an elaborate cape. Lucas stood beside them, watching closely. He then turned toward Amanda and Rory with a covert salute. Amanda watched Rory laugh, looking for signs of pain.

"How are *you* feeling?" she asked in return. "If you aren't up for this…"

"I'm fine." Rory shrugged off the concern and walked over to Cameron.

Amanda hung back, surveying the scene.

Clusters of Leotria had gathered to watch the trial. There were similarities among them. The hooked, white-gold beaks. The lithe bodies and powerful wings. Yet they also had distinctive plumage. Some had similar coloring to Ilta, with pink and lavender feathers transitioning to purples and deep blues. Others boasted hues of yellow and green, or orange and red.

Regardless of coloring, Leotria mingled across the mountain's rocky expanse and in groups perched on higher formations. They reminded Amanda of guests at a party. Flitting from one cluster to another. Chattering together with flapping gestures of their dainty hands and emphatic ripples of their gleaming wings.

The rules of the race were simple. Thorvald explained that Amanda would race against a sand timer, trying to reach the finish line before the sand ran out. The length of the course was under 100 meters and the sand timer lasted 30 seconds. Amanda felt good about that, knowing she could easily run 100 meters in less than half that time. But then she saw the course was a curving incline along the rise of the mountain and was reminded of both the higher altitude and higher gravity of Opt-V.

They walked the course first. Though there was plenty of space to the edge of the mountain, Amanda felt dizzied by the vast sky and long drop to the ground below. As they headed back to the starting line, Leotria fluttered alongside and perched along the length of the course. Their colorful bodies blocked the open view, making it easier to imagine they were standing on lower ground.

"Are you ready?" Cameron asked as they returned to the starting line.

Ilta stood beside them, holding the silver sand timer in one hand and a gold bell in the other. Thorvald explained that the bell would be Amanda's cue to start. She moved into a running stance, as she had learned in gym class, and nodded.

When the bell rang, Amanda darted forward. She kept her gaze on the course, letting the Leotria's colorful feathers blur into the background. Before she knew it, she had reached the top marker and stumbled to a stop. The Leotria spectators cheered by chirping and snapping their fingers. Amanda smiled, sure she had done well.

As she ambled back down to the starting line, Rory hurried up to meet her. Cameron and Lucas flashed thumbs up from a distance.

"You did it!" Rory confirmed proudly. "With plenty of time to spare."

"That was it?" Amanda was pleased but wary. The race seemed too easy, which Thorvald soon confirmed.

"Ilta offers her congratulations on round one."

"Round one?" Rory asked before Amanda had a chance to respond.

"Yes." Thorvald glanced at Ilta warily. "If you remember, Ilta did say the race would be modified based on Amanda's human form and abilities. Round one was the assessment of those abilities."

"And round two will be the actual race?" Cameron asked, but Thorvald pressed his lips together and sighed. He conferred with Ilta briefly.

"Ilta is not that straightforward," he tried to explain. "She says there will be as many rounds as it takes to finish the race."

"What does that mean?" Lucas stepped in, eyes sharp and flashing.

Amanda walked away as they continued to debate. There was more to this trial than a simple race. Ilta wanted her to dig deep and challenge herself.

"It's fine," Amanda called, returning to the starting line. "Let's go again."

As everyone moved into position, one of Ilta's aides brought her a new sand timer. One with a smaller vial of sand. Amanda crouched and nodded, then sprinted forward the moment Ilta rang her bell.

This time Amanda leaned into the run and gave it everything she had. When she staggered across the finish line, she took a few long shuddering breaths and shook out her arms. She wasn't sure how she did this time, but as she walked back, she was again greeted with snaps and chirps of congratulations.

"I passed?"

Rory assured her that she had, but before they could celebrate, Thorvald cleared his throat and announced it was time for round three.

Amanda watched as another aide brought Ilta an even smaller vial of sand.

"You can rest first," Thorvald offered, as Amanda sipped from the water bottle Cameron handed her. "Ilta wants you to listen to your body."

Amanda brushed off the advice. She wanted to go again while her adrenaline was up.

This time, as she crossed the finish line, breathless and shaky, the chirping from the crowd had a different sound. The Leotria she passed on her way back down whistled and snapped with subdued encouragement.

Rory shook her head, and Amanda wasn't surprised.

"Was I close?" But before anyone could answer, Amanda asked, "Can I try again?"

Thorvald relayed the question to Ilta, then told Amanda she could repeat the race as many times as she liked.

"Okay." Amanda handed the water bottle back to Cameron and bounced lightly on her toes.

"Let's go again."

"Amanda…" Cameron tried to caution her, but Amanda wouldn't listen. She crouched and sprinted forward at the sound of Ilta's bell. Her arms and legs pumped. Her mind saw nothing but blue sky. Halfway up, her feet skittered on some loose dirt, but she kept her balance and pushed forward. Despite the slip, she thought she might have had it that time. But when she returned to the starting line, she knew she had failed again.

"It's okay," she insisted, after a gulp of water. "My foot slipped. I'll get it this time."

Ignoring calls for rest, Amanda crouched and nodded grimly. Ilta rang her bell. Amanda shot up the mountain path and lurched over the finish line. She gasped for breath, knees bent, and hands braced against her thighs. She felt sure she had gotten it this time, but she hadn't.

The rounds added up as Amanda tried over and over again. The world was a blur of bright feathers, ringing bells, and disappointment. Her legs and lungs ached. There was a stitch in her side, and it was getting harder to ignore the concern on her friends' faces.

Stumbling down the mountain, her face flushed and legs shaking, Amanda thought she might throw up. Rory started to speak, but Cameron stopped her. He offered water and Amanda dropped to her knees, holding back the bile that swirled in her stomach. After several slow breaths, Amanda steeled herself and got to her feet.

Ilta's bright eyes studied her intently.

Amanda clenched her fists, preparing for another try but sure her times were only getting worse. She looked into the distance, seeing a stretch of blue sky with white wisps of clouds. Snowy mountain peaks towered nearby with a dip into the valley between, and Amanda wondered which direction it was to the sea, remembering the eerie beauty of the lagoon at night.

She wasn't ready to win this race.

The architect's journey would end here. She closed her eyes as waves of disappointment washed through her. She had let everyone down. The High Council would have to find another way to keep the Vertex from revealing psychic travel to the world.

Amanda faced Ilta with a heavy heart. She resigned to forfeit now and ask to try again when she had trained for the challenges of mountain running.

"Do you want to try again?" Thorvald asked, just as he had after previous rounds.

Part of her screamed to say yes, to give it one more try. One final push could be the time she beat the clock. But Amanda shook her head.

"I can't finish this race. I can't run that fast."

Thorvald translated her words. Ilta raised her wings and snapped her fingers, chirping happily as the gathered Leotria joined in. Amanda was stung by their reaction, thinking they were celebrating her failure. But Thorvald quickly reassured her.

"You won!" he told her proudly. "The point of Ilta's race wasn't to beat the time but to recognize and accept your own limitations. And you did it! Eventually."

"I did?" Amanda crouched with her arms on her thighs, dizzy from her exertions. Her thoughts swam as Thorvald reminded them of the Leotria's active lifestyle, darting from place to place to consume enough food to sustain the energy they spent in flight.

"Leotria must always be aware of their abilities and limitations, fine-tuning the distances they can fly based on their current needs for food, rest, and so on. Edmund admired their self-awareness and said it inspired him to take greater care with his own bodily needs."

"And he wanted his successor to understand that as well," Cameron concluded as Amanda stood up, facing Ilta directly.

With her legs shaking and lungs aching, she resented Ilta's smug pleasure. *You could have told me,* Amanda wanted to say. *I would have stopped sooner if I knew it meant winning.* But the imagined words came with a sense of doubt. Her fear of losing was what had made it hard to put her own needs first.

Courage and restraint. As Edmund's words came back to her, Amanda realized the hardest lesson might be learning when to push and when to hold back.

She bowed her head to Ilta and spoke sincerely.

"It's a valuable lesson, thank you."

CHAPTER 15

TEAMWORK AND LEADERSHIP

"We need to cut through these vines if we're going to lower this bridge," Rory stated firmly. Lucas crossed his arms and shook his head.

"Not with these rocks. You've tried. I've tried. It's not working."

They were standing at the edge of a deep ravine. Beside them, a tall wooden drawbridge had been raised and tied in place with thick vines wrapped around massive boulders. Rory held a sharp rock in her right hand and was trying not to cradle her left arm too obviously.

"I can get it. I just need to adjust my angle."

"You're going to rip your stitches," Lucas warned. "If you haven't already."

"My shoulder is fine!" Rory shot back, earning doubtful frowns from both Lucas and Amanda.

"Oh, yeah? Climb that tree." Lucas pointed to one of the smaller trees at the edge of the thick rainforest. Vines dripped from its lowest limbs, which were at least 20 feet from the ground.

"Stop!" Amanda grabbed Rory's right arm to keep her from proving that a recent stab wound wouldn't stop her from climbing to the top of an 80-foot tree.

"Arguing isn't getting us anywhere."

Hours had passed since they started the Nicules' trial. They had been told it was an obstacle course through the rainforest but weren't given a map or set destination. Keah had pointed toward a path through the trees and told them to follow it until they found her. Thorvald and Cameron would be waiting with her. Some of her trusted aides would be following Amanda's team from a distance. They soon realized that by *distance* she meant her aides would be swinging in the trees, far above their heads, and occasionally climbing closer to chatter over their progress.

They had cleared several challenges, including some obvious ones like crossing a rope bridge across a drop of several hundred feet and weaving their way through narrow passages of overgrown plants and vines. There were more puzzling obstacles as well. Rory had figured out how to stack rocks on seesaw beams to raise a series of platforms. Lucas had found a rope ladder hung within a huge hollow tree.

When faced with a path that passed along the base of a small waterfall, Amanda had discovered hidden ropes on either side that raised a barrier to block the flow of water and lifted a narrow log bridge for them to cross. She'd also lost her grip on the rope at the end of Lucas' crossing, dowsing him with water and nearly sending him into the river before Rory caught his arm and pulled him to dry land.

By the time they had reached this raised drawbridge, they were worn down and wishing the course would end. Now, as Amanda glared at them, she lost all patience with their arguing.

"In case you've forgotten," she told them. "I'm supposed to be in charge here."

Lucas crossed his arms and shrugged. Rory leaned against a boulder and gingerly rotated her left shoulder.

"Right." Amanda sighed. "Look, I know you both have more experience with this kind of thing, and you both have really strong ideas about what to do, but we're supposed to be a team. And Keah put me in charge."

Rory sighed as well, then looked back into the dense forest where two Nicules sat high up in the branches, quietly checking in on them.

"You're in charge," Lucas said with another shrug.

This was the fourth time Amanda had pleaded with them to follow her. Each time, Rory and Lucas had stepped back for her to lead the way. But with each new puzzle or fork in the path, they had jumped in with suggestions and arguments until one of them got their way.

"Okay. In that case, I say we take a break to calm down and regroup."

"Fine," Lucas agreed. "I could use some time in the sun."

He climbed onto a cluster of rocks near the edge of the cliff, bathing in the sun that had been mostly blocked under the forest canopy. His shirt and pants were still damp from Amanda's slipped rope at the waterfall.

Rory continued to lean against the boulder, letting the flat rock fall from her hand. There were several like it scattered at the base of the bridge. She had taken that to mean the stones could cut the vines that held the drawbridge in place. Lucas had claimed they were a misdirection.

Amanda climbed onto another large rock, closer to the edge of the forest, and studied the drawbridge from a distance. It was a large but simple structure. A wide platform rose about 12 feet tall, framing a narrow bridge attached on a pivot and raised by vines thread through pulleys at its top corners and wrapped around a winch on the platform. Now, however, the raised bridge was tied fast to a massive boulder below, keeping it in its upright position.

The lifted bridge stood a few feet higher than the platform, suggesting the ravine was over 10 feet across. Too far to safely jump, even with a running start. Cutting the anchor vine with the rocks hadn't worked, and Amanda didn't know how to keep Rory and Lucas from arguing long enough to work on a new plan.

Feeling hopeless, she sent a psychic message.

"There's more than one way to lead headstrong people like Rory and Lucas," Cameron said with an encouraging grin. Amanda could see him in the castle's great hall, superimposed over the clearing before her.

"Try coming at them sideways," he suggested. "Remind them that they're there to help you be a leader and tell them how it feels when they don't listen to you. Be vulnerable. Tug at their emotions."

Taking his advice to heart, Amanda moved to sit in the grassy space between Lucas and Rory. It was time to come clean. After a moment of silence, she cleared her throat.

"I can't do this."

Rory looked up with pressed lips. Lucas grudgingly pivoted his body to face them both.

"I want to be the next architect," Amanda said firmly. "The one who can make new doors and keep the Vertex from revealing everything. I want to learn everything quickly and make you proud, but maybe I'm not ready."

She looked at Rory nervously, before dropping her eyes.

"Trina caught me traveling over a week ago. I tried to deny it, but… Well, she knows. And I didn't tell anyone. I tried to pretend it didn't matter when I know I should have told someone."

Amanda studied the ground beneath her. Fernlike plants mingled with the grass. She mindlessly rubbed a leaf between her fingers, then dropped it when clear sap lightly stung her hand.

"Amanda, we know about Trina."

Rory spoke evenly. Lucas nodded in confirmation.

"Drew told Judy when it happened," Rory explained. "He was worried about how Trina would cope. She arranged for a counselor to work with Trina, under a cover story for her parents, of course."

"We had to assess the situation," Lucas added. "Find out who she had told or who she might tell."

Amanda sat up as if splashed with cold water.

"Well, that's… good," she mumbled, confused by the emotions tumbling through her body. After a long pause she added, "No one told me."

"No," Rory agreed. "We didn't tell you."

"You were waiting for me to tell you," Amanda realized, sounding strangely calm as she said the words out loud. She wanted to know if she was in trouble for not telling. Instead, she asked, "Is Trina okay?"

"Yeah, she's good," Rory reassured. "And we're hopeful she won't tell anyone. The counselor is going to work with her for a while."

"Good." Amanda felt relief wash over her. Lucas was watching her thoughtfully.

"It should have come from me," she added more firmly. "Not from Drew."

"Yes," Rory agreed.

"But we all make mistakes," Lucas said, closing the subject with a return of his usual off-hand charm. "Now, how are we going to cross that ravine?"

Amanda looked back at the towering bridge, then surveyed their surroundings.

"Let's list what we know," she suggested, thinking of how she would approach a math problem. "We weren't allowed to bring knives or other tools, just our canteens and a basic first aid kit. The Nicules would be able to cut those ropes and lower the bridge with whatever is already here. Same for any Erlopes and Leotria who might have to pass this test."

"The Leotria could fly across." Lucas shrugged before quickly adding, "I know, I know. They aren't allowed to fly during the trial, but wings would be handy."

Amanda examined the bridge more closely.

"It's not attached to the winch anymore," Rory pointed out. "The winch is for raising it but once it was tied in place, it looks like they cut the lines to the winch. We just need to release the anchor line."

Amanda visually traced the anchor line from the top of the platform, where it wrapped around a wooden rod, then ran down to tie around a deep groove in the boulder. It was impossible to slide the vine off the rock without cutting or untying it.

"The knots won't budge, and these flat rocks aren't cutting the vines at all," she said thoughtfully. "But this pile of rocks is here for a reason… Did you notice the yellow streaks on this one?"

Amanda handed a rock to Rory and picked up another one. Lucas examined the rocks, too, finding more with yellow centers.

"Some of these rocks have a different shape," he noted. "It's more concave where they're stained with yellow. Or maybe the yellow is etched in."

"Like with an acid?" Rory suggested, flicking at a faint bit of yellow with her fingernail.

"Acid!" Amanda remembered the stinging she'd felt when crushing the fern's leaves and ran to pull some from the ground, explaining as she went.

"Wait, if it's strong enough to burn through that vine, it would burn your hands."

Amanda was already holding the picked fern leaves. The clear sap stung slightly but not enough to mark her skin. She tried squeezing some onto the vine anyway. Nothing happened.

"Look for something yellow," she suggested, then spotted some large flowers growing in clusters on a larger fern at the base of some nearby trees. The flowers had long petals that were swollen near their base.

"We can pick some petals with the rocks. Like this." Amanda held two flat rocks and pressed them together like pincers.

"Here, let me." Lucas pulled off his outer shirt, and Rory helped him wrap the linen sleeves around his hands for added protection. Amanda placed flat rocks in his padded hands, and he carefully pulled a yellow petal from its stem. They heard a faint sizzle as a drop of sap fell toward the ground, shriveling the fern leaves in its path.

Lucas dropped the fat petal onto one of the more concave rocks and used a flat rock to press it into a liquid mash. As sap pooled in the well of the rock, he cautiously carried it to the vine and poured. They all watched as the dribble of sap began to sizzle through the thick vine.

Like Lucas, Amanda, and Rory both wore long-sleeved linen shirts over white tank tops. They quickly copied his wrapped hands and used flat rocks to pick more petals. It was careful work, but before long, they'd nearly burned through the vine.

"Wait," Amanda warned. "What's going to keep the bridge from crashing down and breaking when it hits the other side?"

Rory and Lucas looked at each other questioningly. Lucas shrugged.

"A lot of trees here seem to have more give than back home. Remember how bouncy that long bridge was earlier? Besides, the Nicules built this thing. I assume they know it will work."

"We should step back though," Rory added, "when it starts to go."

They agreed and began crushing a final round of petals, taking turns to carefully pour the sap over the remaining strands of the vine. When the last threads finally split, they all jumped back. There was a brief pause where Amanda wondered if they needed to give the bridge a push, but the vine suddenly uncoiled from the boulder and the bridge toppled toward the ravine.

With an enormous crash, the end of the bridge met the opposite cliff, then bounced before finally settling into place. Small animals and birds scurried from the nearby trees. The watching Nicules laughed and clapped. A moment later, they dropped into the clearing and chattered something Amanda took as praise before hurrying across the bridge.

"Well, it held their weight," Rory observed. "Shall we?"

They uncoiled their stained and burned shirts and slipped them back over their bare arms. Any sap that had touched the fabric had left small holes, but none remained to burn their skin. The tattered shirts fit with the rest of their damp, mud-streaked clothes. Amanda's body felt equally abused and ready for this trial to be over.

Yet, when they crossed the bridge and entered the new stretch of rainforest, there was still no sign of Keah, Cameron, and Thorvald waiting for them. The Nicules who had observed their drawbridge success had also disappeared between the trees.

"Think we should check in with Cameron?" Amanda asked uncertainly. "Find out if we're almost done."

"No," Rory answered wearily. "The trial will be over when it's over."

"But we have to be close to the end by now."

"Not necessarily," Lucas said, peering into his nearly empty canteen. "The Nicules checking up on us are likely reporting back to Keah. She'll decide when we've had enough."

"You think it's an endurance test?" Rory asked. "Instead of being about teamwork?"

"Maybe both." Lucas shrugged.

They walked on, following a wide path through the trees. Amanda considered everything they knew about the trials on Opt-V and what Edmund wanted her to learn from them.

"Courage and restraint," she reminded thoughtfully. "Bravery and boundaries."

Rory and Lucas were quiet. They knew Edmund's goals for the architect's journey as well as she did.

"The lagoon was about self-reflection, which takes bravery," Amanda continued. "The race was to recognize my limits, which is about setting boundaries. So, why this third trial? Is it courage or restraint? And why is it about teamwork and leadership?"

"Teamwork takes courage and restraint," Rory offered.

"Leadership does, too," Lucas added. "Knowing when to speak up and when to shut up."

"When to take charge and when to listen to someone else," Rory countered.

They exchanged smiles that suggested inside stories, and Amanda instantly felt left out. It was like that whenever Rory and Lucas were together. They'd argue, criticize each other, and then suddenly switch to a grudging admiration that hinted at something deeper between them.

Amanda considered the personal time Rory had been taking and how Lucas had often been coincidentally busy at the same time. She stopped walking and decided to choose courage over restraint.

"Are you dating or what?"

Rory and Lucas spun to face her.

"Each other?" Lucas asked in disbelief, while Rory shook her head and made a face that suggested Amanda had lost her mind.

"No," Rory answered emphatically, then softened. "I mean, he's not as awful as I once thought. And, on occasion, he's even been useful to have around. But no."

"Such high praise," Lucas said with a sarcastic bow of his head. "While I hold the great Rory Beck in higher esteem, I'll also answer with a firm no. I'm too focused on work to add those complications to my life. Not that there's anything wrong with that."

He added his last words hastily with an apologetic look to Rory that made her face tense up. Amanda wondered if that meant what she thought it did.

"Okay, fine!" Rory relaxed into a half-smile and said, "It's new and I don't want to make a big thing of this, but, yeah, I have a girlfriend."

The shy joy on Rory's face swept away any jealousy Amanda might have felt over someone else taking up her time. She jumped in excitement, saying, "That's great! Can I meet her? Or do you not want me to meet her? Wait, does she know about all this?"

"Yes, Mia is a traveler," Rory explained. "She knows what I do, and I'd love for you to meet her someday. It's only been a few months though, and I wanted to keep it to myself for a while. It's nice to have some separation between PTS and my home life."

Amanda remembered her time with Drew and how sometimes she just wanted to take a break from anything to do with her psychic travel world.

"It's not that I was shutting you out…" Rory began carefully, but Amanda cut her off.

"No, I get it! Avu yai," she added happily, reminded of the Stellarian wish to live your best life.

"Avu yai," Rory agreed, and they smiled together.

"Cool," Lucas interjected with a casual bob of his head. "If we're done with the kumbayas, I'd really like to get out of this forest."

They started walking again. After a few steps, Amanda said, "Maybe this is part of what Edmund wanted me to learn. The talking and sharing that happens when you spend the day with people, trying to get through a challenge."

"Could be," Rory agreed. "I've bonded with travelers during missions."

Lucas was quiet. Before Amanda could ask what he was thinking, they came to another break in the trees. This time there was no ravine to cross. The ground fell away, opening to a breathtaking panorama of far-off mountains and a lush spread of jungle treetops. Directly beneath the cliff, they saw a clearing beside a river fed by a waterfall.

They paused to take in the scenery, listening to the rush of the waterfall and enjoying a breeze that rippled through their tattered clothes.

Amanda stepped forward with a gasp.

"There!" She pointed at a group of travelers and Nicules who had stepped out from the trees below. It was Khea, Cameron, Thorvald, and a few others.

"This must be it," Rory said, sounding relieved.

"We just have to get down to them," Lucas added, eyeing the drop, which seemed to be about 60 feet. A thick tree branch extended near the edge of the cliff with long vines dangling down to the clearing. Piles of cut vines were scattered near the line of the trees.

Lucas lifted the tail of his ragged shirt, showing two locking carabiners hanging from a belt loop. He raised an eyebrow at Rory, and she paled at his suggestion.

"Munter hitches?" Rory sounded skeptical, but Amanda could tell she didn't hate whatever Lucas was suggesting. "We weren't supposed to bring tools."

"Eh, what're a few carabiners? Keah saw them and didn't say anything. I had a third, but it must not have been locked. I think it fell off when I nearly took a swim in that stream."

Amanda apologized again, while Rory stifled a laugh at the memory, then quickly grew serious.

"Use the cut vines for harnesses?" she asked.

"I'm thinking Spanish bowlines," he confirmed.

Amanda watched as they assessed the cut vines. They each picked up a section, pulling on them and checking their lengths.

"This'll do," Lucas nodded.

"We only have two carabiners," Rory reminded.

"Better to tether Amanda anyway," Lucas said. "Unless she has more training than I think."

"No, that's best," Rory agreed, though she seemed unsure of the plan that was taking shape.

Amanda had heard enough.

"Anyone want to clue me in?"

They both turned, looking as if they had suddenly remembered her presence.

"Rappelling," Lucas explained tersely. "Using carabiners and these vines."

He pointed to the vines dangling over the cliff edge. Amanda's heart skipped as she tried to remember everything she knew about rappelling.

"But there's no belay!" she stammered, thinking of her climbs with Rory. She had always had a top line and had never rappelled, just lowered. She didn't entirely understand the difference in technique, but she knew there was one. The idea of rappelling off a cliff with a vine and no climbing equipment was terrifying.

"It's okay," Rory reassured. "I'll tether you to me and you'll just be along for the ride."

Amanda felt her eyes widen as she looked back at the sheer cliff.

"Uh, Rory?" Lucas called lightly. "Your chest wound?"

Rory glared at Lucas defiantly.

"It's nothing! Barely grazed me!" She shrugged off the injury, but Lucas let his eyes drop to her shirt where blood had stained the white linen.

"Okay, but I think you pulled some stitches."

Rory cursed at the blood before pushing her outer shirt aside to assess the damage. Amanda bit her lip, upset that she hadn't noticed the growing splotches of blood.

"I'll carry her," Lucas said, stepping to the cliff edge to tug on one of the hanging vines. "These seem strong enough. Guess we won't know until we try."

Amanda's gaze darted between them. Rory had pulled off her outer shirt and was folding it into a makeshift bandage. Lucas stepped over to help, wordlessly tying the shirt in a way that put pressure on the seeping wound. He then turned to Amanda, his eyes glinting with humor that seemed entirely out of place.

"What do you say, leader?" he asked with a crooked smile. "Do you trust me to get you down this cliff?"

Amanda took in Rory's pale face and the sight of Keah and the others in the clearing below. They were nearly at the end of the course. If they could just get down this cliff, she would be done with this trial and done with another step of Edmund's quest.

"Will you be okay?" Amanda asked Rory, worried about her injury. But Rory said she only needed one good arm to get to the ground.

"Rappelling on a Munter hitch won't be fun," Rory warned. "Even if you're tethered to Lucas. But it will be over quick, and it's our best bet."

Amanda nodded tightly, knowing she needed to trust Rory and Lucas' experience.

Lucas went to work rigging harnesses out of the cut vines, and Rory helped as much as she could, being careful not to use her left arm too much. Amanda stood back and watched them, trying to breathe slowly and deeply. Before she knew it, they were rigged into vine-made harnesses and standing at the edge of the cliff.

"Okay," Lucas told her. "You're going to be in front of me, like you're sitting across my lap, and put your arms around my neck. Just don't get in the way of my arms once we start down. I'm going to tie you to me, and you'll be safe. I've done this with unconscious men twice your size, so just try to relax, okay?"

Rory was attaching herself to a vine beside them using a carabiner and a special twist of the vine around it. Amanda hesitated before moving close enough for Lucas to tie their harnesses together.

"Wait!" Amanda felt dizzy at the idea of what they were about to do.

Lucas and Rory looked at her with concern.

"I came clean about Trina. Rory told us about Mia." Her voice shook as her eyes were drawn to the edge of the cliff. "Lucas, you need to share something before we do this."

Lucas froze.

Vines wrapped around his body and another vine hung in front of him. Once he securely tethered Amanda, they could begin their descent. His eyes closed for a moment, then he answered with gruff sincerity.

"I may have stirred the Vertex up more than I can handle. I needed them when I was in exile, and I thought they made some good points, but now… They're moving too fast, and I don't know if I can control them."

There was quiet when he finished. They could hear animals chirping in the rainforest and a light wind rustling through branches and leaves. Amanda didn't know what to say, or if she should say anything at all.

Rory simply said, "Thank you."

Amanda echoed her thanks. She didn't know what would happen with the Vertex either, but hearing Lucas' fear somehow made her feel better about him.

Lucas nodded sharply, composed himself, and gestured for Amanda to step closer. In a moment, she was firmly attached to him with her arms around his neck and her cheek pressed against his collarbone.

"Here we go!" Lucas called, stepping off the edge of the cliff.

§

"How can you say that?" Cameron railed at Keah, who chattered back faster than Thorvald could translate. "They finished the course, didn't they?"

"It's about more than finishing the course," Thorvald pleaded, stepping between them as Keah emphatically jumped and flailed her arms. "Amanda's leadership skills were also being tested."

"She led them through the course!" Cameron insisted, then spun to face Lucas. "Tell them that she led you through the course!"

Lucas hesitated. A flash of guilt crossed his face before he said, "Amanda was our team leader."

"See!" Cameron gestured toward Lucas. His diplomatic calm had been replaced by a seething, protective anger. "Translate that! Tell Keah that Amanda was their team leader."

The Nicules who had followed them through the course chattered rapidly until Keah stopped them with a lifted hand. It was clear her mind was already made up.

"They showed good teamwork," Thorvald explained patiently. "But Keah feels Amanda's leadership skills are lacking. She can be tested again at a future time…"

"The other elders say she passed," Cameron reminded hotly, but Thorvald shook his head.

"The overall result must be unanimous."

Keah turned to address Amanda, but silence fell as Amanda sharply turned away.

Rory sat nearby with her back to a rock while a medic repaired her torn stitches.

Cameron studied them both before stepping closer to Keah. Though he towered over her, Keah met his anger with her own menacing glare.

"This isn't over!" Cameron threatened, but his voice wavered as Keah bared her sharp fangs.

Lucas put a hand on Cameron's shoulder, saying it was time to go home.

Chapter 16
Priorities

When Amanda saw Drew waiting outside her Spanish class, she thought he would finally ask about her Opt-V trials. Instead, he pulled her near a row of lockers and said, "This thing with Nick is getting out of hand."

It was their second day back from Spring Break, and Amanda was well aware that Nick had been spreading rumors that she was "one of those travelers." An alien. She had laughed it off to anyone who brought it up but that hadn't stopped the staring and whispers.

The whole thing was an irritation she didn't need after the sting of failing Keah's trial. She already had the High Council negotiating with the tribal elders to overturn the decision, while Rory fumed and took the blame for not letting her lead them through the course.

That left her with no patience for Nick's accusations. She had confronted Trina, who swore she hadn't told Nick anything, and Amanda wanted to believe her.

As Drew hovered over her, his stony expression showed a mix of anger and concern.

"You need to tell Rory or Cameron about this. Or Judy. Someone."

"Before you do?" Amanda's tone was harsh, but Drew only stood taller.

"If that's what I have to do."

Amanda softened, knowing he had been right to call Judy. She checked that no one was close enough to overhear and said, "I'm glad they sent someone to help Trina. You're a good friend."

Their eyes met and some of the coldness between them melted away.

"I already told Rory about Nick," Amanda admitted. "And Cameron. They're looking into it but don't think he's much of a threat."

At lunch, Nick proved them wrong.

When Amanda got to the cafeteria, she saw Drew and Nick arguing next to their usual table. Trina sat beside them, looking quietly at her tray, and Brooklyn watched the fight with interest.

Amanda arrived in time to hear Drew say, "You need to stop running your mouth."

"You know it's true," Nick shot back. "And everyone else is about to know it, too."

"Stop it!" Amanda stepped between them and swept her gaze across the crowd that had begun to gather. Trey stood in front of the others, watching with a heavy frown and clenched fists. Across the cafeteria, a lunchroom monitor started to walk their way.

"There are ways of testing," Nick said, turning to Amanda. "Or you can just admit it."

"Do you hear yourself?" Amanda demanded. "Where do you get this stuff?"

She already knew the answer. Nick had given her links to the message boards he followed, and she had passed them on to Cameron after a quick skim of the most recent posts. Their theories had all seemed ridiculous. Several claimed the aliens wore human disguises to blend in. Some claimed travelers had more powers, like shapeshifting to steal your identity or killing you with a single thought.

Nick's words stirred a memory of those posts. *Ways of testing.* Amanda had seen a thread about testing suspected aliens, shocking them into disappearing…

She noticed the backpack in Nick's hand just as he pulled out a small device. As she jumped to one side, a hard shove sent her sprawling to the cafeteria floor. Screams echoed in the huge room. Some feet pounded toward them while others raced away.

Pushing herself to a seat, Amanda saw Trey flat on his back with thin wires running to a dropped taser. Drew had Nick's arms pinned behind his back. Several students held up their phones while teachers rushed into the fray.

"This is completely unacceptable!" Patty yelled at the principal an hour later.

She and Cameron had rushed to the school as soon as Patty received the call. Nick had been detained by the school resource officer while Trey and Amanda were taken to the school nurse. Drew had stayed by Amanda's side, and no one made him leave. They now sat beside the principal's desk while Patty ranted angrily about school security and consequences for Nick's actions.

"Nick has been expelled and will not return to this school," Mrs. Saunders told them, using her firm principal voice that did not invite questions. "Furthermore, he's been taken to the police station and an officer will speak to you shortly about your legal options."

Watching her, Amanda felt sorry for Mrs. Saunders. She had already spoken to Nick's parents before they left for the police station and Trey's parents before they left for the hospital. Amanda and Drew had sat silently in her outer office the whole time, while Patty fumed, and Cameron tried to calm her down, despite his own simmering rage.

As they waited, Trey's parents had hurled their own complaints, yelling loud enough to be heard through the principal's closed door.

When they left Mrs. Saunders' office, Trey's mother stopped to ask if Amanda was okay. His father only scowled, muttering that he didn't know what Trey was thinking by jumping in front of a taser like that.

"He was protecting my daughter," Patty told him curtly. "You should be proud of a son who would do that."

"What's to be proud of?" Trey's dad grumbled darkly before storming away.

Amanda didn't understand it either. The last time their parents had been called to the school, Amanda had slammed Trey's head into a locker. Luckily, a teacher saw the whole thing and knew it had been self-defense. Trey had gotten a three-day suspension. In her worry over this new event, Patty seemed to have forgotten about that.

By the time it was their turn in the principal's office, Amanda wanted to forget everything and just go home. Patty wouldn't hear of it.

"What's to stop these conspiracy people from coming after my daughter?" she demanded. "You know that boy belongs to some crazy groups."

Drew reached for Amanda's hand. She squeezed back but felt nothing through the eerie calm that had come over her the moment she hit the floor.

"We've asked the students who recorded the incident to delete their photos and videos and remove any live streams they may have posted."

"And I'm sure they all complied."

Mrs. Saunders politely ignored Patty's sarcasm. As she continued to list their initial precautions, Amanda was distracted by Rory's voice in her mind asking for an update. When she tuned back into the conversation in the room, she was caught off guard by what she heard.

"Our virtual academy provides excellent at-home instruction. Mid-year enrollment is not ideal, but we can help ease the transition."

"Wait! What?" Amanda dropped Drew's hand, shifting to the edge of her seat. "I don't want to leave school."

"Amanda, please," Patty said patiently. "We're finding out our options."

"No one's making a decision yet," Cameron added, and Amanda flinched at the authority in his voice.

To the principal, Cameron was there as her mother's boyfriend. Amanda knew he was there as a member of the High Council, protecting their future architect.

"Will I have a say in this?" Amanda directed the question to Cameron instead of her mother.

"Of course, you will," he reassured, but his voice was distracted and his smile didn't reach his eyes.

§

"I'm not moving to Arcadia."

Amanda had a sense of déjà vu as she and Drew talked in the party room. This time, they sat on adjacent couches and were careful to avoid eye contact. Instead, they cautiously took turns studying each other's profiles and quickly looking away.

"Okay." Drew cupped his hands, pressing his curled fingers against his palm to crack his joints. "But you're leaving school?"

Amanda looked at her own hands as she nodded. She had argued with the High Council but lost, finally agreeing to switch to the virtual school as long as she could live at home. Moving to Arcadia for a while would be a backup plan in case any anti-traveler normals decided to believe Nick's accusations. Even Patty agreed not to stand in the way if it came to that.

"I will be in Arcadia a lot though." Amanda reached for her bottled water, then changed her mind and left it on the coffee table.

"I've finished the trials in Terra-V, and we don't know when the tribal elders will let me try again in Opt-V. The research team is still working on a way to improve life in Stellaria. So far, they think mass production is the best option. Machines that will let them make clothes and things more quickly. But I think they like making things by hand, even if it is slower."

Amanda heard herself babbling and stopped talking. She grabbed her water, took a quick sip, and screwed the cap back on the bottle with care. Drew quietly watched.

"Shortwave radio."

"What?" Amanda had forgotten what they were talking about. "Oh, in Stellaria?"

"For communication," Drew clarified. "They could talk to other villages without having to wait for carrier pigeons. They'd need power for the antennas, but maybe you could give them some kind of battery or small generator."

"Or walkie-talkies." Amanda looked at him gently. "Remember our walkie-talkies?"

Drew had gotten a set of walkie-talkies for his ninth birthday and given one to Amanda. They'd talk to each other from their apartments or take them to the park while searching for new specimens for their rock collection.

"Whatever happened to them?"

Drew shook his head and shrugged. "I guess we didn't need them when we got phones."

Their eyes met. Drew's were full of questions. Amanda looked away, taking another sip of her water.

"It's a good idea," she said, once Drew had stopped looking at her. "I'll tell the research team and see what they think. I keep meaning to go see the elders in Stellaria, get some hints about the right answer, but I've been so busy. Some of the researchers have talked to them though, so they'll have a better idea of what would work."

"Yeah, well, communication is usually a good bet."

Amanda agreed, wondering if his words had a deeper meaning. She nearly asked when Drew slapped both hands on his thighs and stood up.

"Yeah, so, my dad wants me home for dinner…"

He brushed his hands against his upper legs again, as if checking for his phone and wallet, then started toward the double doors. Amanda followed him. Her mouth opened to say something, but she didn't know what. At the doorway, he turned back.

"I'm glad you weren't tased." He smiled sadly and Amanda felt a catch in her chest.

"Thanks to you," she said, picturing Drew pinning Nick's arms behind his back while everyone else either ran away or pulled out their phones.

"And to Trey," Drew reminded, his smile switching to a dry laugh of disbelief.

"Yeah, I did not see that coming."

"Cool of him, though." Drew rocked on his heels thoughtfully, then flashed a mischievous grin. "Not funny at all that he got tased."

"Stop!" Amanda slapped at his chest playfully. "It's not funny!" But she couldn't help laughing at Drew's raised eyebrow and evil smile.

"What?" he asked with mock innocence. "I said it's *not* funny! You're the one laughing!"

He shrugged and Amanda laughed harder, unable to stop even as tears rimmed her eyes.

"Wow, that's cold!" Drew teased. "Look at you, laughing at the guy who saved you!"

"I know!" Amanda gasped. "It's not funny!"

The words were hard to get out as she struggled for breath, and then the laughter abruptly stopped. Amanda's hysterical tears gave way to actual sobs as the weight of the experience washed over her.

She stumbled forward and Drew held her, shifting his tone just as quickly.

"It's okay," he muttered while rubbing his cheek against her hair. "You're okay."

They stood together, rocking in the doorway until Amanda's tears stopped. She carefully slipped out of Drew's arms, apologizing for falling apart on him.

"It's okay," he repeated more firmly. "You're allowed to fall apart sometimes. We all do."

"Do you?" Amanda looked up at him, taking in his height and broad shoulders. She'd seen him cry before but not in a long time.

"Obviously." He tilted his head. "Why else would I break up with you?"

"Oh." The air sucked out of the room. Amanda's thoughts swirled without settling on anything she could say. Drew closed his eyes and took a slow breath.

"Forget it," he said at last, brushing away the moment with a swipe of his hand. "It's for the best. But I'm still here for you. Somehow."

He sounded uncertain and Amanda nearly reached for his arm. Instead, she twined her fingers together and took a deep breath.

"So, we're friends?"

Drew winced, looking up at the ceiling before visibly pulling away.

"I don't know, Amanda. We're... something. Can we just not with the labels?"

"Yeah," Amanda agreed quickly, remembering Trina saying something similar about her and Nick. She didn't like that comparison.

"I really do have to go," Drew reminded.

"Yeah, okay. Thanks, again. For your help."

Amanda let him leave first, avoiding the shared elevator ride, and wondered if he really thought their breakup was for the best.

§

Cameron didn't join them for dinner that night. The taser incident had taken up a lot of his time, so he was working late. When Patty relayed that message, Amanda realized he had been at dinner more often than not for several weeks.

"How are you?" Patty asked as they sat down to baked chicken with string beans and baby potatoes.

Amanda didn't know how to answer. Memories from the cafeteria flashed through her mind before settling on Drew's expression as they stood by the party room doors.

"Are you ready to go back to Arcadia?" Patty tried again, sending Amanda's thoughts spinning from Drew to her work with Mitra.

Amanda set down her fork.

"Are you going to marry Cameron?"

Patty coughed and choked, her face turning red as she swallowed harshly and reached for her water. When she recovered, she asked, "Where did that come from?"

"Seems like a reasonable question." Amanda shrugged and began cutting her chicken. "I mean, you're obviously dating, right?"

Patty set down her fork and folded her hands in her lap. She sounded generally curious when she asked, "Would that bother you?"

"Dating or getting married?" Amanda asked, then wondered if it made a difference. She hadn't planned on bringing the subject up at all, it just sort of came out.

"We aren't getting married," Patty clarified, slowly cutting her string beans. "Well, I mean, that hasn't come up. And dating? I don't know if I'd call it dating exactly… but, I guess, I wouldn't *not* call it dating."

"That clears it up." Amanda watched her mom pick at her plate, then decided to give her a break. "I'm not upset. It's just a little, I don't know, weird, I guess. He was my first training agent. He was Dad's partner…"

She stopped talking, seeing a flash of pain, or maybe guilt, cross Patty's face.

"But Dad's been gone a long time," Amanda added. "And it's not like you and Cameron had something going on when he was alive. Oh, wait! You didn't, did you?"

"Of course not!" Patty flared, then took a calming breath. "Amanda, Cameron was just a friend then, and I hadn't seen him in so long. I never expected this."

Amanda nodded and slowly chewed a bite of chicken. She vividly remembered how angry Patty had been when Cameron finally told her about psychic travel and his part in keeping the secret from her for so many years.

She didn't like to remember those days.

"I wish you had told me," Amanda said softly, pushing a potato across her plate. "That you're dating."

"I should have," Patty agreed. "I didn't know how."

Amanda understood that.

"Sometimes I want to talk to you about things," she said slowly. "But I don't know what to say either."

"You can talk to me about anything." Patty waited as Amanda chewed another bite of chicken, then added, "I think getting started is the hardest part."

"It is," Amanda agreed. "It's like, I know I want to talk about something, but I don't know what to say first and all the words in my head sound… wrong."

As she spoke, they both relaxed into the conversation.

"What if you just give me the subject?" Patty suggested. "One word."

"Drew," Amanda said without looking up.

"Ah," Patty said knowingly.

"And Mitra," Amanda added.

"Oh," Patty said in a higher voice, then reached for a quick sip of water.

"Not that there's anything going on," Amanda hurried to explain. "With Mitra, I mean. Or with Drew, now that we broke up. Except there's maybe still something with Drew. And Drew thinks there's something with Mitra, even if I don't. Except Mitra is kind of… attractive, I guess."

Patty watched Amanda eat a piece of potato.

"It can be tricky," she ventured, "when there are two people you might want to date."

"But I don't!" Amanda interrupted, a flash of anger heating her words. "I mean, I don't think I want to date either of them. Or anyone really. Not right now. And you don't have to look so happy about that!"

Patty laughed, shaking off her look of relief.

"No, no, I'm sorry. Look, it's not that I'm happy if you don't want to date. Someday I do want you to date and find someone to share your life with. But right now, you have a lot going on and dating can be complicated. Setting your own priorities is a good thing."

"Exactly!" Amanda ran both hands over her face and through her hair. "The thing is, I have moments where I look at Drew, or sometimes Mitra, and have thoughts of… well, you know, dating stuff. But most of the time, I'm too busy with everything else. My training, schoolwork, the Vertex situation. There's just so much."

Patty nodded, letting Amanda get everything out.

"But then…" Amanda's voice grew small, "I think maybe there's something wrong with me. Because everyone else is so obsessed with dating or hooking up or whatever. Trina. Drew. Everyone at school. Mitra, maybe. You and Cameron. But I barely think about it."

Tears stung as Amanda dropped her hands to her lap and looked down in shame.

"Hey," Patty said urgently, reaching for Amanda's arm and tugging gently until she could wrap Amanda's hand in her own. "There is nothing wrong with you."

Amanda's eyes darted to her mom, making contact once she saw unwavering support.

"You are a normal, sixteen-year-old," Patty insisted. "I know you hear a lot about teenagers having raging hormones, girls being boy-crazy, boys being girl-crazy, and all that. But there's also nothing wrong with not being obsessed with dating and sex. Not now and not at any age. The truth is romantic relationships are more complicated than that. And that's okay."

"Even with Drew," Amanda began slowly, fighting through her embarrassment. "I care about him so much and there were times when it was nice, to kiss him or have his arms around me, but most of the time, I just wanted to talk to him like always."

Patty tensed as she asked, "Did Drew push for more than that?"

"No," Amanda answered quickly. "He never pushed at all, but I think that's why he broke up with me. He said it was because he thinks I like Mitra, but he only thinks that because I wasn't ready to… or wasn't interested in…"

She trailed off, her face flaming. Patty patted her hand reassuringly.

"Amanda, you are an amazing young woman. There's nothing wrong with feeling physical attraction to other people. And there's nothing wrong with not being in a hurry to do anything about it.

"If Drew, or anyone else, has different expectations, then they simply aren't a good match for you. Maybe you and Drew will be on the same page when you're older. Or maybe you'll meet someone else who is a better fit. Life is long, and there's no need to rush."

Amanda agreed weakly. She wasn't sure if Patty was right or if it was just the kind of advice a mom would give, but it was good to hear.

Shadows fell across scattered tables beyond the coffee shop's sunny front window. The narrow space had been designed for aesthetics over functionality. Funky art lined the dark purple walls and painted wood screens divided tables into cozy nooks. Large potted plants crowded any remaining space, while heavy wear added character to the hardwood floor. Overall, the place had a bohemian vibe and was a favorite hang-out in the historic part of town.

Amanda ordered an iced coffee from the barista. She didn't see Trey until he leaned around a screen at the back of the room and held up one hand in a motionless wave. Amanda turned back to the counter where the barista was scooping ice into her cup. The shop was half-empty, which wouldn't last long on a Sunday morning.

Joining Trey, Amanda saw his table was the last nook before a brick back wall separated the main café space from the bathrooms. He slouched against the wall, leaving

Amanda to sit across from him. A yellow wooden screen crowded behind her chair.

She knew from his text that he hadn't been hurt by the taser, but she asked how he was as a courtesy.

"Alright." Trey shrugged one shoulder. The corners of his mouth turned down as his eyes scanned her face. "You okay? I didn't mean to push you that hard."

"Yeah, no, that was fine." Amanda nearly explained that she was already jumping out of the way, and his push only threw her off balance, but she didn't want to take away from his moment of bravery.

They sipped their drinks without talking.

Trey looked down his outstretched arms to the coffee cradled in his hands. Amanda saw one of his hands lightly twitch against the tabletop.

"So, you and Drew are done?" Trey lifted his gaze slowly as he asked, a proposition creeping in.

Amanda shifted back, bumping her chair into the wooden screen behind her. The man on the other side scooted his chair farther away, proving a fault in the café's cluttered sense of style.

"Come on, Mandy. When are you going to give me a chance?"

Trey's tone was teasing but Amanda tensed. She remembered the time he had cornered her at her locker, and then again at the mall where he had kissed her before she could shove him away.

"It's *Amanda*," she corrected coldly, "and I've been very clear about you having no chance."

Trey's mouth curled into a sneer.

"Right. You don't mean that. None of you mean that," he added, leaving Amanda to guess he was including all the girls who rejected him. "I know I come on strong, but you don't want the nice guy. You say you do, but that didn't work out for Drew, did it?"

Amanda felt her jaw harden and her eyes narrow as she bit the inside of her lip.

"I knew I shouldn't have come here," she muttered, then corrected herself. "No, scratch that. I'm not the one who's wrong here. You tried to do a nice thing for me, and I wanted to thank you for that. But I don't owe you anything, no matter what you do. No girl owes you anything."

"Oh, here we go." Trey rolled his eyes. "Tell me how wrong I am. Make up some reason why I'm not the guy girls like you go for. Tell me why you think you're better than me. Better than everyone."

"I do not!" Amanda flared, but Trey was quick to argue.

"You do, too! I see the way you keep your distance, looking down on everyone, playing hard to get. But you aren't different. You just don't admit you're like the rest of us. Look at you, getting all red-faced, breathing fast. Tell me you aren't excited when I'm around. Drew didn't excite you, did he? Not the way I can. Go ahead and ask your best friend. Trina knows how exciting I can be."

He leaned far across the table, his voice low and steady. Amanda's skin crawled as he bit his lower lip and raised an eyebrow suggestively.

"Ugh," Amanda recoiled, bumped her chair against the wooden screen again, and heard the man behind her curse as he got up to leave. Trey reached for her hand, but she quickly pulled away, crossing her arms over her chest to contain her shaking anger.

"You are so messed up!" she told him, disgust clear in her voice. "You don't know me. You don't know the first thing about how I think or what I want. You just can't face the fact that I don't want to be with you. So, what? You throw it in my face that Trina dated you for about five minutes? Like that's going to make me want to date you? Jeez, you're just so… ugh!

"You know what?" she asked, letting her pent-up anger pour out. "I don't think I'm better than everyone, but I do think I'm better than you. Because I accept that people have their own thoughts and feelings. And I respect that. I might get it wrong sometimes and make mistakes, like everyone does, but I learn from them and try to do better. I don't double down on being a jerk and thinking what I want is more important than what anyone else wants for themselves."

Running out of steam, Amanda settled back in her seat and reached for the cold sensation of her iced coffee against her sweating palms. Trey crossed his arms and stared past his right shoulder. He sat very still. His lips were clenched, and his Adam's apple bobbed with a harsh swallow. For a moment, Amanda was afraid he would cry.

"Look," she said with a hint of regret, "if you want to date someone, you don't do that by bullying her into it. And it isn't about putting on an act or making one big gesture. You wait to find a girl who will like you for who you are and have real shared interests and stuff."

Trey rolled his eyes her way.

"Be myself?" he asked with heavy sarcasm. "Be myself and you'll what? Be my friend? Lead me on for a while, maybe date me until you get bored, like you did with Drew?"

Amanda stood up.

"You know what? I don't care what you do. Go on being a jerk. Or work on yourself and maybe find someone who could like you. Just leave me out of it."

Trey didn't stop her from walking away. Amanda waited for it. She expected him to call out, or follow her, but she crossed the café without interruption and opened the door with a sense of satisfaction. Her mom was right. She had her own life to live, and she didn't owe Trey—or anyone—her time or attention. His warped ideas about dating were not her problem.

The satisfaction faded when she saw a familiar figure leaning against the side of Patty's car.

"What are you doing here?"

With a slow smile, Lucas said, "You will never guess where I'm taking you!"

§

Security at the U.S. Capitol was tight but not as efficient as the gatehouses Amanda had moved through on other worlds. She'd been sitting in a nondescript basement room for over an hour, along with Rory, Lucas, and Cameron. During their wait, an aide checked in frequently, offering water bottles and promising the general would be with them soon. Amanda had stopped believing him.

When Lucas had shown up with his plan to tour one of the sites for a new proximal door, she was surprised it was in the Capitol building. During the drive to D.C., she'd asked if the president would be there and been shocked to learn that he didn't know about the Psychic Traveler Society at all. As they waited, she brought up the subject again.

"Our relationships with governments are complicated," Cameron explained diplomatically. "Here in the U.S., it's a case-by-case situation requiring a special security clearance that's carefully buried within the published system."

"But doesn't the president have the highest clearance there is? Even *this* president?"

Rory laughed at Amanda's question, but Cameron only allowed himself a wry smile.

"Speaking as a member of the High Council, I won't comment on world leaders."

"And speaking as Cameron?" Amanda drew a laugh, but he still declined to give an opinion.

"Did past presidents know about us?" Amanda couldn't let the subject go. Clearly, there was a relationship between PTS and the U.S. government, but she didn't understand how that could possibly work without the president being involved.

"Many of them have," Cameron admitted. "But often not until their second term. I believe most one-term presidents were never read in. There are other officials we primarily work with, particularly in positions that don't end when the president changes. It's a relatively small group."

Lucas stood up then, pacing the room in a sign of uncharacteristic nerves.

"He'll be here when he gets here," Rory told him, leaning back in her own chair. She then turned to Amanda and said, "We'll likely have a different president before you make a door."

"But it's like a year and a half until the next election," Amanda reminded. "Why are we here now if we're waiting that long?"

"The person who is president has nothing to do with you creating a door." Lucas stopped pacing and leaned against a square column near their group of chairs.

The door abruptly opened, ending the conversation.

Major General Falkner swept into the room wearing Army Greens with an array of ribbons over his left breast pocket. His aide followed close behind, carrying a stack of folders in the crook of one arm and a stainless-steel travel mug in his free hand.

"You must be Amanda Jones."

The general's smile fled quickly, as if knowing it didn't belong on his gruff face.

Lucas stepped in to finish the introductions, and General Falkner nodded briskly at each name. His eyes lingered on Amanda appraisingly, though it was impossible to tell what he was thinking. He suddenly turned toward the door saying, "Well, let's give you the tour."

They were led down a short hall and into a large room with metal detectors by each door and locked cabinets on its side walls. The room also held two tables with conveyor belts leading to X-ray scanners. The set-up reminded Amanda of airport security, though there were no TSA agents, guards, or other workers in sight.

"This is where you want me to make a door?" Amanda asked, despite it being the room's obvious purpose.

"We are preparing for any eventuality." General Falkner pointed out reinforced walls, biometric weapons cabinets, automatic door locks, and other security features. It reminded Amanda of the secure gatehouse on Stellaria, and she considered who was being protected here.

"Does Congress know about this?"

General Falkner shot Lucas a disapproving frown. Lucas tried to shrug with his usual swagger but couldn't relax the twitch by his eye or the tension in his jaw.

"What?" Amanda asked. "We're in the same building, right? If Congress is upstairs, won't they notice travelers moving in and out of this room all day and night?"

"It's a large building," the general answered shortly.

"Right…?" Amanda didn't understand the warning she saw in Lucas' eyes. "But wouldn't it make more sense to use a less secure building? I mean, have some security, like with doors on other worlds, but look at us today. We needed an escort to get down here, and we weren't allowed to leave that other room. Will travelers be able to pass through with a special badge or something?"

"Those issues do not concern you," General Falkner said firmly. "Your job will be to make the connection. If you can."

Amanda had more questions, but Cameron cut her off, saying they would talk about the politics of the situation another time.

"General Falkner is here to show us the facility and have a chance to meet our next architect."

Realizing she wasn't making a very good impression, Amanda kept quiet for the rest of the visit. She crossed her arms as Lucas explained the progress of her training with occasional clarification from Rory or Cameron.

No one mentioned that she had failed Keah's test, or that she was still struggling to find a solution to the question posed by the elders in Stellaria. Instead, they talked about the experience of the resource team working to complete the architect's journey and the progress they had made together. Listening, Amanda had a hard time picking out any accomplishments of her own.

Back in her room that evening, she settled against her headboard and met Gerald for a scheduled tutoring session. He was still helping her with history, while also adding information about how travelers had shaped world events behind closed doors. They met in the living room of the birdhouse, where Amanda had experienced some of her earliest lessons in psychic travel.

"I don't know what I did wrong," she complained from her place on the couch. She had filled Gerald in on their visit to the Capitol and on Lucas' apparent frustration with her when it was over.

"Don't you?" Gerald sat in an adjacent chair, offering raised eyebrows and a gentle smile.

Amanda shrugged.

Looking around the room, she realized this would be the most logical place for a door to the Capitol. Given that it already held doors to New York, Chicago, and San Francisco. But there wasn't much wall space. Lucas had once suggested she create a new mindspace house dedicated to doors connected to cities on Earth, but it would be years before she had the skills for that.

"I guess I wasn't supposed to be questioning the general," Amanda admitted reluctantly. "But why not? I had good questions! And putting a proximal zone in the Capitol is a really stupid idea. Shouldn't I have some say in where it goes?"

"You might," Gerald agreed, "once you have your full architect powers. But what if this is about something bigger than connecting a single door?"

Amanda frowned in confusion until Gerald sighed wearily and began his explanation.

"We're nearing a tipping point. It's getting harder to hide our society from normals, and a growing number of travelers are pushing to come out of the shadows. It's only a matter of time. Psychic travel is going to go public, and it's going to be messy when it does."

Biting her lip, Amanda pictured the Vertex vanishing from the stage at her school, then thought of Nick and his online conspiracy group. Change was coming.

"There's a reason the International Council made Lucas our director," Gerald continued intently. "He knows how to work the angles. He's promising the Vertex additional doors around our world. More doors means moving more freely when things get ugly after the big reveal.

"But he's also working with the U.S. government to put those doors in places they control. He's staying on their good side, knowing we'll need government support to limit mass panic among the normals."

"The U.S. Consulate in Mumbai," Amanda said softly, remembering the case Lucas had made for moving the Mumbai door to a better facility. "Lucas told the Vertex doors should be in more modern, secure places, like the U.S. Consulate. That's not a coincidence."

"No, it isn't," Gerald agreed solemnly. "Lucas is crafty. The Vertex has members all over the world, but their leadership is currently based in the United States, just like the High Council. It will seem reasonable that he's finding U.S.-controlled spaces for new doors. If he's lucky, no one will question that. But he's probably making deals with other world powers as well."

"Because we'll need government support around the world." Amanda clasped her hands tightly, feeling Lucas' plan coming together in her mind. "That's how he's planning for a more controlled reveal. He's not just buying time to get the messaging together. He's making time for governments to set up more control over psychic travel in our world. Especially for the United States."

The levels of his plan occurred to her gradually, as if peeling back the layers of an onion.

"The Vertex promises to stay secret in return for doors to move more freely, and the government promises to publicly support psychic travelers in return for securing more of our doors."

"Yes," Gerald agreed. "It's a cunning plan. The Vertex is promised more doors and eventual public acknowledgment of their abilities, while the government gets a chance to feel more in control of us all."

"So, this architect's journey is just a distraction? A way to keep people from looking at Lucas' plans too closely?"

Amanda shivered as her part in Lucas' scheme came clearly into view.

"Not exactly," Gerald corrected. "It may help to distract from some of the details, but without your architect skills, Lucas' entire plan falls apart."

Scanning the room again, Amanda saw doors to cities in America as well as Europe. She had made one door herself, from the attic in this house to Terra-V, and it had been an accident. Despite the progress she'd made with Edmund's trials, her architect abilities had hardly changed. It could be months or years before she was ready to reliably create a single door, let alone a series of doors around the whole planet.

"I'm just a pawn in all of this, aren't I?" She didn't like the idea, but it was impossible to ignore. "There's a team moving me through Edmund's journey at their pace. It's not about me learning how to be an architect. They just want to push through and hope I magically figure it all out by the time it's done."

"I don't know," Gerald sighed. "It's unclear what Edmund expects you to learn with these trials. I don't see how elders in other worlds—who aren't psychic travelers themselves—could teach you any practical skills about psychic architecture. The journey appears to be more focused on ensuring the next architect shares Edmund's Victorian values."

"Empathy and perception, creativity and truth, courage and restraint, knowledge and wisdom." Amanda rattled off the values outlined in Edmund's message.

She had read through the transcript of her meeting with the Pyura Elder often enough to have it memorized, but she didn't know how skills in any of those areas would help her build her own mindspace house or purposefully connect doors to new worlds.

"They're not bad values," Gerald clarified. "But the journey is shaping up to be an assessment, a gate to cross, not a training program. I wish we had the letter Edmund referenced." The resource team had never found a letter laying out any specifics of the architect's journey.

"You think it said more about my training? Like a next step after I pass the trials?"

Gerald shrugged.

"There has to be something more than testing your character and view of the world. Though it's fitting. Leave it to a Victorian to make you prove your constitution before letting you in."

Amanda considered what might have been in the letter. Maybe it had important information that was keeping her from learning practical skills during the journey.

Yet, she had accidentally created one door to Terra-V. That made it easier to believe she would be able to do it again in time. That thought led her to a new possibility.

Hesitating over her words, she asked, "What if I learn how to create new doors, but I don't put them where they want me to?"

Gerald pressed his hands against his thighs as a slow smile spread across his face.

"That's why you have Lucas worried."

Chapter 18

The Arcadian Mystics

Vertical rows of flying cars and hover carts skimmed between glass buildings lining the wide city street. Arcadians strolled the spacious sidewalks, scarcely noticing the traffic or the visiting aliens who walked among them. Amanda knew the mystics, like all Arcadians, were human descendants of travelers from Earth, but she eyed the more vibrantly hued aliens they passed and wondered what to expect when they reached Dr. Webb's office.

Before their trip, Lucas had explained that the scientific community in Arcadia—the *civilized society*, according to Dr. Webb—did not freely associate with mystics. It didn't matter that the mystics had been right about psychic travel. There continued to be a divide in the way scientists and mystics approached the matter, which led to animosity on both sides. Still, Amanda was surprised to see extra security guards throughout the science center and posted outside Dr. Webb's office.

She paused just inside the doorway. In her imagination, the mystics appeared as New Age types with colorful clothing and long flowing hair. Instead, the mystics in Dr. Webb's office looked like any other Arcadian she might pass on the city streets.

Halima Burton greeted Amanda and Rory with a warm clasp of their hands. She wore a pale blue tunic and pant suit with a simple silver necklace and matching cuff bracelet. Her dark hair was styled in a pixie cut, much shorter than Dr. Webb's chin-length bob.

Her partner, Argyri Cabrera, wore a white shirt and faded salmon pants. His hair was longer but lifted and brushed back in a soft pompadour. As she shook his hand, Amanda was struck by his subtle resemblance to Mitra. The same angular cheekbones and ice-blue eyes.

They were directed to the seating area in the office's glass-walled corner. Amanda and Rory were positioned across from Halima and Argyri. Dr. Webb sat at an angle between them. A central coffee table held a tea set and tiered trays with fruits and small pastries.

"We've come together today," Dr. Webb began, "to discuss our role in Amanda's training, as it was entrusted by our dear friend Edmund Robinson."

"Thank you for including us," Argyri responded, his gracious tone softening the stiffness of his smile.

When he turned his head to speak, Amanda saw a translator disc behind his left ear.

"You don't have embedded translators?" she asked bluntly, then flushed under Rory's sharp stare. "I mean, sorry if that's rude. It just surprised me."

"It's a perfectly reasonable question," Argyri assured her. "You're very observant."

"We use care with technology and generally avoid elective surgical procedures," Halima explained kindly.

"Yet you are happy to benefit from our technological advances at your own discretion."

Amanda squirmed under Dr. Webb's tight smile, but the mystics weren't bothered.

"Technology and nature can work well together," Halima agreed with a bow of her head.

Birdsong filled the momentary silence, and Amanda looked thoughtfully toward the nearest window. The air felt light around them. The birds and other sounds of the city were muted by the glass but not as much as they would be if Dr. Webb had activated a quiet zone. Given the added security guards, Amanda doubted that was an oversight, though she kept the observation to herself.

"We would love you to visit our research center," Halima offered, turning her gaze to include both Amanda and Rory. "As part of your training."

"Your *research center*," Dr. Webb echoed with a raised eyebrow. "Is it no longer called the Maiorum Shrine?"

Argyri explained that it was both.

"Our research center exists outside of the city, in a location endorsed by Edmund himself, based on lore handed down from our most sensitive ancestors. The research facilities are dedicated to preserving our history, while the shrine commemorates our terrestrial ancestors, the Maiorum. Those who originally came from your world to found our own."

"We believe it was the site of the first psychic door created between our worlds," Halima added. "The one destroyed when the Maiorum chose to stay."

"Do you know how that door was destroyed?"

Amanda wasn't surprised when they shook their heads, saying not even Edmund could find that answer, though he had tried. They said it was a mystery he had spent many years working on, though they did not have access to his personal research.

"It sounds like your research center is lacking in research," Dr. Webb quipped, amusing herself alone.

Amanda reached for a pastry, looking for a distraction from the strained silence.

"We have eagerly awaited our meeting," Halima told her brightly. "Edmund had hoped you would appear while he was still alive, and he worried how you would fare without the guidance of an experienced architect."

Chewing slowly, Amanda knew Halima didn't mean Edmund was waiting for her specifically but for the next traveler to show promise as a psychic architect. Previous High Councils had been charged with eliminating travelers who opposed them, and any of those travelers might have become the next architect. A sadness came over Amanda as she wondered how many were lost and what might have happened to her if Lucas hadn't led a rebellion that exposed the practice and removed the last High Council.

"Amanda?"

Rory said her name insistently but gently, and Amanda saw that everyone was waiting for her to say something.

"Sorry, I was lost in a thought."

"We understand," Argyri reassured. "It is said Edmund was often lost in his thoughts as well."

Amanda smiled weakly, not sure that counted as proof she was Edmund's rightful successor.

"But you didn't know Edmund."

"Not personally, no," Halima agreed. "Though we've read the letters he left behind."

"Letters?" Rory asked as Amanda watched Dr. Webb frown. She wondered if that meant they had the missing letter Edmund had left for her, but Argyri's answer dashed that hope.

"We have many letters Edmund wrote to our scholars. He would often write his ideas while traveling on other worlds, then bring them during his next visit. He said letter writing was a habit he couldn't break, even when he would be delivering the letters himself."

"As to Amanda's training," Dr. Webb interjected. "I believe we have come to an agreement?"

Argyri pulled a blue folder out of his satchel. Halima met Dr. Webb's challenging gaze, showing the power struggle they had navigated while setting up this meeting.

"We have brought the documents you requested as proof that we accept your right to decide when Amanda's trial in Arcadia is complete."

Rory set down the cup of tea she had just lifted from the table. Sensing her keen interest, Amanda brought the pastry she was eating to her lap without noticing the crumbs that flaked across her jeans.

Dr. Webb opened the folder and scanned its contents before turning to face Amanda and Rory.

"In our conversations regarding your training, new information has come to light about Edmund's complete plan for your architect's journey. It seems a key piece of his program was left out of the instructions he left with allies on his chosen worlds."

"Left out?" The pastry cracked in Amanda's grip. She hastily put the broken pieces on the coffee table, as Rory handed her a napkin. Halima was about to speak when Dr. Webb cleared her throat.

"As I've said before, it was clear some information was missing from the documents Edmund left in our care. It appears his instructions for our world were divided between our scientific and mystic communities."

"Like the trials shared by the tribes in Opt-V," Amanda said with a sinking feeling in her stomach. Dr. Webb, who knew about her failure to pass all three of those challenges, quickly shook her head.

"No, as you've just heard, Halima and Argyri have agreed that I will decide when your trial in our world is complete. You will not have to jump through hoops for both of us to complete that part of your journey."

The pointed look she flashed at the mystics raised a warning Amanda didn't understand.

"What does that mean?" Rory asked in a warning tone, her patience clearly waning.

"Edmund helped design our research center," Halima explained. "Beyond approving the location, he planned its architecture, including a special room where he could work and a vault that could only be opened by his successor. After completing the architect's journey."

"A vault?" Amanda was on her feet before she knew what she was doing. Rory quickly stood as well, and the mystics hastily followed suit. Only Dr. Webb remained in her seat.

"We do not know what this vault contains," Argyri explained. "Though we assume it will help Amanda further develop her psychic architect skills."

"This is the first we're hearing of a vault," Rory told them. "Or of anything that comes after the trials."

"We are aware of that now."

Halima and Argyri shared an uncomfortable look. Amanda remembered her conversation with Gerald and couldn't wait to share this development.

"We only learned about the architect's journey when Dr. Webb told us about her instructions from Edmund," Rory clarified, clearly frustrated. "And then we spent months going through Edmund's diaries and checking several worlds he had frequently referenced before we found the message he left with the Pyura Elder."

"Our instructions indicated that Edmund had left a letter for his apparent successor with your High Council," Halima said with regret. "When we heard Dr. Webb was working with a potential psychic architect, we believed you knew about our part in the architect's journey and would contact us when you were ready."

"I knew nothing of this letter or their part in Edmund's plan," Dr. Webb added, one elbow resting on the wide arm of her chair while her hands clasped lightly in her lap.

"I brought what I knew to Lucas when time passed without the High Council or Amanda mentioning the architect's journey. I was only recently informed about the vault, during our arrangements for this meeting."

Rory shook her head in exasperation. Amanda paced toward the windows, processing this new information. Edmund's missing letter would have explained so much. Even without it, they could have known about the vault much sooner if the Arcadian scientists and mystics had a better relationship.

"All right." Rory sighed heavily and resumed her seat. "How is the vault opened?"

Halima and Argyri sat as well. Amanda stayed close to the windows.

"There is a code that will unlock the vault," Argyri said. "We do not know the code yet, but we will once Amanda receives the letters Edmund left for her on completion of his four trials."

"The trials are key," Amanda muttered, recalling a line from Edmund's message through the Pyura Elder.

"Yes," Dr. Webb agreed archly. "Edmund wanted you to work for whatever he left in that vault."

"He wanted to ensure she was ready," Halima corrected, which raised Dr. Webb's eyebrow.

"Edmund did not know Amanda Jones," she responded sharply. "But I do."

She turned to Amanda with a glint in her eye.

"You exhibited your value of truth by bringing Mitra books forbidden by your former High Council. An act which brought the true circumstances of your world to our attention. Upon discovering more unpleasant truths about said council, you aided a peaceful revolution.

"Furthermore, you have displayed creativity through your work with Mitra, bringing you closer than any Maiorum to reaching our separated mindspace. Through you, we have learned more about our own psychic abilities, which shows a capacity to build what already exists. Therefore, your trial on Arcadia is complete."

She reached into a side table, extracting the Pyura relic and a red folder. Rory accepted the items, as Amanda stared in disbelief.

"That's it? My trial is done?"

"In Arcadia, yes," Dr. Webb confirmed. "You still have trials to pass in worlds that have not gotten to know you yet. Hopefully, that will happen soon, as Lucas has impressed the urgency of your completing your architect training. A goal I would like to see you achieve as well."

Amanda faced the mystics warily, expecting them to argue with Dr. Webb's decision, but they both smiled warmly. Rory gestured for Amanda to retake her seat.

"We want you to succeed, Amanda," Halima told her earnestly. "We will not attempt to open Edmund's vault until you have passed the trials set with his other allies, but we will help you as much as we can."

"You can come to our research center," Argyri invited again. "Perhaps something in Edmund's letters would help you with your remaining trials."

"I would like to see where the original door connected our worlds."

"That door no longer exists," Dr. Webb reminded, pouring herself a cup of tea. "Our scientists have checked the location of their shrine and there is no evidence of remaining energy. Nothing like the subtle frequencies that are found in our active gatehouses."

Amanda nodded politely, but she remembered the faint pulse she had thought she felt when Gerald showed her the original door's location in the mindspace. Her heart felt a little flip of hope.

§

In the center of the shopping plaza, children splashed in a play fountain while parents watched from shaded tables. Amanda adjusted her sunglasses and took a sip of her mango smoothie.

"Take a walk away from the crowd?" Trina suggested, and Amanda agreed.

They walked along a row of newly opened shops and past a fenced-off construction site where large equipment sat idle in the Saturday sun. This was a relatively new town center with large open spaces that would eventually hold a mix of office and apartment buildings.

In minutes, Amanda and Trina had left the busy retail center, moving beyond construction zones and into an open area slated for later development. A man in the distance walked his dog. Otherwise, they were alone.

"I heard a mini-golf place is coming in over here." Trina gestured toward the empty lots around them.

"That's a rumor," Amanda told her. "But a traveling carnival is supposed to set up for a few weeks this summer."

"Cool."

A cloud slipped across the sun, and the plastic smoothie cup felt cold in Amanda's hand.

A month after Trina's discovery and confrontation, the anger between them had settled into stiff politeness.

"How's it going?" Trina asked uncertainly, then added, "The psychic traveler stuff."

Amanda didn't know how to answer. Trina knew about PTS in general. She'd been told that psychic travel was an ability some humans developed later in life and that Amanda was the only teenage traveler. She had not been told about Amanda's potential as a psychic architect.

"It's… okay." Amanda glanced at Trina as they walked. She was sipping a raspberry smoothie and her eyes were hidden by large sunglasses.

"It must be pretty weird," Trina observed. "Though I guess you've had time to get used to it."

"I guess." Amanda thought about that, then shook her head. "I don't know that I'm used to it exactly. It's still a thing I'm figuring out. Sometimes, I think I know where I fit in. But then, I step back and it's like I'm just bouncing around, reacting to what everyone else is telling me to do."

"Like what?" Trina sounded genuinely interested, then quickly backpedaled. "I mean, if you can tell me. I know it's secret and all."

"Well, there's this training they have me doing," Amanda answered carefully. "It's supposed to help me learn more about my abilities, but it's nothing like I expected. Instead of teaching me to do things, these trials are set up to prove I'm ready to be taught. Or something like that."

"Are the trials hard?"

They were a few blocks from the town center. The streets were mostly finished but covered in dirt and gravel from the cleared lots. A large sign announced that lots were still available and displayed the developer's name and number in bright red letters.

"That's the thing," Amanda answered with a puzzled frown. "They're not. I mean, one part of them was hard—and I'm still working on that—but the rest of it…" She trailed off, looking for the right words.

"So, it's been mostly easy?"

"No." Amanda flashed back to Rory being stabbed in Terra-V. "Not easy, but… Well, it's more about how I see things instead of teaching me new skills or testing me on anything I can do. I didn't expect that."

"I didn't expect any of this," Trina said with a sigh. They were nearing the edge of the development. A narrow retention pond ran between the farthest lots and a nearby highway. It was edged by cattails and wildflowers. Some ducks skimmed the surface.

"I met Trey for coffee," Amanda said, changing the subject. "I kinda felt like I should, after what happened."

Trina didn't say anything.

"He was a jerk about it. Like, he thought it changed everything. Because he saved me or something."

Trina scoffed. "You were moving out of the way before he pushed you."

Amanda agreed, reminded that Trina was there.

"I didn't know what Nick was going to do," Trina added firmly. "And I didn't tell him about you. I said I would keep your secret and I did."

"Yeah, I know." Amanda hung her head, knowing she'd doubted Trina, and questioned her when Nick started with his accusations. Since then, an investigation by PTS agents had determined Nick had been working on his own. They also believed Trina had kept her discovery to herself.

Trina studied Amanda questioningly.

"Okay, I was freaked when Nick started those rumors," Amanda admitted. "I was afraid you might tell him. Maybe I would even deserve that, after the way I treated you. But I should have trusted that you wouldn't tell anyone. And I'm sorry I didn't."

Trina sipped her smoothie thoughtfully.

"Plus," Amanda rushed on, wanting to get everything out, "I didn't think you would care what happened to me, now that Brooklyn's around."

Amanda's face flamed as she watched the ducks glide across the pond, serene on the outside as their little feet flapped frantically under the water.

"Hey," Trina said lightly, drawing Amanda's attention. "Brooklyn's fine when you're not around. And maybe she's kind of fun. But she's not you. You know?"

"Yeah?" Amanda blinked back tears.

"Yeah," Trina repeated, then changed the subject. "Now, tell me about this coffee with Trey. He just expected you to fall all over him in gratitude? *Quelle surprise!*"

"Basically," Amanda laughed as they resumed walking. "I told him one gesture didn't make a difference."

"You've gotta look at the whole relationship," Trina agreed. "Not one moment."

"Or one secret?" Amanda asked carefully.

They walked along the retention pond, looping the far side of the undeveloped lots. Once they turned, the finished portion of the town center towered above the expanse of half-finished roads and empty dirt.

"I know why you didn't tell me," Trina said slowly. "I've talked to that counselor and to Drew about it. It hurt that you told Drew and not me, but he explained how he was there with you when you found out. So, it wasn't like you chose him over me. And, yeah, we've been friends for a long time… that counts for something."

"It does!" Amanda insisted. "We have history."

"We do," Trina conceded, then stopped walking and faced Amanda directly. "Look, I'm glad we're talking again, and I know you can't tell me everything. Just don't shut me out, okay? And I won't let Brooklyn or anyone else come get in the way. We can have other stuff going on, but making time for each other is what matters. Right?"

"Definitely," Amanda choked up, realizing she wanted Trina in her life. Even with their ups and downs, they had built a friendship, and that had value. Amanda straightened, a look of wonder shining in her eyes.

"Trina! That's it!" She hugged Trina impulsively.

"What's it?"

"One of the trials!" Amanda exclaimed, thinking of Stellaria. "They gave me a problem to solve, and I just figured it out. Thanks to you."

"Thanks to me?" Trina asked proudly. "Well, *merci pour moi!*"

CHAPTER 19
LESSONS LEARNED

"**W**hat do you think?"

Amanda nervously looked around the dining table. Cameron, Patty, and Rory gazed back with shining eyes, but she didn't trust their expressions alone.

"I think you're brilliant." Cameron's answer brought a sigh of relief.

"We'll call off the research team," Rory added.

"Are you sure?" Amanda had shared her idea for how to improve Stellaria, but she wasn't confident it was the answer the Stellaria's elders expected.

"Absolutely," Cameron answered for Rory. "Now that you say it, it's obvious."

"Mom?" Amanda turned to Patty. She was the only one who hadn't responded, and Amanda wasn't sure what to make of the hint of tears in her eyes.

"I'm so proud of you!" Patty gushed, bringing a flush to Amanda's cheeks. "You really are growing up so fast!"

Cameron reached for Patty's hand as Amanda ducked her head to stare at the table. She was embarrassed but pleased by their strong show of support.

Still, her confidence flagged when she was in Stellaria's town hall, seated across from the village elders.

"It's nice to see you again, Amanda," Niane offered.

"Finally," Anra added, doing nothing to ease Amanda's trembling discomfort.

"Amanda has been very busy with the architect's journey," Rory reminded, "though she has been working on a solution to the question you proposed."

"Yes," Anra said. "We've had many visits from people asking questions on her behalf."

"They've surveyed the village and taken measurements with their devices," Mardin told them, wrinkling his nose at the word *devices*.

"We needed more information," Rory explained. "The scientists we sent were asked to be discreet."

"They were polite," Kasper allowed. "Though we had hoped Amanda would visit us herself."

Amanda lifted a hand to stop Rory's response.

"They're right," she told Rory quietly, then turned to address the elders. "I should have come back myself. That's what I came to tell you."

As the elders waited to hear more, doubt washed away Amanda's brief flash of courage. It felt like she was standing at the top of that rainforest cliff, strapped into a makeshift harness and about to make a terrifying descent, only to have Keah say it wasn't enough.

That *she* wasn't enough.

Rory nudged Amanda's leg, bringing the elders back into focus. Amanda wondered if it was too late to switch gears. She could still offer them a radio system like Drew had suggested. Her support team had researched that option and drawn up a plan.

But after remembering the cynical way Mardin had said *devices*, she decided to step off the cliff.

"Two months ago, you asked me how I could improve your way of life. You also invited me to your apple festival, which I missed. You invited me to come back and talk to you about the task, too, which I didn't do. Instead, I sent my research team, and I think that was a mistake."

Amanda cleared her throat. She hoped one of the elders would say something encouraging, but they sat quietly as she tried to think of another way to express her answer.

"There are technical ideas I could suggest for your village. Like devices that would let you send messages across long distances or artificial lights that would be brighter than the flowers you use to see at night."

Anra's eyes narrowed. Kasper frowned lightly. Seeing their reactions, Amanda hurried on.

"But I don't think that's what you want. Or what Edmund wanted. I think you gave me the answer when you gave me the question. You invited me to come back and talk to you. You said you would help me find the answer, and I didn't give you a chance."

"You are here to ask for help with the answer?" Niane asked, her face unreadable.

"No," Amanda said shakily. "I think I have the answer. But you can tell me if I have the right idea."

When Amanda hesitated, Niane folded her hands and asked her to share her answer.

"I can improve your way of life by being part of it," Amanda said haltingly. "I can come to visit you the way Edmund did, listen to your stories, and tell you stories about me and my experiences. I can make time for you and build a friendship. So, I guess that's my answer. I can improve your lives in some small way just by being part of them."

Amanda knew she had made a horrible mistake the moment she stopped talking.

Silence stretched and her words echoed in her head. A taunting thought asked, *Who do you think you are? Why would they want your company over a radio system or TVs or any of the cool things you could offer?*

She couldn't bring herself to look at Rory. She could only wait with trembling hands for one of the elders to tell her that she had failed their test.

Instead, Niane studied her thoughtfully and asked, "What led you to that decision?"

It felt like a trap. They wanted to tear apart her idea before telling her she failed. But Amanda took a deep breath and answered honestly.

"I was talking with a friend… someone I've been having trouble with lately. Well, not trouble exactly, but we haven't been as close as we used to be. And there was this other guy, not a friend but someone who wants to be, and he… Well, he tried to do one big thing for me, and it was nice, I guess, but it didn't suddenly make us friends…"

She trailed off and regrouped, trying to remember how she had explained her idea at home.

"Also, the trials Edmund set up in the other worlds haven't been what I expected. I thought someone would teach me a new skill and I'd have a test to show I learned it. Instead, they've been more about me. The way I see the world and the way I see myself.

"I'm learning to trust myself. To do my best, even if I can't know how every single thing will be affected by my choices. I'm figuring out that strength isn't about stepping in with the right answer, but about being present and part of the team…"

Breaking off again, Amanda's thoughts turned to Keah's trial in Opt-V. She realized how unfair it had been for her to fail when trusting Rory and Lucas' expertise had been good leadership.

"Amanda?"

At Rory's sharp nudge, Amanda saw the elders now murmuring among themselves. The day was overcast. Clusters of Stellaria glowed from wall planters and large bowls scattered around the room. A beautiful quilt on the wall behind the elders showed an orchard with two children gathering fruit. *Avu yai,* Amanda thought wistfully.

"You have learned quite a bit on your journey," Niane observed as Mardin gleefully tapped his fingers on his knee. "Edmund would be proud of your progress."

Glancing at Rory, Amanda's heartbeat quickened. Even Anra looked pleased.

"Does that mean I'm right? Is that the answer Edmund wanted me to give?"

"You are very close," Kasper said with a sly grin. "Edmund did not want you to offer changes."

"No changes simply for the sake of change," Mardin clarified, straightening his sweater with a proud air. "Edmund understood that about our people. We don't rush into change."

"Though we do appreciate the richness and joy outside perspectives can bring," Niane added. "Your friendship would improve our lives in that way. Avu yai."

"If you take the time to visit," Anra said pointedly, before adding her own *avu yai* to the chorus offered by the other elders.

"I will!" Amanda promised. "Avu yai! Oh, and I don't expect you to say I've passed your trial until I've proven that by spending more time with you."

"Have you completed your other trials?" Mardin asked, leaning forward as he spoke.

After filling them in on her progress in the other worlds, and the vault that awaited the end of her journey, the elders held a brief discussion in their own language. Rory quietly cracked her knuckles. Amanda studied the glowing hearts of the nearest Stellaria blossoms.

"Edmund Robinson was a kind, wise man," Niane said, resuming their meeting. "We grew up with his stories and have read the letters he left in our library, as well as the instructions he entrusted with us for your training. After speaking with you today, we feel you are ready to proceed with your training."

"Once you have completed your other trials," Anra corrected hastily.

Amanda shot Rory a questioning look, but Kasper was quick to explain.

"Edmund's letters refer to our world as your fourth trial. You have passed two trials on other worlds. Come back once you complete your final trial in Opt-V. We will then consider your trial with us to be complete."

§

After a quick check with the research team, Amanda knew there were a few hours of daylight left in Opt-V. She wanted to visit Keah right away, while she was fired up and ready to argue her case.

Rory wasn't sold on the idea.

"The High Council is working on setting up a meeting with her through Thorvald. We can't just barge in and expect her to see you without any notice."

"Why not? Maybe that's what Keah wants. Maybe it would be a sign of leadership."

"Or as a sign of disrespect," Rory countered.

"Okay, then let's just talk to Thorvald. Now that we know more and are so close to finishing, we can ask him to help us with Keah."

"I don't know…" Rory wavered.

"Look, I know I'm sixteen, and I have a lot to learn, but this is supposed to be my journey. I need to start making more of the decisions myself. I'm the one who's going to be a psychic architect. Not anyone else. I need to step up and take charge, even if it means making mistakes."

Rory closed her eyes. When she opened them, she and Amanda were standing in the castle's great hall beside the doors to Opt-V.

The outpost was quiet when they arrived.

Only a half-dozen travelers lived in Opt-V year-round, though teams of visiting scientists often came through to conduct studies on the planet or visit an observatory set high in the mountains. Thorvald had been assigned to Opt-V the longest, and his team often helped researchers navigate the diverse world. When they were out, a few travelers stayed back to guard the outpost. Today, the outpost appeared to be empty.

Rory warned Amanda to stay close and quiet as they searched the building. There were no travelers in any of the bedrooms or common rooms. They expanded their search to the immediate grounds, then moved from the dappled clearing onto the worn path that led toward the meeting place of the tribal elders. Within minutes, they were startled by rustling bushes.

"Halt!" A traveler stepped onto the path with her weapon drawn, then lowered it with a sigh of relief when she recognized Rory and Amanda. "Well, you've picked a great time to show up."

"Mel?" Rory lowered her own knife, remembering Mel from a previous visit. "What's happening?"

"We have a situation," Mel told them, darting her eyes around the dense rainforest. "A researcher from a team out at Emerald Ridge wandered out of bounds early this morning and interrupted a ritual with the Nicules. Thorvald took a team out to intervene."

"Have you sent for backup?" Rory sounded worried, but Mel shook her head.

"That'll only make it worse. We'll give Thorvald a chance to talk Keah down first."

She and Rory reviewed logistics and concerns while Amanda peered deeper into the rainforest. She could see branches rustling in far-off trees.

"And here come her scouts to make sure we're not calling in the cavalry." Mel nodded toward the approaching movement. "I'll tell Thorvald you're here."

While she sent a psychic message, Rory turned to Amanda and said, "This is why we don't show up off-world unannounced."

"Got it," Amanda said firmly. She was about to ask if they should leave when Mel said Thorvald wanted them to join him.

"Keah wants to see you," she added, before offering to lead them to the meeting.

During their thirty-minute walk, Amanda wondered what Patty and Cameron would say when she got home. Rory had messaged them, then been evasive about their reaction, saying, "Let's just get through this and deal with it when we're home safe."

As they neared the meeting, Amanda could hear excited chattering from the Nicules. Her fear only grew when they saw two Nicules standing guard over a scientist, a large metal box perched on a flat rock, and Keah presiding over the gathering from a large bolder.

Thorvald, his team, and several Nicules stood before Keah in opposing groups.

"Well, this is a surprise," Thorvald greeted, his words light and his smile grim.

"For us, too," Rory returned, while Amanda forced herself to meet Keah's sharp gaze.

"She wants to know why you have come here," Thorvald translated Keah's grunts with a weary sigh.

Rory gestured for Amanda to answer.

They were meeting at the scene of the scientist's crime: a cliffside clearing where a narrow river tumbled over the mountain's rocky edge. Keah's boulder perch was backed by a blue sky that seemed impossibly bright against the enclosing rainforest.

Amanda squinted against the light and said, "I came to ask Keah for a retrial."

Thorvald translated and the Nicules laughed heartily. Keah laughed the loudest, though she quickly stopped to pass Thorvald her reply.

"She says you have come at a good time to prove your leadership," he relayed uneasily. "She wants to hear how you would handle this case if you were her."

He then explained the details of the situation. The research team had been set up in a nearby location known as Emerald Ridge for the last six weeks, with Keah's permission. They had been cautioned to stay within a set boundary, but one of the scientists had gone outside of the approved zone to set up more equipment near the crest of the waterfall in this clearing. While retrieving his equipment, he inadvertently interrupted a sacred rite-of-passage trial for two young Nicules.

As punishment for his disrespect, the Nicules' parents wanted the scientist put to death and his equipment smashed to pieces. Thorvald was pushing for a lesser punishment, where they could destroy the equipment but send the errant scientist home and ban him from returning.

"You cannot destroy that equipment!" the scientist argued hotly. "It will set my research back two years!"

"But you'll be alive," Thorvald snapped angrily.

Amanda stared from Thorvald to Rory with wide eyes. "They want to kill him?"

"It's a matter of honor," Thorvald said with a heavy sigh. "But we won't let that happen."

"Why doesn't he just travel home?"

"He's refusing to leave that damn device." Thorvald shook his head.

Keah jumped down from her rock and bounded between them, chattering warningly.

"She doesn't want me to advise you," Thorvald translated, lifting his hands to appease her request. "Now that I've told you the facts, I can interpret only."

"Rory?" Amanda looked for help, but Rory gauged the menacing look on Keah's face and said she should try to stay out of it, too.

"Just tell Keah you side with Thorvald."

"Don't let them destroy that device!" the scientist pleaded, earning a shove from one of his guards.

Amanda brought templed fingers to cover her mouth. This morning she'd been having a quiet meeting in Stellaria and now she was in a rainforest being asked whether a man should live or die. She had wanted to take charge, but this didn't seem real.

For a wild moment, she wanted to simply fade back into the house and leave Thorvald and Keah to manage without her. But now that she was here, she was afraid of what leaving might do.

"Is this rite-of-passage ritual the same as the trial I went through? An obstacle course?" She asked Thorvald, gesturing for him to translate.

Through Thorvald, Keah said that it was similar, and the scientist's interference was a serious act of disrespect. Amanda considered that, then posed another question.

"Has anyone asked the young Nicules what they want? The ones whose ritual was interrupted?"

Thorvald relayed her question and Keah narrowed her eyes. She then waved her arm, barking a request that brought two young Nicules forward. Nudging them toward Amanda showed Amanda could ask them herself.

"Do you think the scientist should be punished for interrupting your trial?"

They Nicules chattered at each other, then pointed at the piece of equipment sitting on the flat rock and gave Thorvald a lengthy answer.

"They are angry that they were disrespected," Thorvald translated. "They say the scientist doesn't think their ritual is important, and he looks down on them because they do not understand his device."

"I create medicine!" the scientist called out. "The data in that equipment could save lives! Ow!" He moaned as a guard smacked the side of his head. One of his teammates stepped forward, but Thorvald held him back.

Looking between the desperate scientists and the angry Nicules, Amanda thought quickly.

"Agree with Thorvald," Rory hissed, seeing Keah's lips press tight in contained impatience. Amanda waved her off and turned to face Keah.

"I have my answer." As Thorvald translated, Amanda took a deep breath. "I learned to respect the tribes of your world by sharing in your trials. You're angry that this man disrespected your culture. I get that, but instead of punishing him, I'd send him through a trial like the course I finished. He could bring two travelers from the outpost."

Grumbling complaints began to ripple through the gathered Nicules. Rory edged closer as Amanda hurried to build on her answer.

"I'd also have him teach your young about this device and about his work as a sort of cultural exchange. Then he will see that your people are smart and worthy to share in his knowledge."

The Nicules' agitation grew. They grunted and shifted angrily. Some hit their chests with one fist or shrieked their disapproval either at Keah or toward the scientist who was beginning to show fear.

"They aren't buying it," Thorvald warned. He and Rory tightly flanked Amanda, their eyes darting warily between the nearest Nicules.

"Wait!" Amanda called, waving her arms overhead until Keah let out a shriek that silenced the clearing and gave her space to continue. Swallowing hard, Amanda glanced at the scientist and tried to add something that would appease the Nicules.

"If he does not meet those challenges, I would ban him from this world. And his team, too."

The clearing remained eerily silent as Keah considered Amanda's answer. She tilted her head and asked a question through Thorvald.

"You won't give my people the satisfaction of punishing this man here and now?"

Amanda focused on Keah's eyes, her most human-like feature, and hoped they had more in common than their outward appearances suggested.

"I think it's more satisfying to build respect through friendship than with fear."

Keah nodded thoughtfully after hearing Thorvald's translation. Her next words brought relief to his face.

"She says you have shown good leadership and have now passed her trial."

Rory grasped Amanda's arm, but before they could celebrate, Keah made a pronouncement that chased away Thorvald's joy.

"What is it?" Rory asked as the Nicules began to shout and beat their chests.

"She says she's a different kind of leader," Thorvald answered hoarsely. Then, as chaos erupted around them, he shouted, "We've gotta go! Now!"

CHAPTER 20

OPENING THE DOOR

Lucas drove the hover cart at its maximum speed, smoothly skidding along the air while Amanda took in this unfamiliar part of Arcadia. A proximal door on the far side of the city had brought them close to the mystics' research center, but there was still a short ride through the woods to get there. Rory sat beside Amanda, across from Cameron and Elma Anthony, the head negotiator for the Vertex movement.

Amanda slouched in her seat, looking at the scenery and ignoring Elma's bright eyes. She knew Lucas had been using her progress to negotiate with the Vertex, so it wasn't all that surprising Elma had been invited to witness her success. Amanda didn't like it though, and neither did Cameron or Rory.

"Are you excited?"

Amanda rolled her eyes toward Elma, hoping someone else would respond for her. When they didn't, she shrugged and turned away. Out of the corner of her eye, Amanda saw Elma frown, but she tried not to care as she focused on their passing surroundings.

The forest was cool and shady yet dappled with golden sunlight. They rode down a wide road paved with a dark substance that blended into the natural forest floor. Rays of sunlight broke through the leafy canopy at regular intervals, creating shafts of light that glinted off the shells of flying beetles and the wings of shimmering butterflies.

While Amanda was used to hearing birdsong echo throughout the city, calls in the forest were an unbroken melody bouncing from tree to tree. Looking up, she saw graceful branches forming an archway that sheltered the road. The trees here were old, housing an ecosystem that functioned in parallel to the neighboring city, each area offering its own benefits to its inhabitants.

Sneaking a look at Elma, Amanda wondered if this was her first visit to Arcadia. The Vertex was focused on gaining visibility on Earth, but that didn't stop them from using their abilities to visit other worlds. Though, that was likely harder in worlds where PTS had established gatehouses to limit access, like in Arcadia or Stellaria.

Off-world travel drew Amanda's mind back to Keah's trial in Opt-V. She still had nightmares about that day. Just when she had thought she succeeded, Keah had barked an order, and the scientist was gone. Amanda had looked back in time to see it happen, even as Rory pulled her into the rainforest at a stumbling run. The Nicules guarding the scientist had simply picked him up like a doll and tossed him over the waterfall.

My fault. The words whispered through Amanda's mind before she could block them out. Thorvald, Rory, Cameron, Lucas, Patty, everyone said Keah's decision was not her fault. And the scientist hadn't died. He was in the hospital, hooked up to machines, and in serious condition, but he was alive and that was something.

Later, facing Keah with the other tribal elders had taken all of Amanda's strength. She had stood rigid, refusing to acknowledge Keah, as they presented her with a letter from Edmund and the returned Pyura relic. Sitting across from Elma now was nothing compared to that.

Amanda pushed the pain of that day away as Lucas slowed the hover cart. They rode into a large clearing where a wood and glass building rose as if it had grown from the forest itself. The structure featured dark wood and large windows in a sprawling, multi-level configuration.

Rose bushes sprawled around the foundation. Lush flower beds also grew wild with vining plants winding their way up lower portions of the wood siding.

Arcadians who Amanda assumed to be mystics were scattered throughout the area. Some tended plants. Others sat quietly on stone benches or strolled paths that led deeper into the woods. In an adjacent pond, a trio was catching fish with handheld nets.

As Halima and Argyri came outside to welcome them, Amanda made an effort to be pleasant. The atmosphere was relaxed as their party toured the research center. Its many tables and stacks of books reminded Amanda of a library, while its massive windows brought the nurturing feel of the forest into every room.

"We can show you the Maiorum Shrine while we wait for Dr. Webb to arrive," Argyri offered when the tour of the building's main rooms was complete. "The site of the original door to your world."

Amanda was about to agree when Dr. Webb swept into the room with Mitra and two aides by her sides. Her hair was stylishly pinned back on one side and the brooch she always wore caught the light from an overhead fixture. "No need, we're here now."

Mitra stepped forward to meet Amanda as the others made their greetings and introductions. His hair was longer than usual, and he brushed it away from his eyes before taking hold of Amanda's hands.

"It's been too long."

"It has," Amanda agreed, her surprise at his presence and the warmth in his eyes chasing away her dark mood. "I didn't know you'd be here today."

"I wouldn't miss it."

As their eyes held, Amanda let go of the justifications that were bubbling up inside. She had been avoiding Mitra since Drew's accusations, which hadn't been fair, but instead of showing hurt or confusion, Mitra seemed genuinely happy to see her. That was his way, Amanda realized. She let go of what other people might think and let herself be glad to have a friend with her on an important day.

"Shall we open the vault?" Dr. Webb asked, and all eyes turned to Amanda.

Now that she was so close to opening Edmund's vault, she didn't feel ready to know what was inside. Especially when she would be opening it with an audience.

"Or we could see the shrine first?" Mitra suggested hopefully, after seeing Amanda's hesitation. "I'm curious to see it myself."

Though the walk through the woods was brief, the fresh air helped clear Amanda's mind. She ignored Dr. Webb's impatience and listened as Halima related the history of the shrine's construction.

She explained that the shrine had been built long before Edmund arrived in Arcadia. Their ancestors had handed down stories of the Maiorum, people who had traveled from another world to found their civilization.

"The Maiorum had mystical abilities that let them move between worlds," Argyri said, picking up the story. "Those abilities faded as they formed families with the natives of our world."

"Natives?" Amanda looked at Rory and Cameron, seeing they were confused as well. "But our historians say Arcadia was uninhabited back then."

"And our leaders would never lie to us," Lucas said with heavy sarcasm. This didn't seem like news to him, though Elma was listening with a furrowed brow.

"It's speculation," Dr. Webb said dismissively. "Based on a centuries-old claim that the mystics among us are more closely related to your travelers than most Arcadians. There's no evidence of this native race."

"We have evidence," Halima said in a measured tone. "Our anthropologists have found skeletons that—"

"And our anthropologists refute those claims," Dr. Webb interrupted. "More importantly genetic testing does not support your theory."

"Perhaps," Halima began uneasily, but Argyri put a hand on her arm, saying that this might not be the best time to get into a scientific debate.

They had stopped talking just short of the shrine. Small animals scampered in the trees around them while birds sang in the upper branches. Amanda wondered if there could have been a native Arcadian race when the first travelers arrived. Selective breeding was a leading theory of how the Arcadians had lost their psychic abilities, given that traveler genes were not always passed to children, but adding in another non-traveling race seemed like it would answer some of those questions.

"Sophie Stavros," Amanda said the name without thinking, drawing everyone's attention. This time the mystics were confused. Elma's intense interest worried Amanda.

"She was my fellow exile," Lucas said smoothly, "and she allowed Dr. Webb's team to test her genetics. They've tested mine as well."

"Along with other modern travelers," Dr. Webb added, "strengthening our conclusion that all Arcadians are descended from the Maiorum."

Amanda nodded along, remembering that Sophie's story was a secret. Very few people knew that she had married an Arcadian and was raising Lucas' child, who was the genetic offspring of Lucas and Sophie's wife.

They resumed walking and Amanda tried to hide how awful she felt about bringing Sophie into the conversation. As Elma moved ahead to speak to the mystics, Lucas hung back and gave Amanda's shoulder an encouraging bump. "It's okay," he whispered, "No harm done."

Stepping into a clearing, the small group spread out to allow a better view of the Maiorum Shrine.

The heart of the shrine was a simple archway made from woven branches. Flowers were planted around its base and wooden benches had been placed nearby, but the arch itself was strikingly plain. Amanda's eyes drifted over its intertwined branches. She studied the shadows of each bend and the texture of the bark.

As she stepped to the edge of the arch, Amanda closed her eyes and pictured the work she had done with Mitra. She could see his lab and remember how it felt to sit at an energy table, shifting her mental focus enough to control the lights it displayed. After finding the right frequency, she had come close to connecting with Mitra in the Arcadian mindspace. She had seen him, at least, separated by a glossy film that she hadn't been able to break.

If she could shift her frequency now...

Gently cracking her eyes open, Amanda kept half of her attention on the open archway and let another part of her mind drift into a void that could be the Arcadian mindspace or something deeper. Maybe it was the pure mindspace, running beneath everything. Her eyes watered as they focused on a single curved branch at one side of the shrine. In the void, she saw a faint glow. A pale blue energy that she could just barely feel. Thready and weak.

Then Elma's voice broke her concentration.

"Last year, we thought Amanda might connect our two mindspaces. As a sign of her progress."

The sharp details of the surrounding forest came into full focus as the void slipped away. Amanda blinked rapidly, realizing that the rest of the group had broken into side discussions, unaware of her psychic experiment.

"Our work with Amanda has been quite helpful," Dr. Webb told Elma.

"Has it?" Elma sounded skeptical. "If she can't connect our mindspaces, I suppose you're hoping she will be able to build a house and connect doors in your mindspace as well as ours?"

Her voice rose above the other conversations. Amanda stood very still, pretending not to hear, though the silence told her everyone else was now listening, too.

"This isn't the time," Lucas cut in smoothly, and Elma laughed him off.

"Oh, we're just having a friendly chat. I'm learning so much during this visit."

"Good," Lucas said, though his dark tone sounded like a warning.

"Maybe we should head back?" Rory suggested, stepping to Amanda's side. "You good to go?"

Amanda agreed but Rory hesitated, carefully studying her face, and narrowing her eyes at what she saw.

"I said I'm good," Amanda repeated, then turned to the others. "Let's go see what's in Edmund's vault."

As they walked back to the research center, Mitra fell in step with Amanda. They were quiet, listening to the birds and letting the others gradually get ahead of them.

"What did you feel?" Mitra asked softly.

"I'm not sure." Amanda kept her eyes forward and her voice low. She wasn't surprised that he had noticed.

"But it was something?"

Amanda didn't have to answer. Mitra nodded and they took a few more steps. Ahead, Lucas had pulled Elma to one side of the group. He was saying something that made her cross her arms over her chest.

"Why didn't you tell me about this place before?" Amanda had wanted to ask Mitra about the mystics' shrine since she'd first learned about it, but he only shrugged and said it hadn't seemed important.

"Not important?" Amanda couldn't understand his answer. "You wanted me to connect our mindspaces and you didn't think it was important that I know about the original door between our worlds?"

Mitra's lips parted as he looked at her with a genuine mix of surprise and confusion.

"The original door no longer exists. Tests at this site have shown no discernible energy signature. It was just an idea the mystics believed."

It was Amanda's turn to be confused.

"Then why did you ask if I felt something?"

They were nearing the research center. Mitra stopped walking and Amanda paused beside him. He gazed deep into her eyes with an intensity that left her feeling shaky and exposed.

"Because you see things that we don't."

Birds sang overhead, flitting from tree to tree, as a ray of sunlight fell across their path. Looking ahead, they saw the others had neared the research center and turned back, waiting on them.

"I don't know what Edmund left for me," Amanda admitted quickly. "In the vault."

Mitra's mouth twitched into a half smile and his eyes softened with their familiar light. In his face, she saw his unshakable confidence in whatever she chose to do. He extended one hand in invitation and said, "Let's find out."

§

They followed Halima and Argyri to a room at the back of the research center. Amanda was immediately struck by its similarity to the small den in the birdhouse, the room where Edmund placed all the doors he'd connected to Arcadia. There was a green velvet loveseat beside a pink upholstered armchair and a roll-top desk decorated with inlaid wood. There were fewer windows in this room than in the rest of the center, giving it a cozier feel.

The windows it did have were in roughly the same place as the doors in the mindspace den. The only exception was one space where a solid metal door presumably led to Edmund's vault.

Stepping closer, Amanda examined a cluster of golden symbols set into the metal. There were four triangles, some intersected by lines. The symbols were familiar, though it took a moment to recognize them as the same design stamped on the lower corner of the letters Edmund had left for Amanda with the completion of each trial.

Below the design, a large dial was marked with numbers like a typical combination lock. Below the dial, four openings held wheels like a slot machine, showing designs that matched each of the triangle symbols from the design above. Lower still, an inset shelf was empty but illuminated by a soft glow.

As requested, Cameron had brought the letters from Edmund as well as the returned Pyura relics. He gave them to Halima, who thanked him with a bow of her head.

"This day has been long awaited," she said to them all. "As guardians of the vault and friends of Edmund Robinson, our people are pleased to help your next psychic architect in her training. However, the contents of the vault are for her alone. We will help her unlock the door, as instructed by Edmund, then leave her to proceed alone."

There was a murmur, though no one spoke out. It was well known that psychic architect abilities—like those of psychic engineers—were shrouded in mystery.

"If you'll please move to the hall, we will activate a quiet zone so you can observe the opening of the vault." Complaints were voiced, but Halima was quick to shut them down. "The quiet zone is to protect the integrity of the vault. Edmund's instructions are clear that his successor is to be the only psychic traveler to know how to open it."

"The only psychic traveler," Dr. Webb repeated. "Since I am not a traveler, I presume I will be allowed to stay?"

Halima and Argyri debated the point briefly before leaving the decision to Amanda. She decided Dr. Webb and Mitra could stay, while the other Arcadian scientists moved to the hall with the travelers. The room was separated from the rest of the research center by a wide archway, allowing plenty of space for those in the hall to watch. Yet, Argyri rolled a low screen into place to shield the combination locks as they were opened.

"There are three locks on the vault," Halima explained, once the quiet zone had been activated. "We will start from the bottom. This small shelf holds the Pyura relics. They emit radiation that allows the next locks to move."

"Radiation?" Amanda held two relics at arm's length and glanced nervously at the two in Mitra's hands.

"It's perfectly safe," Dr. Webb assured. "Our tests show a slight energy that is harmless."

"As do our tests," Argyri confirmed, then gestured for Amanda and Mitra to place the relics on the shelf. "The order does not matter for this lock. Any four relics will generate enough energy."

The light on the shelf intensified as each relic was set in place. By the fourth, the light had turned from pale white to a pleasant blue. The same blue light now glowed from between the reels above the shelf as well. These reels were the second lock.

"As you can see, these reels show the same symbols as the vault door. Edmund refers to this design as the psychic architect insignia. The four triangles represent the four elements: water, air, fire, and earth. Edmund assigned a symbol to each of the worlds where your trials were held, and they are to be selected in order on the lock."

"In what order?" Amanda hadn't expected to solve puzzles to open the vault.

"All of the answers are here," Halima reassured. "The symbols for each world are highlighted on each letter. The order was given to you by the Pyura Elder, which is the only information we do not know."

She showed Amanda how the insignia on each of the letters showed one triangle darker than the others. It was a subtle difference she hadn't noticed.

"The message from the Pyura Elder listed their order as Terra-V, Arcadia, Opt-V, and Stellaria," Amanda recited, nervous despite knowing the answer.

Halima shuffled the letters, showing each highlighted symbol as Argyri turned the corresponding reels.

"Terra-V is air, the triangle that is pointing up with a line towards the top. Arcadia is water, the triangle points down. Opt-V is fire, the triangle that points up. And Stellaria is earth, the triangle that points down with a line toward the bottom."

Once the reels locked in place, the blue light glowed at the center of the combination dial. Amanda shuddered in anticipation and Mitra reached to give her hand a quick squeeze, saying, "One lock to go."

Dr. Webb stayed quiet, watching the process intently. Amanda sensed her resentment of the mystics' authority in this moment. Halima glanced her way, sensing it, too.

"The final lock is a combination requiring numbers associated with each world. Dr. Webb, perhaps you could help us with this one?"

"Of course." Dr. Webb quickly hid her surprise, though her hand needlessly smoothed one side of her hair as she waited for more information.

"The number of sentences in each letter is the number for that world, and they are entered in the same order as below. Dr. Webb, would you please count the sentences? Amanda, would you like to turn the dial? You will spin four times to the right before the first number, twice to the left before the second, once to the right before the third, and then turn left for the fourth."

Dr. Webb dutifully counted the sentences in each letter, relaying the numbers to Amanda. She then turned the dial with Argyri's guidance. When the last number had been entered, Halima said it was time to open the door.

Amanda paused before reaching for the wheel that would spin the locks open. She turned toward the hall, seeking Rory's nodded encouragement. It was strange to take this final step of her journey without Rory standing right by her side.

The wheel spun easily, and the door creaked open. Amanda turned to see a silent celebration in the hall and laughed in triumph. But when it was time to enter the vault, she hesitated.

While she was glad Elma had been kept outside, it felt wrong to go in without Rory, Cameron, and Lucas. She remembered what Halima had said about the contents of the vault being for her alone. She would be expected to keep the psychic architect mysteries secret, just as the psychic engineers guarded their knowledge of the pure mindspace and the way their energy was used to maintain the houses and doors. Except, they could share their knowledge with each other while she would be expected to keep everything inside that vault to herself.

"Amanda?" Mitra spoke softly, his tone conveying the concern she saw on the others' faces.

"I'm okay," she said with a deep breath and shaky laugh. "It's just a big moment."

The door to the vault was only partially open, allowing Amanda to enter while concealing its interior from view. She slipped inside and let her eyes adjust to the dim light.

The air was cool and dry. A table and chair sat at the center of the small room. A narrow table along the back wall was lined with objects. As Amanda neared, she saw a series of glass cases covering books and strange instruments.

At the center, a glass case covered a single sheet of paper. Wiping away a film of dust, she saw it was a letter from Edmund. With trembling fingers, Amanda opened the glass lid. She wasn't sure if it was safe to pick up such an old piece of paper without gloves, but she lifted it carefully by the edges.

To my rightful successor,

You have completed the architect's journey. No doubt you are impressed with my ingenuity in designing such a trial, just as I am impressed by your aptitude in its completion.

I cannot know how much time has passed since my departure from the mortal coil, yet I can anticipate your many questions about the skills you will develop in your role as a psychic architect.

I have compiled detailed instructions in the books within this vault. You will also find instruments used to bring forth and strengthen your skills. These are lessons I had hoped to teach you myself. I must now be content in my belief that my written instructions and diagrams will be enough.

There was a time when many psychic architects lived together. I cherish the hope that an increase in our numbers will occur, allowing you to share in our great responsibilities. Until that time, I must impress upon you the importance of keeping our mysteries sacred and secret. These instructional materials are for you alone.

Among the books I have written, you will find mention of psychic engineers. They will work with you to maintain the psychic houses and doorways you create. Yet they are not psychic architects. You are above them, just as you are above all psychic travelers. Remember that as your skills increase and you take your rightful place on our High Council.

Yours with esteem,
Edmund Robinson

§

"It's not enough."

Elma sat at the High Council's conference table, flanked by two Vertex members. Nearly a week had passed since Amanda opened Edmund's vault, but the Vertex was not ready to officially stand down.

"You wanted to see Amanda make progress," Lenora reminded. "You watched her open Edmund's vault. That's progress."

"She opened a vault. I don't know what was inside or if it will help her make the doors we've been promised."

Lucas grit his teeth, upset that Lenora had taken over his negotiations. As head of the High Council, Lenora was also upset that Lucas hadn't been able to close the deal.

"Amanda's training has moved into deeper mysteries. We must trust that she will continue to show progress with the training materials she has inherited."

"That's not enough," Elma repeated. "We know Amanda has shown promise, but now you are conveniently using tradition to string us along with no end date in sight."

"What do you propose?" Lenora asked coldly. Lucas shook his head, already rejecting Elma's input.

"I have two propositions," Elma answered. "Amanda has created a proximal door before. It was an accident, but the ability is there. We want her to create a new door by the Fourth of July. You can choose the location."

"July?" Amanda felt her stomach drop as discussions broke out around the table. "That's just over a month!"

"You've done it before," Elma pointed out again. "This time you have the precious instructions you worked so hard to unlock. You don't have to create a new house, just add a door to an existing one."

Just add a door! Amanda had begun to look through Edmund's books, but his dense writing style and lengthy tangents were not easy to understand. He often included anecdotes about his travels, burying any useful instructions within stories of the people he had met and the adventures he had survived. She hadn't found any explanations for the instruments and nothing about them was intuitive.

"What is the second proposition?" Cameron asked, while Amanda sat in stunned fear.

"Amanda's focus could be divided between creating doors in our mindspace and a house in the Arcadian mindspace. Connecting our mindspaces would remove the conflict."

"I can't even get into the Arcadian mindspace yet!" Amanda sputtered.

"Yet," Elma repeated pointedly. "But Dr. Webb would like you to work on that, and I now see how influential she can be. Especially if you regularly work in Arcadia."

"But I'm not working on that…" Amanda stopped as Lucas held up a hand.

"Connecting the mindspaces is off the table."

"It was an option before," Elma reminded. "What's changed?"

Everyone looked at Amanda for an answer.

One of Edmund's books was devoted to the Arcadian mindspace. It outlined his theories of how the original door had been destroyed, why their travel abilities were lost, and why some mystics seemed to access a separate mindspace. It was more complicated than Amanda could grasp, relying heavily on concepts she was not allowed to share. Such as the existence of the pure mindspace.

"I don't have all the answers yet, but from what I've read so far, I do know that the thing I was going to try before would have failed. It just doesn't work that way."

"So, you are spending your time on the Arcadian's problems." Elma smirked knowingly.

"What? No. It just came up as part of the training… There's a lot of information to sort out."

Elma raised an eyebrow and dropped her smirk.

"We have plans for a reveal you won't be able to explain away." She held Lenora's gaze as she spoke. "If Amanda creates a new door or connects the mindspaces by the Fourth of July, I call it off. Otherwise, we'll give up on your promises and change our situation ourselves."

CHAPTER 21
A NEW ERA

Iveryn's breath bellowed as he tramped from an easy lope to a slow trot. His downy body was matted with sweat from their run through the desert and his red plumed crest drooped as they neared the waiting troughs at the edge of the stone forest. When they came to a stop, Amanda slid to the ground and uncapped her canteen. She watched a ripple shiver through Iveryn's peacock-like tail as they both enjoyed a long drink of water.

Horses on Terra-V loosely resembled horses on Earth. Though they had four long legs and horse-like heads, their elongated bodies were more reminiscent of a big cat, like a cheetah or leopard. They were also covered in short feathers that lay flat like scales, as well as plumes and tail feathers that lifted and unfurled when they were angry or afraid. Iveryn's feathers ranged from pale rose to deep red with tinges of gold that glinted in the sun. His tail feathers relaxed as he drank, hanging just above the dusty ground.

"You could use a bath," Amanda told him affectionately, seeing the sand that clung to his feathers.

Iveryn turned at the sound of her voice and lightly nuzzled her shoulder.

"I know what you want." Amanda offered a chunk of pineapple from her bag and Iveryn whinnied in pleasure. "One more, then drink some water. It's hot out here."

"He missed you."

Amanda turned to see her friend Caeph emerge from the stone forest.

"You could scare a person, sneaking up like that!" Amanda laughed, moving in for a hug. Caeph held onto her hands as they stepped apart, sending a tremor of vhe tingling up her arms.

"We are safe here," Caeph reassured.

A team of knights had come to the desert with Amanda and Iveryn. They patrolled the area, knowing their horses would warn them if danger was near.

"I could use a safe space," Amanda muttered as she absently patted Iveryn's soft flank.

"Alira told me you were having some trouble at home." Caeph moved to a bench in the shade of a stone spire. Iveryn settled on the ground beside her, ready for a nap.

"I'll figure it out." Amanda joined her on the bench, trying not to mind that Iveryn had chosen a spot closer to Caeph. Horses loved the Vherahna, but Amanda knew Iveryn loved her, too. Especially when she had a full bag of pineapple.

On the far side of the stone forest, the knights had made great progress in transforming the former Churukh royals' hidden fortress into a traveler outpost, and it was slowly becoming something of a cultural center. Several Vherahna adepts, like Caeph, had taken up residence. They tended the tuntum tree the royals had kept hidden and isolated in the fortress courtyard, as well as the tuntum saplings they had planted after the royals were overthrown.

Transplanting tuntum trees was a delicate and largely unknown process. Some Churukh farmers had also come to the outpost, curious about the young trees, and offered their expertise in helping them grow.

The former fortress was also the site of the one proximal door Amanda had created.

"Is it strange for you to have powers the Churukh will never have?"

Caeph tilted her head as she considered Amanda's question. After a weighty pause, she said, "I don't think of it as my people having *power* or their people not having power. We simply have different roles in our world."

"Sure," Amanda frowned, second-guessing her choice of words. "I don't mean you're more powerful than the Churukh. Just that you can create vhe, which they need to live… So… Well, maybe that does make you more powerful…"

Caeph patiently waited for Amanda to finish her thought, her purple eyes steady beneath her double-blink. *Blink-blink. Tuntum.* The same rhythm. Amanda thought about how closely connected the Vherahna were to the tuntum trees and to all life in their world. Yet they never tried to take over the way the Churukh royals had. They simply wanted to live in harmony.

"Some of the people on my world have psychic travel abilities. Like me and the knights," Amanda began again. "But the vast majority of people don't. Most of them don't know anything about psychic travel or that we can visit different worlds."

"Does that bother you?" Caeph asked, reminding Amanda of the PTS therapist she had seen for a few weeks after she had been drugged and kidnapped by the former High Council.

"No, it… Well…" Amanda had been thinking about that a lot lately. "See, there's a group of travelers who want everyone to know about us. Because they want everyone to know they have more power. They think that people with our abilities—travelers—are more evolved. Special."

"Is that the only reason they want people to know?"

Amanda didn't expect Caeph's question.

"I don't know. Some of them say they just don't want to hide who they are, and they don't want to worry about being found out."

"It's hard to hide your true self."

"Yeah, I get that part," Amanda agreed. "But people who don't have our abilities are going to be really upset when they find out about us."

"How so?" Caeph reached to stroke Iveryn's head as his feathered crest brushed against her legs.

"Well, they'll be afraid," Amanda said. "Afraid of what we can do and by the idea of our visiting other worlds. Most of them think our world is the only world there is. Some of them have already heard rumors about us and think that we're aliens. Not human, like them."

"Travelers are afraid, too, then," Caeph observed. "Afraid that they won't be accepted."

Tears stung Amanda's eyes. It wasn't a new idea but hearing it said out loud struck a nerve.

"Perhaps there is a reason some travelers want to find a sense of power," Caeph went on. "They want to protect themselves from rejection."

Amanda nodded, unable to speak.

"Your people are much like the Churukh. You want to fit in and be the same as everyone else, but you also want to be special and stand out from everyone else. That is a difficult balance to maintain."

Amanda bit her lip, feeling that truth.

"It could get really bad for us," she said thoughtfully, "because people can't find that balance. And you know what's crazy? I'm the only one with a chance to stop that from happening, but I can't because I don't know how to do the things that are supposed to make me special."

Iveryn dozed beside them, snuffling in her sleep.

"Maybe it isn't about being special," Caeph suggested. "Maybe you need to find balance, too."

§

"This is what I'm thinking…" Amanda sat across from Trina and Drew at a covered picnic table. She had spent the last hour catching Trina up on what it meant to be a psychic architect and sharing the highlights of her training so far. Drew had jumped in with brief explanations, referencing notes he had been compiling in a binder for over a year and a half.

Once Trina understood the situation, Amanda laid out her plan for handling the Vertex's Fourth of July deadline. They all sat back, considering the possibilities.

"Well?" Amanda asked when no one spoke. "What do you think?"

"I'm not sure you should have told me all that," Trina said uneasily.

"That's kind of the point."

"I'm glad you did," Trina quickly reassured. "It's good to know. To be included."

"That's kind of the point," Drew echoed Amanda with a wry smile that warmed her heart.

"But what do you think of the plan?" Amanda pushed, including them both in the question. "Do you think it's a good idea?"

"It's hard to say," Drew hedged. "I mean, you never know how other people will react. But it makes a lot of sense to me."

Some kids raced by, screaming happily on their way to the nearby play area. Amanda tried to remember when her biggest worry was being the last one on the swings.

"Can you do it?" Trina asked cautiously. "Will these engineer people have your back?"

For weeks, Amanda had been working closely with the engineers. Initially, Elaine had been reluctant to hear anything about Edmund's training materials, but Gerald and Elaine had insisted that the Vertex's deadline overrode the usual mystery around psychic architect skills.

Together, they had considered both of their options, connecting the mindspaces or creating a new door. They had also considered the political fallout from either route. Despite their personal opinions, they agreed the choice ultimately fell to Amanda.

"They'll support my decision," Amanda said, wishing she felt as confident as she sounded.

§

On June 27th, the High Council convened a special meeting to resolve their conflict with the Vertex. They were more than halfway through 2019, nearing the end of a decade. In the general public, there was already a sense of change in the air. The feeling that 2020 would begin a new era. Amanda was well aware of that feeling as she sat at the High Council's large conference table.

For this meeting, she had a place at the center of the table with Gerald and Rory on her right side and Dorothy and Elaine on her left. The seven members of the High Council, including Cameron, sat across from them. Lucas was positioned at one end of the table, while Elma sat at the other. Additional members of Vertex's leadership sat in chairs along the wall behind Elma, while Lucas' assistant sat against the wall behind him. A stenographer took notes from his small desk in a back corner of the room.

As council chair, Lenora Nagy would officially lead the discussion, yet the meeting had been Amanda's idea. After gaining the engineers' support, she had approached the council with her idea and convinced them to approve her plan as well. Elma and the other members of the Vertex were the only ones in the room who did not know what was coming.

"Good afternoon," Lenora began solemnly. "We are here to discuss the terms of a binding treaty with the Vertex over the proposed disclosure of the existence of psychic travel and our organized society to the world at large. On this matter, Elma Anthony will represent the Vertex with the consultation of her leadership team."

Elma then introduced the four people she had brought with her, though Amanda was too nervous about her upcoming speech to hear a word she said.

Amanda had made this pitch several times now, starting with Drew and Trina, then the psychic engineers. She had moved on to Rory, Cameron, and Lucas, before getting the plan approved by the High Council. It had begun to feel like a settled matter, but she knew it still hinged on Elma agreeing on behalf of the Vertex.

"You'll be great!" A message from Judy filtered through Amanda's mind and she smiled at her printed speech.

Judy and Patty had been the last to learn of Amanda's plan. Judy had flown in and was waiting with Patty back at the apartment. They had been a test audience for Amanda's speech—which had been edited and polished by Rory, Gerald, Cameron, and Lucas. Both Judy and Patty had praised her mature approach to the conflict.

"Amanda Jones will now present her proposal."

Snapping to attention, Amanda saw Elma's disgruntled expression and realized Lenora had said enough to suggest that neither of the Vertex's ultimatums was going to be accepted.

Amanda thanked Lenora and cleared her throat before addressing Elma directly.

"As I've navigated the architect's journey and moved deeper into my psychic architect training, I've learned a lot about myself, our society, and relationships in general. I've also come to appreciate the concerns the Vertex have raised in a new way."

Glancing up from her speech, Amanda saw curiosity on Elma's face, despite her team's deep frowns. She took a quick sip of water and continued reading.

"Our previously proposed deal for you to hold off on exposing our secret society to the world at large hinges on my ability to create a network of new proximal doors around our world. This is a large undertaking. You have asked that I prove my skills with the creation of one new door or by connecting the Arcadian mindspace to our own. I have another suggestion."

Grumbling from the Vertex leaders was quickly silenced by a word from Lenora, but Amanda felt tension mounting from their side of the room. Elma was harder to read.

"Before I get to my suggestion," Amanda said shakily. "I would like to say something about the current state of the Psychic Traveler Society. I have been aware of our secret organization for less than two years. Yet, in that time, I have already seen great unrest, including a rebellion that has reshaped our leadership."

"Amanda," Elma interrupted gently but firmly. "We are aware of the state of this society."

"Let her speak," Lucas said, his voice steady and eyes flashing. He then shot Amanda a look that suggested she pick up the pace.

Amanda searched for her place in her notes.

"Uh, yes, you are," she stammered as her leg shook beneath the table.

"*You're doing fine,*" Gerald silently encouraged.

"*Don't let them bully you,*" Dorothy urged, before Elaine added, "*We're with you.*"

The room was quiet as Amanda gathered her courage.

"Right," she said resolutely before setting aside her speech and looking Elma in the eye. "You want the world to know about psychic travel, so you won't have to live in secret and hide who you really are. I want that, too.

"The thing is, this whole deal has come down to me proving my skills. But I don't think this should be about me. It should be about the mysteries psychic engineers and architects keep from the rest of our society."

Members of the Vertex murmured to each other freely. Hushed discussions broke out among the council as well, and Lenora gave it a moment before calling the room back to silence. The whole time, Amanda kept her eyes on Elma and watched a smile begin to form.

"What is it that you're proposing?"

Amanda took a deep breath.

"I think we should get rid of the secrecy inside PTS before telling the rest of the world we exist. Look, everyone who is identified as a psychic traveler goes through basic training to understand their abilities and learn how to live with them. But special abilities, like for psychic engineers and psychic architects, are hidden behind this tradition of mystery. I think that's a mistake."

The chatter resumed, but Amanda didn't wait for Lenora to intervene.

"Hear me out! You're focused on normals learning about us, and I agree we should work toward that. But you're missing something important. There aren't a lot of engineers anymore and architects are down to only me. I think we may be missing travelers with potential."

"You think there could be undiscovered engineers and architects among us?" Elma asked in genuine surprise.

"Maybe," Amanda answered honestly. "We wait until travelers show potential before they're tested, or even told about those abilities. But what if they experience strange things and just don't know to tell anyone?"

As a ripple of conversation again passed through the room, Amanda shook her head in frustration. It seemed so obvious to her, but only because she had information that had been kept from others.

"You're proposing some kind of screening for enhanced abilities?" Elma asked.

"No," Amanda said firmly, knowing that was what the council had suggested. She had pushed for more. "I want the engineers and I to reveal our so-called mysteries to all travelers. We can make some secrets part of the general classes all travelers take, and share others in special classes for experienced travelers who want to learn more.

"I'll also share Edmund's architect training materials with the engineers and figure out how we can make that information more widely available, too."

"You all agree with this?" Elma turned to the psychic engineers doubtfully.

They each agreed in turn, before sharing more about their own thoughts.

"I would like to identify travelers with potential psychic engineer or architect abilities more easily," Gerald agreed. "Teaching deeper concepts of psychic travel in general classes will offer travelers information to self-test their own abilities and come forward if they discover they have additional skills."

"Though it may be frustrating," Dorothy conceded, "for those travelers who can only learn about certain concepts in theory, without being able to experience them for themselves."

"Which is why I was initially against this plan," Elaine added honestly. "I believe there are some good reasons our mysteries have been kept secret. However, Amanda has convinced me that times are changing, and transparency may be more valuable than tradition."

Quiet fell as Elaine's last words hung over the group.

"Amanda has put a lot of thought into this proposal," Lenora said with clear admiration. "She has convinced this council that a decision to move forward with the Disclosure Protocol, our plan for revealing our existence to the world, should not rest with our members alone.

"We are prepared to discuss a timeline for our public disclosure with your organization, including input from travelers in our general community."

Stunned delight began to show on the faces of Elma's team. They looked at each other in disbelief, while Elma released a slow, shaky breath.

"However," Lenora continued while she still had their full attention, "improving our internal relationships should come first. To that end, would Amanda's proposal of sharing these advanced mysteries be enough assurance of change that your organization will not reveal our existence before we collectively decide the time is right?"

"Instead of meeting our deadline to create a door or connect the mindspaces?" Elma asked, trying to conceal her happiness with an air of professionalism. "I'll need to discuss it with my team."

"Of course." Lenora called a recess, where the Vertex members would be shown to a private meeting room and refreshments would be available in an adjacent area.

Yet, as they all stood up from the table, it was clear Amanda had already won their support.

§

On July 6th, Amanda woke with a smile on her face. After two days of additional meetings, the Vertex had officially agreed to call off their efforts to reveal psychic travel to the world. Vertex leaders would work with the High Council to finalize the Disclosure Protocol. There would also be a joint effort to spin past Vertex stunts as part of an elaborate hoax by internet pranksters, and the Vertex leadership would deal harshly with any rogue members caught revealing their abilities.

The deal had been finalized and announced to the PTS community on June 30th, but Amanda had still felt uneasy in the days leading to the Fourth of July. Even as she watched fireworks with Trina and Drew, Amanda had been on high alert for signs of the Vertex. The next day, she had scoured the news for any mention of a Vertex stunt, but all was quiet, and her fear began to fade away.

Padding out of her room, she found Judy sipping coffee at the dining table. The sun shone through the sliding glass doors, picking up the blue streaks in her aunt's hair. It was good to have her home.

"Looks like we're in the clear," Judy greeted, looking up from her phone. "Not that I didn't trust your deal."

"It wasn't *my* deal," Amanda corrected. Sharing the mysteries might have been her idea, but she needed the psychic engineers and the High Council to pull it off.

Judy gave her a knowing smile but didn't respond. Amanda grabbed a bagel from the counter and sat cross-legged in the chair across from her.

"Do you really have to leave today?"

"I've been here two weeks," Judy said with a sigh. "I can't stay forever."

"Twelve days," Amanda corrected. "You're going back to Phoenix?"

"For now. I can hop to San Francisco and pick up a flight from there. You know, the Vertex aren't the only ones looking forward to some new doors. No pressure!"

They laughed, though Amanda still felt some pressure to finish her psychic architect training. Even if the deal with the Vertex had bought her time.

"It could be years before I can create a new house with doors all around our world."

"I know," Judy said, patting Amanda's arm. "But there's a chance you won't have to do it alone."

It was possible that another psychic architect might appear once more travelers knew how to identify potential skills, like an ability to access the pure mindspace. Before,

Amanda had been threatened by the idea of another psychic architect stepping forward. Now, she was starting to like the idea of sharing her responsibilities.

"Your origin point will still be set here," Amanda muttered, liking the idea of Judy being linked to their home a while longer.

"Until I get to Phoenix and have to travel from there," Judy reminded gently before changing the subject. "What are your plans for today?"

"Stellaria," Amanda answered, checking the clock. "There's a flower festival. Rory's going to bring Mae."

"Avu yai," Judy said, holding up her coffee in a toast to their best lives.

"Avu yai," Amanda echoed, raising a piece of bagel. She was looking forward to spending more time in Stellaria, and finally meeting Rory's girlfriend, but Judy's departure hung over the day like a dark cloud.

"Hey, none of that," Judy said, seeing Amanda's sadness. "I know! Ditch that bagel. We'll wake up your mom and go out for pancakes."

"Just us?" Amanda asked, brightening slightly. "No Cameron?"

"Just us," Judy assured, then gave Amanda a searching look. "Does it bother you? Your mom and Cameron?"

"No, I'm happy for them. And I'm getting used to the idea of Cameron as a stepdad or whatever he is. It's just… Sometimes it's nice to be just me and my mom. Or me, my mom, and you. You know?"

"I do," Judy agreed. "Your mom knows that, too."

Amanda stood to wake Patty, but Judy held her back.

"As you get older, you'll see that relationships always change and grow. Because people change and grow. You aren't the same girl you were two years ago. You might even miss things about the life you had before all this psychic traveler stuff. Just like you'll look back in two years and miss some things about your life right now.

"All we can do is appreciate the good we have while we have it, and then take parts of that with us into our new adventures."

Memories of the past two years washed through Amanda's heart and mind. How simple her friendships with Drew and Trina had been, her first steps into Terra-V, Judy's early lessons in psychic travel, and discovering the beauty of so many new worlds.

Amanda's future stretched before her, sparkling and uncertain. She didn't know how long this truce with the Vertex would last or how many years she could deepen her skills before the world found out about psychic travel. For now, it was enough to build on the relationships she had made and live her future day by day.

Chapter 22

Five Months Later

For breakfast, Amanda had a bowl of cranberry sauce and a piece of pumpkin pie. Patty eyed her plate with a raised eyebrow but kept quiet, glad the Thanksgiving leftovers weren't going to waste.

"In another year, she'll be an adult and eating what she wants anyway," Cameron laughed.

Ever since Amanda turned seventeen, they had been making jokes about how soon she would be an adult. It was just like her fifteenth birthday when all the adults' jokes revolved around there only being a year left before she would be driving. Which had seemed particularly strange to Amanda, since the discovery of her psychic traveler abilities had pushed driving way down her list of priorities.

Remembering that time, Amanda marveled at how far she had come. Two years ago, she had spent Thanksgiving weekend on her first off-world mission, stumbling through Terra-V and hiding psychic travel from her mom. Now, she could move confidently through proximal doors without a hint of psychic travel sickness. She had traveled to six worlds beyond her own, made close friends in Terra-V and Arcadia, and was forming new friendships in Stellaria. Not to mention the bonds she had made with Rory, Cameron, Lucas, and the psychic engineers.

Watching Cameron now, as he teased Patty over coffee and oatmeal, Amanda recalled her first glimpse of him in the house. He had been dressed as a knight, entering the attic from a trip to Terra-V. He had looked in her direction and her fear of being discovered had knocked her right out of the mindspace. She had felt something beyond fear though. Looking back, it had been a sense of destiny, of knowing she had met someone who was meant to be in her life.

The jokes about her soon becoming an adult were unsettling, but Amanda was more focused on the present. She still had to finish high school, and she wasn't sure if she had made the right choice by going back to her local school this fall. It was nice to be in class with her friends but finishing her sophomore year in virtual classes had given her a lot more freedom.

"Are you nervous about this afternoon?"

Amanda brought her attention to Patty's worried face and shook her head before cutting her fork into a second slice of pie.

"Thinking about school actually."

She watched as Patty and Cameron exchanged a meaningful look. They did that often, sharing silent support. It was nice to see, especially when Amanda remembered what a jerk her mom's last boyfriend had been.

"You can go back to the virtual school after winter break," Patty reminded. "If you decide it's easier."

Amanda nodded without commitment. She would miss seeing Drew and Trina every day, but it was strange to be back at her old school. Talk of time-traveling aliens had largely stopped—now that some of those so-called aliens had come forward to admit it was a hoax—but the students still whispered about the cafeteria taser incident.

The idea of switching back to the virtual school in January was tempting. A fresh start for a new decade, and more flexibility for whatever might come in 2020.

§

Later that afternoon, Amanda hovered in the void of the pure mindspace with Gerald, Dorothy, and Elaine. Her body was in the Capitol building, guarded by Rory and Lucas, in the room that was ready for her proximal door.

In the six months since she had opened Edmund's vault, Amanda's psychic architect abilities had grown. It would be a long time before she could build an entire mindspace house of her own, but she had created a few small objects. She had also removed a bookcase from the birdhouse living room, making space for another door. The High Council had decided that a connection to the U.S. Capitol was the most logical choice, and Amanda had agreed to try, despite her early protests about that location.

"Are you ready?" Dorothy asked, squeezing her right hand gently.

"Are you sure about this?" Elaine added with a more urgent squeeze of her left hand.

They were in a circle, holding hands to share their energy. Gerald stood across from Amanda. His hands were held by Dorothy and Elaine, but his eyes met Amanda's searching gaze.

"She's sure," he answered for her with confidence, and Amanda nodded quickly.

They had created this plan together. Sharing Edmund's research had let the engineers be a larger part of her architect training, though none of them—or any other traveler—had yet shown any architect aptitude of their own.

Gerald winked at Amanda, and she closed her eyes, feeling for any threads of energy around her. While her physical body was in the Capitol, and part of her consciousness was in the mindspace living room, she felt untethered from both. It was like floating in a large body of water on a cloudy night. The energy around her felt like currents in the water.

I am the sea, she thought, recalling the seer in Terra-V. *I am a cricket.* Mhevek's lesson slipped in, bringing doubts about what she was about to do, but Amanda firmly pushed them away. *Feel the energy,* she repeated to herself as her breath settled into a slow, steady rhythm.

The door she had accidentally created from Terra-V had formed in a chaotic swirl of emotion. It was born of panic and her inexperienced attempt to send a psychic call for help. She had now learned from Edmund's books that creating a door was meant to be a slow, calm process. Gently tapping into a thread of energy from her place in the pure mindspace and guiding it to connect with a wall in a mindspace house.

Edmund's description of the process answered the question of how a door could be made to a new world, a place where no architect had visited before. It followed logical steps, despite being rooted in sensations that couldn't entirely be explained. In contrast, her door had been a fluke. Though she *had* created it, showing there was more than one path to success.

Amanda pushed those thoughts away, too, realizing that she was thinking about the process instead of opening her senses to whatever she might feel.

With her eyes still closed, Amanda focused on the energy pulsing from the psychic engineers' hands into her own. She imagined it as a gold circle in the dark around her. To the left, she sensed a line of orange-pink energy trailing into the distance. There was a pulse in the energy, a rhythm, telling her it was a line to the location of her physical body. She could pick up that thread and weave it into the energy of the mindspace house.

That was what she was expected to do.

According to Edmund's books, it was the simplest way of creating a proximal zone. Linking her body's location to the mindspace. But Amanda let the orange-pink line glow in the distance as she cast a wider net.

I am the sea, she silently chanted. In the darkness, a pale-yellow line flickered into existence. A lavender line followed, then more colors of energy radiating in every direction. Amanda's breath sped as she saw herself at the center of a multi-hued starburst.

She wanted to touch each strand, but her hands were held fast by Dorothy and Elaine. She nearly pulled free before remembering that her physical hands were with her body back in the Capitol. The hands she clasped were only a mental image, a representation that appeared when a traveler interacted with the mindspace. She could leave her imaginary hands in place, feeling the engineers' grounding support, while touching her attention from one strand of energy to another.

A few lines of energy were familiar, each connected to worlds she had visited. Others were unfamiliar but had a strength that told her they were established connections. The orange-pink line was weak in comparison, lightly flickering in and out of existence.

Another faint line pulled her attention. It was pale blue with a hint of green. An almost turquoise color that reminded Amanda of the phosphorescent light that shone from Cordrowr's lagoon, though the energy didn't feel like a connection to Opt-V. The energy felt more comfortable. Safe and welcoming.

Amanda found her mind reaching for the blue line, exploring it from all angles until a sense of certainty washed over her. As she focused on the blue light, the other lines of energy began to fade from her awareness. Soon, all had disappeared except for the pink-orange line to the Capitol and the golden ring of light from the engineers.

For a moment, Amanda shifted toward the pink-orange line, but it didn't call to her with the insistence of the blue energy. She pictured the bare spot on the living room wall, the place she had chosen for her new door. She imagined pulling the blue line toward it, plugging it in like a cord to a socket. The space around the wall resisted the connection.

Amanda felt a quiver run through her being—or whatever she was in this bodiless state—and she heard the squeal of a high-pitch whine.

The golden ring glowed brighter as she visualized the blue energy suffusing the empty wall. *A door,* she thought madly, trying to picture the dark wood of the living room doors without losing focus of the flickering blue light. *Almost there.* She could see the outline of a door taking shape on the wall. A blue glow growing brighter as the whine whistled louder.

And then a slash of pain as everything went dark.

"*Amanda!*"

Someone was leaning close, repeating her name, and slapping her cheek lightly.

"Stop that," Amanda mumbled, pushing the hand away.

"She's okay!"

Rory's face came into focus as Amanda blinked blearily. "Did it work?"

Amanda sat up, ran her hands over her face, and took a read of the room. Rory's face showed relief. Lucas smirked as he shook his head. Cameron stood across the room, arguing with General Falkner in harsh but hushed words.

"Depends on what you were trying to do," Lucas answered cynically, then rolled his eyes and went to lend Cameron his support.

A fizz of excitement sharpened Amanda's focus. She mentally felt around the room, suppressing a grin when she couldn't detect a proximal zone. Rory beckoned toward the back of the room and two paramedics swooped in to check Amanda's vitals and ask a series of questions. Rory hovered behind and thanked them when they packed up their equipment.

"But I did make a door?" Amanda asked hopefully, seeing the answer in Rory's eyes.

"Strangest thing," Rory said, stepping closer as the paramedics moved away. "As soon as you passed out, Lucas hopped into the mindspace and tested your new door. It led to an empty construction site by that new development, the one not far from your apartment. And you'll never guess who happened to be there."

Amanda didn't have to ask. She imagined Lucas' face when he stepped through the door to find Drew and Trina innocently sipping on lattes as they took a walk away from the main shopping area.

"How mad is he?" Amanda asked instead.

"He says he'll have to buy that lot," Rory answered, trying to sound stern.

Amanda began to smile, then saw Rory's serious expression, and asked, "How mad are you?"

Rory studied her carefully. So carefully that a cold sweat broke out across Amanda's collarbones. She began searching for the right words to explain until Rory's mouth shifted into a half smile.

"Mistakes are bound to happen, right? I mean, it must be hard to feel out a location based on energy. We're lucky you didn't lock in on your mom instead of your best friends, who happened to be standing in an empty lot."

"Right," Amanda answered with a sigh of relief, then looked over to where Cameron and Lucas were likely trying a similar argument. As she watched, General Falkner threw up one arm and stormed out of the room. Lucas said something to the general's aide, who nodded briskly before leaving as well.

Cameron was still tense from the argument as he walked over to Amanda, but his jaw relaxed as he saw that she was awake and alert.

"You're all right?" He crouched in front of her and peered into her eyes.

"Are you mad?" Amanda asked, still unsure of where she stood after the decision she had made.

"I'm glad you're all right." Cameron sidestepped the question and exchanged a questioning look with Rory. She nodded and crossed the room to talk with Lucas, giving them time to talk alone.

"You're probably ready to get out of here," Cameron began. "I know I am."

"Yeah," Amanda agreed uncertainly. She did want to leave, but even more, she wanted to know that Cameron wasn't angry with her. He sensed her worry and offered a tired, but kind smile.

"I'm not mad. You know, there's a saying some people like to quote: *It's better to ask forgiveness than permission.* Have you heard that one? Well, I understand why that can seem like the best approach sometimes, especially when you're young and still learning how to stand up for yourself. But it's not my preferred way of doing things. I would rather be upfront with people. Particularly with the people who are on my side."

Hanging her head, Amanda heard disappointment in his voice. She could have told him what she had planned to do, but it had seemed better to let him think the location was a mistake instead of a choice. *Plausible deniability,* Gerald had called it.

"But I'm not mad at you," Cameron repeated firmly. "I'm proud of you."

Amanda looked up, tears shining as she saw the truth in Cameron's face.

"You have accomplished so much in such a short time," he went on. "And I'm looking forward to seeing what you'll do as you continue to learn and grow."

They clasped hands and lightly touched foreheads.

"Besides," Cameron added, leaning back with an impish smile. "How could I possibly be mad about having a door so close to home?"

Amanda laughed and let him help her to her feet. She gazed around the room as Rory and Lucas turned to join them. *I did it,* she thought, and her sense of accomplishment was about more than creating a new door.

Teetering on the edge of adulthood, Amanda knew her life would be a mix of mistakes and successes, but she felt ready for whatever the future might bring.

DISCUSSION QUESTIONS
Spoilers ahead

1.   In *Elders and Aliens,* members of the Vertex want to reveal their psychic travel abilities to the world. If psychic travel was real, would you want the world to know? Would your answer depend on whether or not you personally had psychic travel abilities?

2.   While Amanda has feelings for Drew, and a possible attraction to Mitra, dating is not high on her list of priorities. How do you feel about Amanda putting her personal growth and current interests (off-world travel, architect training, etc.) ahead of romance?

3.   Early in the book, Aunt Judy moves out of state, yet she stays involved in Amanda's life as much as she can, often with the help of psychic travel. Have you had a close relative or friend move far away? If you were psychic travelers and could meet them anywhere in the world (or off-world) where would you choose?

4.   In *Healers and Thieves*, Lucas Flynn is introduced as an enemy of the Psychic Traveler Society. By the end of *Family and Foes*, he has become Director of PTS. What do think of him after reading *Elders and Aliens*? Can Amanda fully trust him?

5.   Stellaria is described as a peaceful, perfect world. Why does PTS protect Stellaria with secure gatehouses? Could the world's lack of modern conveniences like phones or electricity be related to that protection?

6.   The tribal leaders in Opt-V foster respect by putting their young through trials that teach them about the other tribes. Do you like learning about other cultures in our world? If you had to complete one of Amanda's trials in Opt-V, which would you choose?

7.   In Arcadia, the scientists and mystics have an uneasy relationship. How do you think their shared experience of helping Amanda complete the architect's journey might affect their future relationship?

8.   The interpreter in Crystal Caverns looks down on the Ooliani's limited vocabulary, without knowing they are telepathic and think English is a limited language. Do you speak more than one language? What do you think about people who speak multiple languages?

9.   At the end of the book, Cameron tells Amanda he doesn't like the old adage, *it's better to ask forgiveness than permission*. Have you heard that saying? Do you think it's good or bad advice? How so?

Acknowledgments

When I began writing *The Psychic Travel Society* series, I hoped to release a new book each year. Despite a four-month delay on the second book due to the pandemic, I was able to release *Healers and Thieves* in 2019 and *Family and Foes* in 2020. Yet, I'm releasing *Elders and Aliens*, the third and final book in the trilogy, three years later.

Like many people, I found myself more affected by the pandemic than I first realized. Both physical and mental health issues made it challenging to give this novel the attention it deserved. After more than a year of managing complications from Covid-19, I then needed surgery for endometriosis. It's been difficult, to say the least.

I would not have gotten through the past few years without the support of my family and friends, particularly my amazing husband, Peter Quilty.

As an indie author, I was also running into business challenges due to choices I had made when publishing my first few novels. I decided to shift my focus to publishing, learning from my early mistakes and correcting them by releasing second editions of my novels.

With all of that going on, I was still working on *Elders and Aliens*, but the writing was slow. I was having trouble pulling such a large story together and wasn't sure if I wanted the series end after three books or four.

This book finally came together in the last year. With my health improved, it was easier to spend long stretches researching and creating worlds for Amanda's travels.

Many people helped with this book, either with direct feedback and suggestions, or by keeping my spirits up on the hardest days. Special thanks to Jen Pool, Michael Cherry, Brian Dunne, Angel Fischer, Wendy McMullan, and Gretchen Schutte. Michael, Lucas would never have suggested those Munter hitches without you!

Thank you to the owners of Comic Logic Books & Artwork who support local authors and artists. And thanks to those who connect with me on social media. Writing is often solo work, and taking a break for some shared memes and quick chats can be a great boost in a quiet day.

Amanda Jones has become a daughter to me. Thank you for sharing in her adventures!

About the Author

Susan Quilty loves creating fictional worlds and has particularly enjoyed helping Amanda explore *The Psychic Traveler Society*. The series began with *Healers and Thieves* in 2019 and continued with *Family and Foes* in 2020.

Previous novels include *The Insistence of Memory* (2017) and *To the Left of Death* (2018). In 2020, Susan also wrote a genre-bending choose-your-story gamebook called *Audrey and Esther Geekify Greenville*.

You can learn more about Susan and her upcoming projects by following her on social media or visiting her website: SusanQuilty.com.

Freely Written: A Podcast

Are you ready for a story break?

Join author Susan Quilty as she uses simple prompts to free write her way into strange, silly, or poignant tales. Weekly episodes offer new stories, while bonus episodes share behind-the-scenes commentary. Episodes are short, about 10 minutes each, and suggestions for future writing prompts are always welcome!

Find **Freely Written** on your favorite podcast app.